DEJA ORTEGA: ODDSBREAKER

SARAH BYLUND

Immortal Works LLC
1505 Glenrose Drive
Salt Lake City, Utah 84104
Tel: (385) 202-0116

© 2021 Sarah Bylund
www.sarahbylund.com

Cover Art by Ashley Literski
http://strangedevotion.wixsite.com/strangedesigns

ISBN 978-1-953491-19-0 (Paperback)
ASIN B092VBJ84P (Kindle Edition)

To Mandy, who taught me what it's like to have a dear sister who is unbelievably giving, strong, supportive, and funny. (And I suppose to Aaron, too, because he's the brother who somehow succeeded in catching her.)

H er face was all made up—but, then, so was her identity.

However, the deception was altogether justified. As an oddsbreaker, if Deja Ortega wanted to pull off a dare and get paid, she had to know how to sell an identity customized for every situation —like to the horned gatekeeper barring her from entering the hallowed halls of The Wrinkle, the galaxy's hottest and snootiest fashion club.

"Are you certain, ma'am?" asked the bouncer, brow furrowed between the horns on either side of his massive head.

"*Yes*," said Deja with a put-upon tone.

"And your name is Shaylone Redd?" he mumbled, eyes searching the screen of his data pad.

"No," she replied, sighing. Peering up at the large fellow with feigned indignation, she said, "It's 'shay-LO-nee.' But Lady Redd is my stage name. Now what's this about me *not* being on the list of today's designers? How could that possibly be? Get someone important out here *immediately* or—"

"Your credentials seem to be in order, Lady Redd, but scheduling difficulties *can* arise," he said in an even tone, though his orange-gold eyes darted left and right as if looking for backup. Of course, Deja had ensured that his "backup" was otherwise engaged.

"Yes, and unemployment *can* happen as well, Qort" she warned, tossing her head with irritation, causing the multicolored, crystal ornaments in her intricate hairdo to jangle and chime. Micro cameras were hidden in a few of them. She also wore a few biopatches beneath her clothes because the client had requested the Deluxe Virtual Package. All her biofeedback data—blood pressure, heart rate, perspiration, adrenaline, cortisol levels, etc.—would be relayed to the client, whose vitals would then be matched with hers thanks to the client's Virtual Biofeed device.

Deja gestured to her entourage of models of varying species. "Look over there," she commanded. "Do these *stunning people* look as though they are on the cleaning crew? Or perhaps they are here to raid and pillage The Wrinkle?" she scoffed, flicking an elegant hand toward the somewhat wrinkled-looking, multi-tiered building behind him. You just never knew what the eccentric building would look like from one week to the next. Constructed like a puzzle with moving parts, its floors, rooms, and staircases were often shifted and shuffled to suit the owners' fashionista whims. Even the club's outer and inner walls were an oft-changing canvas of colors, textures, lights, images, and sounds. Sometimes, the whole place trundled a few miles or so to a new location. Deja paused; it reminded her of some Old Earth books. Something about Howl's Harry, a castle, and Rumble Doors or something?

She focused again on her adversary, who seemed just about ready to fold. "If my show is cancelled because of *you*, sir, I'll make sure you never guard more than the clearance aisle at Fabric Fix." Really, she wanted to wince at her own words. *Poor fellow. Hope I don't cost him his job.*

"A moment, a moment," Qort protested, touching a comm device nestled in one tufted ear. "Helston, I have a Lady Redd here, but—"

Deja didn't need to strain to hear the reply: "But what? Let her in. Her show's on in two turns!" A few colorful words followed that. But Qort was already waving her and her people in.

Deja breathed deep, striding toward the assigned staging room, leading a posse of ecstatic models and two assistants towing in all the clothing and accessories.

Okay. I'm in. Hope my "fashions" will be too.

DDEJA MOVED RAPIDLY, dressing her models with a speed that bespoke all her years helping her carnie mates change costumes backstage. She tried not to laugh at how ridiculous everything looked. But the client had, after all, dared her to use only junk and reclaimed items to create her masterpieces. He had something against the elitist fashion lovers in this establishment.

That grudge was fine by her. Now she had a way to add more to her stash—the precious bribe money that would soon, with any luck, be enough to free her father from that horrid debtor's prison on Gredlar, a backwater planet. Once again, she tried not to worry about his safety. If only her papá hadn't become a degenerate gambler after losing his wife. If only her mamá hadn't been murdered along with the rest of the carnie troupe. If only. Maybe then he wouldn't have sunk so low as to visit gambling's worst armpit (or mecca, depending on your viewpoint). If only.

Gritting her teeth, Deja took another drink from her flask. *If onlys are stupid.* She needed to focus all her efforts on this latest dare, or she was going to fail and lose the promised credits. She surveyed her models with a sharp eye, seeing reclaimed shower curtains, heat shield shingles, old pipes, horrid upholstery fabric from public transit seats, used bolts and washers and other hardware, bits of porcelain and other materials from bathroom fixtures, fake feathers and animal skins from old purses and bags, and even a little burlap from sacks of root vegetables she'd found in the dump. All of it was trash, but she had crafted the refuse into beautiful and exotic outfits. She hoped.

The furry Oxortian wore a dress of "scales" made from washers and porcelain. The tall Ramelite with his graceful limbs wore an armor-like outfit from heat shield shingles, hinged with pipes and accented with color-changing paint. The squat but curvy Twellish woman wore draped burlap and upholstery festooned with glittering stones from the floor of a gutted bathroom. All the others wore similar masterpieces of recycled goods. Some even had props like a live reptile or a fuzzy rodent or the occasional shoulder bag. And they all wore jewelry—if one could call it that given the source.

Her short aide ran up to her. "Lady Redd, you're on in the lower levels in five minutes. The upper levels start in ten."

"Wonderful," she acknowledged, then turned back to her models and started shooing them to their proper places. "Make them *feel* your fashion, people! We want to sell, sell, sell!"

"Yes, Lady Redd," they all answered, strutting or shuffling or even slithering off to their positions. Well and good. Now she just had to watch her work glide down the runway while she worked the crowd. She would only get creds from her daregiver if she managed to sell some of these crazy designs. And sell she would. Her papá's freedom, and maybe even his life, depended on that. Prison, the one in which he resided in particular, was *not* a cushy place.

She surveyed the club's guests on multiple floors until the lights flared and the music blared, then she chose her first marks and approached them with her most charming smile. "Hello, gorgeous ones. I am the Lady Redd. So, how do you like that number on the Ramelite? I believe you long-limbed lovelies would be stunning in that one, don't you agree?"

The guests in question perked up, swiveling their ears in her direction. She continued her flattery mixed with truth, selling four units. After that, she continued to work the rooms, exuding confidence and mystery and, of course, sex appeal.

Deja wasn't the most gorgeous human ever, but she did turn many a head. Her luscious black curls weren't too long, but that was the fashion at the moment. Her papá's Hispanic and Latino heritage and her mamá's French and Mediterranean lineage had graced Deja with light brown skin that had a hint of an olive tint. Her eyes were green and slanted just a bit. Her nose was somewhat long and yet elegant, just like her face. Her lips were perhaps not as full as could be desired; yet they were wide and formed a cupid's bow on the top. Her chin was just a bit square but in a charming fashion. And her cheekbones—well, they were high enough to satisfy any standard of beauty. Her neck, lengthy and slender, lent her even more grace and beauty.

She was five foot nine, too, so she wasn't lacking in height. And her mamá's genes had endowed her well in the cleavage and other-important-curves department. Today, she wore a minimal disguise. She wasn't dealing with a dangerous crowd, so she hadn't felt the need to conceal herself too much.

As she worked the rooms, Deja capitalized on the showmanship she developed over the many years of her youth. While Deja was growing up, her papá, Patricio Ortega, had served as the ship's spitfire chef for the planet-hopping troupe of carnies in which her mother, Esmira Kanathredies, had been an illusionist, escape artist, aerialist, and a lot of other "-ists."

As Deja worked over the next few hours, her heart sped up. When she was nearly done, she stopped a moment to tally her sales.

Yes, this next sale should do it. I think I'll meet the daregiver's challenge!

Her whole body felt light and buzzing with energy. To celebrate, she took another drink from her trusty flask. She tucked her sales tablet under her arm and raced up another flight of stairs to the last level. There, she charmed more buyers. She almost felt bad she wouldn't actually be filling any of these orders for her "masterpieces." No, this dare was about showing the fashion set just how gullible they could be. *I mean, a dress made from a shower curtain or some burlap and a few well-placed baubles? Come on.*

Still, it felt good to be desirable, no matter what the situation. So off she went to complete the dare and skedaddle before anyone realized she had invented the up-and-coming Lady Redd just weeks ago. Deja could already imagine the money being transferred into her account.

*

"Wait, now, Lady Redd or whoever you are. Your bio says you showed your designs on planet Rodon at the Telwan fashion show. Yet I was there, and never did I see *any* of your creations." The reptilian speaker eyed her with his red irises and flicked his tongue in disdain.

Slag it all! Think of something, she ordered herself. She'd done her homework; now she just had to embellish on it.

"Well, that's because my *mentor* stole my ideas and presented them as his own. You're familiar with Monten Talrathius, I presume?"

Her challenger sat back in surprise, forked tongue flicking in and out. "But of course. Who isn't?" He still didn't seem convinced. And everyone at the table awaited her reply. The whole dare could crash down around her if word got around that she wasn't whom she claimed to be.

"Look, the man is brilliant, but he gets bored. He was upset with me because I suggested some changes to his latest line. And we *all* know how well he takes critiques." She paused for effect. A few of the onlookers nodded or huffed in agreement. "So, in retaliation, he took six of my designs and passed them off as Talrathius designs. And what could I do? I couldn't defy him. Not then. I didn't have enough clout. So I just let it be." She conjured a small tear in one eye, which trickled down her face at just the right moment. Then she offered a shrug for effect and sat down on the nearest chair as if the whole conversation had deflated her fragile sensitivities.

"Well, Lady Redd," said the reptilian alien, leaning forward. "I am most sorry to hear of your troubles. It is a story all too common these days. And I, for one, will not let Talrathius spoil these proceedings any further. Where's that sales pad of yours?"

"Why, thank you, dear friend," she said with an air of relief, treating him like her rescuer. She handed over the sales pad, which was soon passed on to the others at the table.

Nailed it, she thought, relieved. Besides, her legs kind of hurt after all that standing and walking and climbing. The shoes she was wearing were killer. Thus, sitting on the chair for a moment was altogether welcome. Fashion was slaggin' hard work.

C a-ching! *There it is,* she thought, watching the credit transfer go through. Her daregiver just paid her for winning the last fashion-intensive dare. She tapped the email button on her PalmStar, a handy device that fit well in her human hand. A data pad with a blue, oval-shaped screen, her PalmStar had many functions. She swiped over to the message app to see if she had received a letter from her father yet. A smile bloomed on her face as she saw a letter from Patricio Ortega. Savoring the words, since he rarely got mail privileges, she read through the message twice.

Querida Hija,

¿Como estás, mija? I hope you are taking good care of yourself. Nothing too risky for my sake, I hope. Do you have any good news for me? Maybe *un hombre guapo* in your life? Now, do not make that face at me. I just want you to be happy. I know you must be lonely. I am sorry I got myself in this awful situation.

I am still working in the prison galley. Of course, it is primitive. But I make do. Do not concern yourself too much with me. The warden has requested me to make *toda su comida.* I have a nicer cell now with only two cellmates. And I don't have to go out on the labor trips. *¡Por fin, un poco de suerte!* And yet...*estoy cansado.* I am too old. However, I will carry on, *mija.* I cannot wait to see your beautiful face once again. *Cuídate.*

Con Mucho Amor,
Tu papá

Poor Daddy, she thought, breathing out a long-held lungful of air. She knew he kept a brave face for her most of the time. But he was an old man, and prison life was not an easy one by far. She debated on what to write back. While she thought, she sipped a drink of rubarlo nectar with a shot of gehut. It was early, but she couldn't help feeling stressed about her father's predicament. Finally, she began her letter:

Querido Papá,

Estoy muy bien. I am glad you are top dog in *la cocina ahora.* You deserve that and so much more.

I just completed a dare in which I created fashion masterpieces from, get this, *basura.* Yes, it's true! I used all sorts of crazy materials that people had chucked out. And the fashionistas just ate it up! It was quite a difficult job, though. It took me weeks to prepare. But, *Papá,* I made good money. I hope to have you out of prison soon. Maybe even by the end of the year. Never give up hope.

As for me finding a man, don't start! You know I don't have time to date anyone. Besides, I don't attract the good ones in *mi profesión.* I am always on the run from the law, especially the Coalition. You know how it is for me. One day, I will have time to settle down. But not right now.

I am getting ready for another dare. Nothing too dangerous. Don't worry. *Estar segura, también.*

Con Mucho Amor,
Tu hija

When she finished typing, Deja tapped the send icon. After thinking about her papá a while longer, she tapped the sleep control on her PalmStar. Her father had always enjoyed two things: cooking and gambling. But it wasn't until his wife, Deja's mother, had been murdered that his need to gamble had evolved into an all-consuming obsession.

Deja sighed and tucked her PalmStar away inside her special vest. Made of black hydrathermex fabric—its magno-tabbed pockets keyed to her genetic signature—the vest kept everything in place and safe from galactic pickpockets. Well, safer than most. All told, the custom-made vest had nine pockets, but only four of those were on the outside. The front featured glossy, ebony buttons in the shape of tiny barrels. Those were just pleasant diversions, however. Her fingers found the much more practical closure hidden beneath the button flap: a magnetic, watertight seal.

Straightening her vest in front of a cracked mirror in a cramped room on planet Be'Voya, she felt much more protected, not to mention sexier. Impeccably tailored, the garment swept past her waist and over her hips. That, combined with its construction from several vertical panels of fabric, lent her an even taller, curvier physique. Stars and suns, but she loved that part. And the front plunged into a V-neck. For safety's sake, she'd also paid for shield lining. The tough, dual-layered material could stop just about any blade and most projectiles of moderate size. The inner pockets concealed her flask, PalmStar, CredChips, lock-picking tools, knife, micro binoculars, comm-tapping gizmos, and other useful implements.

Deja needed to prepare for a dare that involved swimming with grutch sharks. Tomorrow, she'd swim with the fearsome creatures and, she hoped, come out alive. For now, though, she wanted to soak up some local color first. Taking a day or so off after a dare always helped her center herself.

Looking around her room, she debated on what to bring with her to the nearby marketplace. The room had old-fashioned plaster walls and was only big enough for a small cot, a closet, a primitive yet flushable toilet, and a sink mounted on the wall. The establishment was sort of like a youth hostel back on Old Earth. She was lucky to have a private room at all. Of course, the room smelled a little bit like old urine and sweat and, alas, had no window. The showers were communal; as such, she had no desire to use them until she really needed to. Even then, she'd be sure to wear some flip flops to avoid any nastiness on the shower floor.

Her compact blaster was already strapped in the holster on her thigh. Her blue duffel bag rested on the cot at the moment. Deja didn't like the idea of leaving it in her room unless she took her valuable items with her. Walking over to the bag, she opened it and checked to make sure most of her pricey equipment was in her vest already. Her clothes could be replaced without much bother. Her shoes weren't the costly kind. She'd left her more expensive clothing, footwear, and other items back on the Blythrian Space Station in her private locker.

Sure, the duffel also contained some basic makeup and toiletries. Yet such stuff shouldn't be all that tempting to any thieves. She paused, placing a hand on her med kit, which included some bandages, bone vaccine, flesh sealant (for light wounds), sutures and curved needles (for heavy-duty wounds), various drugs for a variety of purposes, and a bunch of other basic supplies for a medical emergency. Better take that with her, just in case someone raided her room while she was away.

Reaching into a pocket inside her duffel, she pulled out a sleek, folded backpack. Unfolding it, she packed her med kit inside as well as an extra pair of pants and a shirt. She also stowed some sunscreen and a water bottle in a side pocket. At the last second, she decided to toss in a wide-brimmed hat in case the sun got too hot later in the day. Satisfied with her gear, she walked over to the door and opened it. Locking it behind her, she tromped down the long hall and over to the outer door. She exited the front entrance only to find an unexpected visitor loitering on the other side.

A young, human girl stood with her dirty hands clasped in front of her. She was leaning against one of the many palm trees. One quick look and Deja could tell the kid was probably homeless. Her light skin was freckled and sunburned, and her red hair hadn't been washed in a long time. Any haircuts seemed to have been performed with a dull knife. It sort of looked like she was wearing a fuzzy, scarlet nest on her head. About eight years old, she had blue eyes that seemed much older that her physical age. Her lips were thin, as was her body, which was clad in a baggy, shabby dress that used to be a pretty yellow shade. Her feet, covered in dust, were clad in simple sandals suitable for the tropical climate.

The child bobbed her head at Deja and spoke in Common. "How do ya do? Might ya be needing someone to show you 'round and run errands an' such? My rates is cheap. An' I don't cause no trouble."

Deja wouldn't mind a little company, especially if it helped out a child in need. She flashed a little smile at the willowy girl. "Well now, that could be nice. What do you call yourself?"

"Name's Maizie," said the child with a small smile of her own, showing uneven teeth.

"Hi, Maizie." Deja held out her right hand. "I'm Deja. Nice to meet you."

The small street urchin reached out and shook Deja's hand. "Would ya like to go to the market today? Lots of stuff to see over yonder."

"Actually, that's right where I'd like to go. What's your going rate for the day?"

"Oh, just fifty dorems, is all."

"Fine by me," Deja replied, fishing in an inside pocket of her vest for a preloaded CredChip. "Here's twenty-five for right now. Where do you think I should start?"

Maizie took the chip and tucked it away in a pocket on her skirt, smiling big now. "Well, that depends. You hungry, Miss Deja?"

"You read my mind! I'm famished."

"OK," said Maizie, "come this-a-way."

Obliging, Deja followed the girl out of the hostel's courtyard and onto a busy, cobblestone-paved street in the coastal town of Ginyo. The street was lined with houses made from a variety of materials, wooden or plasticrete walls and simple thatched roofs or tin roofs.

Some buildings were made from a bamboo-like material. All in all, this world wasn't too technologically advanced. So it was still rustic in many ways. Some people had fancier houses and possessions, but most didn't. And many people (human and alien alike) walked or rode bikes. Some rode in rickshaws while others drove vehicles powered by the sun or fossil fuels. The morning air was already moist and warm, making Deja feel a bit sticky. But her skin didn't mind. No clouds obscured the cornflower blue sky.

"Maizie," she asked, "where are we headed?"

"Oh, just the best café 'round these parts—The Red Claw. You'll like it plenty."

"Sounds great. Lead on," Deja said, walking behind the child and wondering how long Maizie had been without a home.

LIEUTENANT COLONEL GEOFF THORNE of the Galactic Justice Coalition sat with his back to the wall in a small restaurant called The Red Claw in the bustling town of Ginyo on the coast of the Ikenama Sea. He was on holiday, so he wasn't wearing his uniform, though he did have an off-duty blaster strapped to his thigh and a good hunting knife on his belt. He was wearing a many-pocketed fishing vest over a short-sleeved, gray shirt and camo cargo pants in blues and grays. As per his usual habit, he was evaluating his surroundings, making sure he knew all the exits, the possible threats, and so on.

Six feet, three inches tall with a muscular frame, Geoff was in his early thirties. But he looked younger than his age; everyone said so. Perhaps it was his deep-set, blue eyes? He also had a square jaw and a cleft chin. The soldier's brown hair was cut in a short, military style. His nose had a hawkish outline and was a bit crooked after getting broken and reset too often. His hands were large, but his fingers were somewhat slender and strong despite having broken his hands and some of his knuckles a few times. Modern medicine could do wonders—most of the time. His white skin had a deep tan from hours and hours spent outside.

The restaurant wasn't much to look at. The bar as well as the tables and chairs were all simple but sturdy. Some chairs or stools were larger or smaller than his own chair to accommodate other species. At the moment, several two-armed, four-legged, amphibian Zooxes were standing by the bar, talking vociferously, and drinking alcoholic yogg. Geoff didn't care much for the drink himself, but most humans didn't. At any rate, it was a bit early to be hitting the yogg. He himself was nursing a cup of black coffee and eating a savory pastry in a leisurely fashion. Behind the bar, a hulking human male stood doing inventory and washing mugs. A young, Be'Voyan female with bluish skin and long, black hair was just going back to the kitchen to get an order. Geoff began to study the other patrons of the restaurant. A trio of male humans looked like they were down on their luck, all of them in threadbare clothing.

Four native Be'Voyans, three males and one female, were dressed in the local police garb: rugged boots and green-gray camo uniforms. They spoke to each other in hushed tones, their bodies rigid and their eyes often roving their surroundings. He knew how formidable Be'Voyans could be, what with their combat training. This group also wore menacing rifles and truncheons, not to mention a few knives. The Coalition had rated this planet as a low-risk zone, but he wondered if something might be going on judging from the behavior of this assembly of officers in the café. He had heard some rumors that the planet was trying to join the Coalition.

His gaze moved on to other café patrons, including a one-eyed Tondwian who occupied a sizeable wooden chair near the far side of the café. She had blocky features like most of her kind, but her elegantly draped clothing made her seem sleeker. A porcine, tusked Orinkk in a jaunty white hat and loose clothing lounged in a wicker chair reading something on a data tablet and munching on some jarberry tartlets. Those Orinkks sure loved sweets. He paused. Too bad a small number of them also had the unfortunate tradition of eating part of their deceased friend or family member before the burial ritual. *Cannibals.* The thought made Geoff shudder a bit. Of course, the vast majority of that species didn't practice endocannibalism, which was reassuring.

In any case, the most unlikely occupants of the café were two Evuutans, one male and one female. Both were obviously warriors, what with all the tribal tattoos on their crested heads, thick necks, and impressive arms. Their skin was albino, of course. And they both wore tight-fitting clothes that highlighted their muscles with ease. Most Evuutans were big on honor and sacrifice but didn't always have the best manners. As a result, Geoff generally classified them as the "Klingons" of the galaxy. Anyhow, these two were typing up something on their PalmStars. They also had wicked-looking spears leaning against their small table.

Somewhat bored with his vigil, the lieutenant colonel fought the urge to yawn. He hoped he didn't have long to wait before the captain of his upcoming deep-sea fishing trip showed up. *I'd better catch some real whoppers on this expedition.* A pity his adoptive father couldn't come with him on this occasion. But he hadn't been able to get away from the non-profit he ran with Geoff's birth mother.

Geoff startled when one of the larger Zooxes roared in laughter and announced, "Well, let's just go ask the hog then!"

The Orinkk spared a sidelong glance at the green, rubbery-skinned Zoox who had issued the insult, sniffing in disdain with his pig-like snout but saying nothing. Unfortunately, the group of Zooxes wouldn't let the matter drop.

"So, my piggy friend," said Zoox Number One, "have you eaten any friends and family lately?"

"You are no friend of mine. And I am sure you do not mean to insult me with such a question," said the offended party, straightening his hat.

"Come on. Don't put on airs. I know your kind loves munching on your fallen relatives and comrades," sneered the drunk Zoox.

The two other Zooxes, equally intoxicated, chimed in with, "Yeah, oinker!" and "Tell the truth!"

Geoff sighed. Things were getting ugly. Technically, this planet wasn't part of the Galactic Justice Coalition. So he didn't have any jurisdiction here. Yet he didn't like to see people being mistreated. The Evuutans seemed to feel the same because they perked up and set down their PalmStars with a dual *thwack*. The four Be'Voyans looked in the direction of the speaker, but their expressions were amused, not outraged.

"Look," said the Orinkk, "you are obviously drunk. Apologize and I will go on my way." He stood and waited for a response.

"Ohhh, we're soused, huh? Doesn't mean you get to ignore a perfectly good question!" exclaimed Zoox Number One, walking over to the Orinkk. The other two Zooxes followed him.

"What I eat is none of your business, you slaggerous scum."

At such an affront, Zoox Number One punched the porcine alien in the face. The portly guy fell back into his chair and tipped backwards, sprawling on the floor.

A few things happened quite fast after the Orinkk went down. The Tondwian turned her head in the direction of the fight, but didn't move. The bartender reached beneath the countertop and pulled out a sizeable blaster. Both Evuutans sprang from their chairs, grabbing their spears, and hustled to the Orinkk's side. The three Zooxes chuckled loudly, shaking their heads, and one of them kicked the prone alien. The Be'Voyans all stood up, poised to spring. Geoff himself came to his feet in a swift motion and then sprinted the short distance to the scene of the disturbance.

A bar fight...in a café? Really? he thought.

And then all heck broke loose. The bartender fired his blaster on stun at Zoox Number One, who swayed but didn't drop to the floor. The male albino warrior jabbed the butt of his spear into the stomach of Zoox Number Two, who reared onto his back legs in shock. The female Evuutan yelled out, "Soldiers, do your duty or face my wrath!" This prompted all the Be'Voyans to unsling their truncheons and join the fray—against the Evuutans and Orinkk.

The Orinkk lumbered to his feet and slugged the Zoox who had started all this in the first place. The amphibious alien collapsed like a sack of butchered meat. Geoff unholstered his blaster and leveled it at Zoox Number Two, who dodged the blast. But the male Evuutan whipped his spear around to whack him in the side. Zoox Number Two tried to deliver an uppercut to the male Evuutan, yet the warrior was decidedly *not* intoxicated and *quite* spry. So he danced out of the way and kicked the Zoox in the stomach. That was enough to take out Zoox Number Two.

The four male Be'Voyans advanced on the female Evuutan warrior, who snarled and attacked with her spear. As Geoff turned to help her, the hardy Orinkk and Zoox Number Three grappled with each other, falling to the ground.

Geoff swept the feet of one Be'Voyan and punched another one in the face, jumping aside to avoid a truncheon. *This is no good*, he thought, wishing his whole team were here to back him up. No use wishing for that, however. So he trained his blaster on a slender Be'Voyan and pulled the trigger, stunning the soldier, who dropped to the floor. A truncheon slammed into Geoff's wrist. His blaster spun across the floor, and he teetered for a bit. But Geoff used the motion to swivel and bring up his other arm, landing a solid fist into the throat of the Be'Voyan who had attacked him. That fellow staggered and fell, grasping at his neck and coughing, which left just one Be'Voyan officer facing off with Geoff and the female Evuutan.

The Orinkk and the male Evuutan were holding their own against the remaining Zoox and the female Be'Voyan. Geoff and his unexpected partner in combat stood back to back to deal with the remaining male Be'Voyan and two of the humans who had decided to join the brawl. The third human went to assist the Zoox and Be'Voyan squaring off against the Orinkk and the male Evuutan. Geoff wondered why the humans had decided to fight against him, but he didn't have much time to spare for thinking. Instead, his instincts and training took over, and he dealt out some decent punishment right up until a blow landed on the base of his skull. He went down but rolled, preparing to get to his feet.

Mid-roll, the front door crashed open and several gunshots rang out. Rolling into a crouch, he spared a glance toward the door and saw five uniformed Be'Voyans streaming into the small café. They were led by a tall soldier with his gun pointed at the ceiling.

"Stop this idiocy now!" demanded the leader.

Geoff raised his hands immediately, head still ringing from the blow he'd taken and the shots the leader had fired. The mayhem quickly wound down, though not before some participants landed a few more punches, kicks, and whatnot.

"I said stop!" roared the Be'Voyan commander, and finally everyone was still. Geoff kept his eyes on the newly arrived leader but evaluated the damage in his line of sight. Various humans and aliens alike were on the floor and most tables and chairs were overturned.

Great. This is gonna be fun. And where is the captain I was supposed to meet?

"Mister Rowan," said the lead officer to the bartender, "who started this mess?"

"That," said Rowan, "would be these three Zooxes here, who assaulted the Orinkk. But your Be'Voyans jumped in and made things worse."

Several outcries arose from the named parties, but the leader just fired another few shots into the ceiling. "Enough. Soldiers, line up over there. Humans, over here. Zooxes, go stand by the bar—if you can stand. And the rest of you just stay where you are."

Geoff marched off to stand with the other humans, the ones he'd been fighting just moments ago. Once everyone was in place, the police sergeant strode up to the bartender. "Please tell me what transpired. And do it quick. We have other things to be dealing with besides ridiculous brawls."

Rowan, who bristled at the word "ridiculous," pointed at Zoox

Number One and began telling a not-so-short tale of what had transpired.

Sigh. Geoff decided to hold his peace unless the guy in control asked him a direct question. After all, he was reluctant to tell anyone he was a Coalition operative. He couldn't share that he was in black ops. But he sure didn't want to gain extra scrutiny by saying he was with the GJC.

The soldier in charge questioned a few people, and Geoff thought he might be off the hook. Sadly, that was not the case.

"You, sir," the commander said to Geoff, who groaned inwardly, "what brings you to Be'Voya?"

Geoff cleared his throat. "I'm just here for a deep-sea fishing expedition. I was supposed to meet the ship's captain about ten minutes ago."

"And the captain's name?"

"Captain Hunshi, sir," Geoff replied.

"That tracks," admitted the sergeant. "Do you agree with this establishment's proprietor as to the cause of this disgrace?"

"Yes, I do. The Orinkk was insulted and did not take the first swing. Your soldiers did not seem, uh, motivated by the Orinkk's plight, sad to say."

"Understood. Will you accompany us to the station to make a statement?"

"Well..." Geoff paused. He wanted to do the right thing, but he also didn't want to do the stupid thing.

"Is there some reason you would not wish to visit our local constabulary?" asked the officer in a sharp voice. His golden eyes regarded Geoff with keen interest.

"No, sir. I just don't want to miss the captain. But I suppose I can simply message him."

"Good answer," the man said with a brisk nod. "Everyone, let's go. Stay orderly or else." And with that, the new bunch of soldiers escorted everyone out of the café.

Well, this sucks.

"Whoa, hold on, Maizie," Deja said, putting her hand on the girl's left shoulder. "It looks like some local color has been mixing things up at the Red Claw."

They had just arrived at the café only to find a group of native soldiers escorting a bunch of natives, aliens, and humans out the front door and into two open-bed trucks. Deja and Maizie stood across the street, where a crowd had now formed. As an oddsbreaker, she had no desire to run afoul of the local police. So she was not about to head into the café now.

"Oh," Maizie declared. "You is right about that. I wonder what went on in there?"

"I don't know, and I don't care to know. What?" Deja asked when Maizie made a small sound. "Do you recognize any of them?"

"Yes. That shorter Be'Voyan there is my brother," Maizie said quietly.

Brother? "But he's a native," Deja pointed out. "How is he your brother, if you don't mind my asking?"

"Uh, well, we kinda adopted each other, you see."

"Okay. So...you've got *connections* then," Deja said, looking down at the child with a grin.

"Yup. Looks like I'll hafta ask him what happened after his shift rolls up."

"Yes. It appears that he came with the team that arrived after things got interesting. I mean, it doesn't seem like he's in trouble," Deja ventured.

"Nope, he is real good at keeping outta trouble."

"I'll bet. That's good to know. What's his name?" Inwardly, Deja wondered why Maizie was still on the streets if her adoptive brother was making good money in the local policing unit. But maybe he had just joined or something. Maybe Maizie didn't like to be tied down to one place. Well, she'd leave that be for now.

"Oh, it's Officer Sef Doljang."

"Nice. Well, how about we find somewhere else to get some grub?" Deja proposed.

"Sure thing, Miss Deja. Let's go see Pen over at his place."

Nodding, Deja was about to turn away when she caught someone watching her. It was a young human male walking out of the café, following the lead of those ahead of him. For some reason, he was staring at her, though he quickly averted his deep-blue eyes. Whoever he was, the stranger was slaggin' handsome. She could tell he was taller than her. A short-sleeved shirt clung to the defined muscles in his biceps, while a multi-pocketed, tan vest highlighted his slim waist and broad chest. His hair was buzzed short in a military-style cut. Plus, he walked like a fighter, and his somewhat crooked nose added to that impression. *Huh. I wonder why he was staring at me.*

Shrugging it off, she turned to follow Maizie, who had started weaving through the crowd, heading east toward the market. Hopefully, Deja's belly would be nice and full soon. Also, she could use another drink.

Deja finished eating and wiped her mouth with a paper napkin. She'd just devoured a simple but tasty meal of roasted meat and vegetables tossed in noodles with a spicy sauce accompanied by some local wine.

"Pen," Deja said, "would you mind sharing your recipe for that delightful dish?"

The Be'Voyan looked up from his grill, turning some meat on a skewer with an expert movement of his hand. The blue-skinned male laughed, showing his bright yet crooked teeth. "Well, suppose I do. Would you still come visit me shop?" He winked one golden eye at her.

"Oh, I'm sure you have plenty for me to taste test besides what I just ate," she said, smiling back. "What do you think, Maizie? Should your friend give me his recipe?" Deja waggled her eyebrows at her young companion, encouraging a yes.

Maizie giggled. "You's payin' me, so I says yes."

"Good point," Deja said. "But that's the right answer."

"Okay then. If you insist," Pen surrendered. "Come on over." He motioned for some other customers to move back so Deja could approach. "Just watch while I make the next order." He returned his attention to the grill as well as the portable stove and workspace he had set up.

Deja swept her hair back in a ponytail with an elastic and moved around the setup to Pen's side. Pen commenced showing her how to prepare the meal, starting with what type of meat he had used: yuffa quail. Since her father was a chef, Deja had developed the habit of asking for recipes just about everywhere she went. She had therefore made lots of friends in the culinary field. Additionally, she could pick up on new recipes pretty fast. Papá always said she had a talent for tickling the taste buds.

As the cooking lesson progressed, Deja asked a few questions here and there, excited to be learning something new. Meanwhile, Maizie sat at a nearby table, munching on the food Deja had bought her and watching with some interest. As soon as they were done here, she wanted Maizie to show her around the marketplace. She'd heard it had quite the variety of goods, including some useful equipment, neat art and jewelry, and decent icewine.

GEOFF CHECKED his PalmStar while he waited for someone to take his statement. A new message from Captain Hunshi awaited him.

Hunshi: Sorry to hear you got caught up in some local shenanigans at the café. I can't meet you until later in the day. Could we meet in four hours at the marketplace downtown?

With a few quick taps on his keypad, Geoff confirmed that he would be happy to meet the captain then. He asked where in the marketplace they should meet. Then he stowed his PalmStar in his vest and sighed. It had been at least an hour and he still hadn't been debriefed. He began to worry a little as he saw officers having hushed conversations throughout the precinct. Not all of the officers were Be'Voyans, but most were. Tension seemed to be hovering over everyone like a raincloud about to burst. He just didn't know what was causing that angst. He remembered how the commander had said, "We have other things to be dealing with besides ridiculous brawls."

"Excuse me, sir," Geoff said to a passing officer, "is something wrong?"

The person in question, a short Be'Voyan who appeared rather young, paused in front of Geoff.

"We are dealing with a...situation at the moment. But we cannot release any details at this time," said the Be'Voyan in a level tone. Geoff nodded, knowing the officer was towing a careful line.

"OK, I understand," Geoff responded. "Could you tell me how much longer before I can go? I'm just here to make a statement about the altercation at the Red Claw this morning."

"Ah, I see. Let me check and get back to you." The younger alien checked the data pad in his hand. "What's your name?"

"Geoff Thorne," he replied, still deciding to guard his connection to the Coalition. "And may I have your name?"

"Yes. It's Officer Sef Doljang. I'll be back."

"Thank you, Officer Doljang. I appreciate it." And with that, Geoff leaned back in his chair to wait some more, pondering what drama was unfolding on the planet. His thoughts also flitted to the striking young woman he had seen when he was leaving the café. She had beautiful, brown-olive skin and curly, dark hair. He didn't know why, but she stood out from the small crowd that had assembled on the other side of the street. She seemed to be accompanying a young street urchin with matted, red hair. The woman had glanced at him for a moment before the pair of them moved on. He wondered what she was doing in Ginyo.

He stopped his pondering when he saw the same young officer approaching. "Mister Thorne," he said, "we are ready for you now. Come with me."

"Wonderful," said Geoff, standing in one smooth motion.

He followed Doljang to a back office, weaving back and forth through various desks topped with semi-ancient computers. The commander's office was a bit cramped, but it made up for it with a more comfortable chair for a guest and vertical privacy blinds on the windows. The young officer stepped into the office as well and stood against the inside wall next to the door. The sergeant who had been at the café earlier sat behind a simple wooden desk. He motioned for Geoff to sit down.

"Hello, Mister Thorne. My name is Sergeant Yong Chouf. Thank you for waiting while we shuffled through various matters. I trust you weren't too bored?" The middle-aged Be'Voyan had black hair with a salt-and-pepper look, yet his golden eyes were still bright. He steepled his hands together, awaiting Geoff's response.

"Oh, I found things to occupy myself with. I'm no stranger to waiting," Geoff said affably.

"That's good. Now, can I get your statement in your own words please?"

"Of course." He went on to summarize his actions and what he had witnessed, ending with, "And I'm afraid to say I was surprised that your people sided *against* the Orinkk."

Chouf furrowed his brow in irritation. "Yes, that was indeed unfortunate. They will be reprimanded. My apologies for their involvement in all this."

"Thank you, sir," Geoff said with a nod. He admired a person in power who could handle criticism of his underlings—whether or not that criticism was warranted.

"You're welcome. Pardon me for asking, but you seem to have some...military training. Am I right?" asked Sergeant Chouf.

Geoff tried not to sigh. He'd known the line of questioning might go down this route. But he'd answered similar questions on many other worlds. "Well," he said, "you're not wrong there. But I'm not here in any capacity for a foreign power. Why do you ask?"

"Good question, Mr. Thorne. I'm not at liberty to discuss much. But I will say that you should remain alert during your visit here."

"I gathered as much," Geoff said.

"Ah. I imagine you noticed the anxiety here, trained as you are."

"A bit, yeah," he demurred.

"No doubt," nodded the sergeant. "Well, those are all the questions I had for you. Officer Doljang will record your contact information should we need to be in touch. Thank you for your time."

"Not a problem, Sergeant Chouf. I hope whatever is going on can be resolved quickly," Geoff said, getting up from his seat.

"Our hopes, too," said the commander.

"This way, sir." Sef opened the door for Geoff to exit first. And that was that. Soon, he'd be at the marketplace and meeting up with the ship captain in preparation for his trip. Hopefully nothing else crazy happened between now and then.

Deja followed Maizie through a crowd and past pushcarts and stalls in the marketplace in a thriving downtown area. Something pulled at Deja's right sleeve. She yanked her arm back, preparing to throw a punch. But she stopped when she saw a little boy in front of her cowering away.

"Sorry, missus! I was just wondering if you had a few creds to spare. I wasn't meaning no harm, I promise." The boy was a native Be'Voyan, about seven, with dark hair, an upturned nose, grubby clothes, and bare feet.

Maizie twirled around when she heard the boy speak. "Hey, you. Don't you be botherin' my payin' customer, Rip!"

"Maizie, it's okay," Deja said in a soothing voice. She looked around, making sure no pickpockets were lurking behind her while she talked to the kid. Satisfied, she looked down at the child and smiled. "Rip, is it?" The boy nodded. "Well, I think I can shell out a few creds if you promise to keep all the pickpockets away. Do we have a deal?"

His gold eyes lit up with admiration. "You got a smart one here, Maizie," Rip announced. "Sure, I can do that," he told Deja.

"Then I've got some money to spare. Here you go." She reached inside her vest and took out a preloaded CredChip. It was enough for him to buy some sandals and a handful of meals.

The boy reached out his little blue hand and grabbed the small white chip. "Thank you, missus. I won't let you down!" Then he took off, weaving into the crowd.

Deja and Maizie went on their way. They walked for another ten minutes before they reached their destination.

"Ta da!" Maizie pointed at the large stall loaded down with all manner of aquatic gear. "This here is the best place to buy flippers an' such." The proprietor was a middle-aged Be'Voyan female with a charming gap between her front teeth and braided, black hair. Deja smiled at the woman, who grinned in return.

"Hello, Maizie," said the stall owner. "Who have you brought to me this time?"

"Kanicha, I brought ya Miss Deja. She's needing some gear for a dive t'morrow."

"Wonderful, Maizie. Nice to meet you, Miss Deja. What are you looking for?"

"Good to meet you," Deja replied. "I need the works: A wetsuit, a headlamp, a tank and regulator, some flippers, and a dive knife with a gas cartridge."

"Excellent. I can outfit you in no time! Let's get you measured, and then I can show you some options."

"Perfect," Deja agreed.

Kanicha took out her measuring tape and started taking Deja's measurements for the wetsuit. While the shopkeeper was busying herself, Deja looked around at the other booths and pushcarts. Her wandering eyes passed over a tall, muscular figure and then returned back to it.

The man from outside the café? The one who stared at me. What's he up to?

Dressed like a cross between a fisherman and a soldier, the brown-haired man was talking to someone smaller whom Deja couldn't see from this angle. He stood at a pushcart stocked with some kind of meat pies and fruit. A few moments later, the pushcart vendor handed over a sack of meat pies and a sack of produce to the man. Deja watched as the mystery man squatted down and handed both bags to a small figure in front of him who had previously been obscured. Deja squinted, surprised.

It's Rip! That fellow just bought the poor kid at least a week's worth of food!

The stranger reached up and ruffled the boy's dark hair. Rip said what looked like "Thank you" and then darted off with his loot. The large man watched the child go and straightened up. At that moment, Kanicha brought out a heap of wetsuits in her arms. Deja stopped watching the kind gentleman and turned to the store's proprietor.

"Here are a few suits that should fit. All are good, but some are extra special," she said.

Deja quickly evaluated the merchandise. "Oooh, these are nice. Do you have a place I can try this one on?" Deja asked, picking out a black wetsuit with gray spots.

"Excellent taste. And, yes, follow me into my shop at the back. There's a changing room in there."

"Maizie," Deja said, "come with me and help?"

"Sure," said the girl.

Deja slipped past the stall's table and followed Kanicha into the store, which was small but full of many sorts of goods on shelves and counters. The stall owner walked around to the back and motioned toward a simple changing room with a fabric curtain strung across the opening.

"Great," Deja told her. "Maizie, wait here until I need you, okay?" The girl nodded, smiling.

"I'll just be right outside watching my stall," Kanicha said, leaving.

Deja stepped inside the room and closed the curtain. Stripping down, she then worked to put on the wetsuit, which took quite some effort. The fabric had to be skin-hugging because the suit was meant to insulate the body against the cold water. But, naturally, this quality made a wetsuit rather difficult to put on.

Oomph. There we go, she thought. She pushed the curtain aside.

"Maizie, zip me up, would you?" Deja asked, turning around and crouching down a bit so the child could reach the zipper. Maizie had no trouble with the task. After that, Deja pulled on the gloves. Then the oddsbreaker started stretching and bending, testing the fit of the suit. It fit brilliantly.

"What do you think, Maizie? Do we have a winner?"

"Oh, yes," she said with a grin.

"My thoughts as well," Deja announced. "Unzip me now, would you?" That done, she stepped back into the changing room and slid the curtain shut. After a bit of a struggle, she took off the suit and started putting on her own clothes again. Just as she did so, her ears picked up a tremendous racket outside and the entire store shook.

BOOM!

Something just blew up! Rushing to lace up her sandals, she heard other sounds: the *ratatat-tat-tat* of old-fashioned gunfire. And a lot of it. Screaming reached her ears soon after. The shop's front door opened and slammed shut. Worried that Maizie had gone outside, Deja snapped the curtain back and found the child cowering on the floor with her hands to her ears. Grabbing her backpack, Deja knelt down before the girl. "Are you hurt?"

"No, but what's goin' on?" Maizie squeaked.

"Just stay here," she instructed. She raced to the shop's door, where she found Kanicha bleeding from a head wound. Grabbing a child's T-shirt from a nearby shelf, she pressed it to the woman's head.

"Thanks," the other woman said, wincing.

"What's happening?" Deja yelled over the noise.

"Some religious nut detonated a bomb, and his buddies are shooting up the place!" Kanicha said.

Oh, great! The oddsbreaker unholstered her blaster and set it to kill. "Do you have a weapon?" she asked Kanicha.

The Be'Voyan nodded, grabbing a shotgun from under a shelf.

"Good. You feel like being my backup?"

"Yeah, fine by me. Gotta protect Maizie and the shop."

"Okay, stay behind me and stay low," Deja ordered through a dry mouth. Her heart rate shot up. She stood and spoke to Maizie. "Get in the back and hide, now!" The kid jumped up and scrambled toward the back.

Crouching low, Deja and the shopkeeper headed out the door and then kneeled behind the heavy-laden counter. The gunfire was more sporadic now. Deja took a quick peek over the table. A few bodies lay amidst rubble from some of the stores and pushcarts in the street. Other people, most wounded, were trying to escape. The gunfire came from about four hundred yards away where two huge, Be'Voyan males with automatic rifles fired into the crowd.

She was just about to hustle herself and Kanicha back into the store when she saw *him*—the mysterious stranger. His bloodied and motionless body was slumped backward over a pushcart. The blast must have taken him out before he could fight back, because he still had a blaster strapped to his right thigh. *Gravgummit! Is he alive?*

If he was, he wouldn't be for long. The gunmen were moving in closer. Deja looked at the man's chest, waiting to see if it would rise and fall. *Yes. There. He is still breathing!*

Preparing to do something that was most likely stupid, she shouted to Kanicha, "You stay here and cover me. I've got some hero stuff to do!"

"No problem," Kanicha agreed.

Deja sped out to the unconscious man. A bullet whizzed by, lodging in the pushcart just left of the injured fellow. With a leap, Deja tackled the prone figure and pushed him to the ground out of the line of fire. A spray of bullets hit the cart where the man had just been.

She spun off of him, whipping her blaster up. Without letting herself think, she aimed at the shooter and fired off two shots, hitting the Be'Voyan in the chest, and he went down. Her first kill; at that thought, her stomach reeled. But she shook her head—she couldn't let the horror of that fact stop her now. She fired two more blasts at the other insurgent, who staggered but didn't drop. Just as Deja was about to fire again, two shots rang out—one from an unseen person in the rubble to her left and one from Kanicha to her right. The last gunman fell dead. Deja whipped to her left, looking for the source of that other shot. It was a kneeling Be'Voyan police officer—and she knew him. Maizie's brother.

"Officer Sef Doljang," she called out, "are you okay?"

"Yeah, one second. Who's there?"

"I'm Deja, a friend of your sister's."

"Maizie?" he asked with urgency, standing up with a wobble. "Do you know where she is?"

"Yeah, over in this shop. And she's fine, don't worry," Deja added. "But this guy isn't. Can you help?" Deja knelt beside the huge man and started examining his wounds. *He's in really bad shape*, she thought, looking at a large gash on his torso, a head wound, and what looked like a broken left tibia. Plus, he had a bullet wound in his right forearm. Lucky for him, he was *still* unconscious.

She took off her backpack and opened it, digging for her med kit. Sef arrived at her side.

"Hey, I know this guy," he said.

"Who is he?"

"His name is Geoff Thorne. He was in a fight earlier today. Defended an Orinkk's honor."

Deja spared Sef a glance. "What, really? I don't know him, but I saw him giving a street kid some food earlier."

"Oh," Sef replied, "and for that you risked your life to save his? Impressive."

Deja shook her head. "Nah, just doing what any decent person would do, you know?" She pulled out a pouch of medications from her backpack and selected a pain killer plus a bone booster serum that would help his leg heal. She administered the meds and then looked over at Sef, who was also bloodied.

"How are you? Any broken bones? Gunshot wounds?"

"Don't think so. Just had a building fall on me is all. Whoa, Thorne looks really bad off."

"Yeah, it's not good," she said. "Help me set the bone in his leg?"

"Of course," the officer said, kneeling down.

With his help, Deja carefully but expertly set the bone, silently thanking her papá for letting her shadow the troupe's doctor so often.

Deja took some scissors out of her kit and started cutting Thorne's shirt so she could get to the injury on his stomach. "I've gotta stop the bleeding."

"Right," Sef replied. "I'll call for help." He grabbed the small radio at his waist, pressed a button, and spoke into it, "Precinct One-Three, this is Officer Doljang reporting. Multiple casualties and wounded at the downtown market. Requesting assistance. Over."

As he spoke, Deja looked around, trying to determine if any other survivors were in need of help. *Dang it. Most everyone else looks dead*, she thought.

Sef released the button, waiting for a response on the radio. All they heard was static. The Be'Voyan looked at her with sad, gold eyes, and Deja sighed.

"Nothing," Sef announced. "I don't think we can expect help. I'm guessing these fanatics hit multiple targets at once. We've been tracking some chatter about a possible attack, but couldn't pin down a location. I'm guessing that *all* the locations were targets—including my precinct."

"Slag it all," Deja cursed. "Can you help me roll Thorne? I need to look for wounds on his other side."

Sef gripped Geoff's right shoulder and upper arm while she put her hands on his right hip. "One, two, three, roll." They both pulled, rolling Thorne onto his left side. "OK, no other wounds. And the GSW in his arm is a through-and-through," Deja said, relieved. "OK, let's roll him back." She counted again, and they eased him down.

"All right. You want to handle Thorne?" Sef asked.

"Yeah. Why don't you go find Maizie and Kanicha? Do you know Kanicha?" He nodded. "Good. They're over there," she added, pointing.

"OK," said Sef, standing up with a groan. "I'll be back." His blue skin looked a bit ashen.

"Thanks, but take it easy," Deja called as he walked away. "You definitely look like a building clobbered you." She turned her attention back to the handsome stranger, grabbing some gauze from her med pack. "Hang in there, Geoff Thorne. You're not dying on *my* watch." She pressed some gauze over the wound in his side and on his forearm, pushing down hard.

With a jerk, Thorne's blue eyes flew open. "Ohhh. What's... where am I?"

"You're in the marketplace. You've been hurt. Just lie still, OK? I've got you."

"Who...wait, I've...s-seen you b-before," mumbled Thorne, his eyes focusing on her face.

"Yeah. Over at The Red Claw. Don't talk, just conserve your energy, got it?"

"Yes, m-ma'am. But who are y-you?"

Deja paused, deciding if she should give her real name. She didn't know who this guy was. And in all likelihood, they were both in a war zone now. "Just call me 'nurse,' okay?" she proposed, still putting pressure on the wounds he had sustained.

"O-okay, Nurse. Ouch!"

"Sorry. Hang in there, friend." She had saved his life; now she just had to keep him alive.

"Damage report?" Thorne asked, squeezing his eyes shut against the pain.

Deja paused, wondering what to say. She decided to be honest. It seemed like he could handle it. "It's bad," she confirmed. "But you're gonna be fine. Just breathe for me, OK?"

The man blew out a shuddering breath. "Right. I c-can do th-that."

Deja heard some noise to her right and turned to see the officer leading Maizie and Kanicha over, picking their way across the rubble.

The two Be'Voyans looked battered, but Maizie, who came to Deja's side, seemed unhurt.

"Hey," Sef said, "Kanicha and I will start looking for other survivors."

Deja voiced her agreement, while Maizie just licked her lips and looked down nervously at Geoff. Tears had made little tracks on her dirty face from her eyes to her chin. "Is...is he gonna be okay?"

Deja looked back at her patient. She had *killed* to save this man. So she hoped he was worth it. Thorne had passed out again. Well, she couldn't blame the dude. It was preferable that way. They just had to find some way to get him and any other survivors the hell out of there to someplace safe, wherever *that* was. Then she'd have to patch him up, find food, and so on.

"*Gravgummit,*" Deja said. "I need a slagging drink."

G eoff struggled to open his eyes. His body felt light and numb but also sticky from humidity. He couldn't really move. Worry ignited in his mind like a flame, burning through his consciousness. He opened his eyes at last and found himself looking up at a yellowed, plaster ceiling with a naked light bulb hanging from it.

Where am I? What happened?

"There you are. Welcome back," said a pleasant female voice.

Geoff managed to turn his head toward the voice and saw a young, human female with short, dark curls and green eyes. She seemed...familiar. But his brain was too scrambled to remember where he had seen her.

"Hello," he croaked. "Who are you? Where am I?"

"Easy, easy," she said. "Uh...call me 'nurse.' And you are in my room at a hostel on Be'Voya. You kinda got in the way of a bomb *and* a bullet. Not so smart of you, I might add."

"Oh," Geoff said, absorbing that information. Now that she mentioned a bomb, he had a vague recollection of an explosion throwing him against something hard. But he didn't remember anything after that. "How bad is it? What happened?" He looked around, taking in a small room with a porcelain sink and toilet. He appeared to be resting on a cot. None too comfortable, but he was used to such things. He tried to move and groaned instead.

"Whoa. No moving around, Mr. Thorne. You're in bad shape.

You have a deep laceration in your side, a bullet wound in your right arm, and a broken bone in your left leg. Plus, you're bruised all over. So just be still."

"How," he coughed, "do you know my name?" He laid still, realizing he must be on some powerful pain meds what with the loopy, numb feeling.

"Well, I ran into a friend of yours: Officer Sef Doljang. He helped me get you back here where we are holed up. The marketplace was attacked as was the local precinct and some other places, including the local hospital. There's a rebel force terrorizing the whole city in coordinated attacks. Something about not wanting their religion 'polluted' by infidel outsiders, namely, the Coalition. Yeah, the Coats can be super meddlesome. Still, I don't think blowing up innocents in the name of a cause is a good way to win the people's hearts and minds."

Ah, so she doesn't trust the GJC, Geoff noted. And we're caught up in the middle of a holy war. Crap. "I see. Well none of that sounds especially good. Can I, uh, get some water?" he asked.

"Oh, of course. I'm not being very nurse-like, am I?" The woman picked up a metal water bottle and positioned the straw near his mouth. "There you go. But don't drink too much at once."

He took a few sips and sighed. "Tastes good," he acknowledged. He raised his head a little and looked down at himself. He was swaddled in a dark-green blanket. "What meds do you have me on?"

"Just some pain meds and a bone-healing serum. Still, your leg is gonna need the splint I put on it for a while. And I had to stitch up your wounds. I'm afraid it's not too pretty, Mr. Thorne."

"But you got the job done," he said, not caring. "And call me Geoff. No need for formalities, Nurse. You've earned that and much more."

"Okay then, Geoff. Do you feel up to eating anything?"

"I...no, not right now. My stomach feels off," Geoff confessed.

"Well, then I am prescribing some sleep, and don't argue with me," she replied.

Geoff cleared his throat, then smiled. "Yes, ma'am." He took another look at his rescuer and closed his tired eyes, wondering how he could've gotten so unlucky and lucky at the same time.

Deja took another drink from her flask. It had been a day and night of nursing the sick man, and she was running low on spirit and spirits. She'd had to use some of her alcohol to clean Geoff's wounds when her disinfectant ran out. She knew she shouldn't be obsessing about alcohol right now. The oddsbreaker ought to be checking on Geoff again. Going over to the cot, she put her hand on his forehead.

Gravgummit! He has a fever.

She went to her med kit and pulled out a gizmo that could test BP, temp, and so on. She turned it on and held it over his forehead. It beeped, then read: 104°. That was *so* not good. With careful motions, Deja untucked the blanket around her patient. She and Sef had stripped him down to his boxers because of his wounds. With care, Deja peeled back the dressing on the gash in Geoff's side, hoping it wouldn't be inflamed and red. Her hopes were futile. It didn't look good. At all. Then she checked the bullet wound. It looked pink, but not puffy or gooey. Still, his gut wound must be infected.

Deja went back to her med kit and rummaged around, looking for the antibiotics. She came up empty and cursed her stupidity. She'd forgotten to restock those! She grabbed her PalmStar and typed up a message to Officer Doljang.

Deja: Geoff has a fever and infection. Need antibiotics, stat. Could also use some more food, a bedpan, and disinfectant.

She waited for an hour before she got a reply.

**Sef: Sorry to hear it. Both hospitals are in the hands of the rebels. But we just reacquired control of my precinct and a few other areas. I'll see if I can get you

some antibiotics and food. Not sure about the other items. Be in touch.

While she waited for a reply, Deja paced. Her limbs felt shaky. She hated to admit it, but she was afraid. What if the rebels attacked the hostel? What if Geoff died on her watch? She'd never been responsible for another life before. And she had never killed another person before.

Where was her flask again? Oh, right. On the sink. She grabbed it and unscrewed the lid. But a weak voice made her come up short.

"Sir, reporting for duty, sir."

She whirled around. Geoff was awake, staring off into space, and, apparently, talking to himself.

She kneeled down by the cot. "Geoff. I'm here. You're safe."

"Sir," he said, "Lieutenant Colonel Geoff Thorne reporting for duty."

Holy crap! He's military! The blood leeched from her face. She cleared her throat, determined to see if she could get more information from him without jeopardizing his health.

"Lieutenant Colonel Geoff Thorne," she said, "what is your serial number and outfit?"

"I am officer 234APW50 of the Galactic Justice Coalition."

What? She had rescued a slagging Coat! And he might die if she didn't get him the right meds. Worse, he might find out about her, uh, colorful line of work and turn her in. Deja chewed her lip, then bent closer to Geoff.

"Shh, you're okay, Geoff. You're safe. Nurse is here. Come back to me."

His eyes wandered and then turned in her direction, finding her face at last. "Nurse?" he ventured.

"Yes. I'm your nurse. What do you need?"

"Th-thirsty," he whispered.

"Here," she raised the water with a straw to his lips, "take a drink." He sucked down a bunch of the liquid. "Hey, hey, not so fast," she coaxed.

"Sorry, Nurse."

"It's okay. How do you feel?"

"Really...cold," Geoff mumbled.

"I'm sure you are. You're running a fever, but I'll take care of you, don't worry." Just then, her PalmStar pinged. She pulled it out of her vest pocket.

Sef: OK, I scored some antibiotics and other supplies. I've given them to Kanicha. But you'll have to meet her over by the courthouse. It's too risky for her to pass through the disputed territory.

Deja: Right. Got it. I'll meet her in three hours. Thanks a bunch. Oh, by the way, I just found out that Geoff is a COALITION officer!

Sef: Really? Well, I knew there was something more to him. He said he was on holiday. So he must not be here in an official capacity.

Deja: I know. But it makes me wonder what to do. I probably should've let you take him to the field hospital. But I thought he'd be more comfortable here. And the field clinic was already strained. Anyway, do you want to contact the GJC about him? Maybe they can do an exfil?

Sef: I'll speak with my superior about it.

Deja: OK, great.

Deja tucked away her PalmStar and looked at her patient. Geoff's breathing was ragged. She hoped she could get the antibiotics plus some other supplies and get back before he got worse. She hated to leave him, though.

"Just rest, Geoff," she told him. "I have to go out for a while. Don't try to move."

"You're leaving?" he muttered, eyes focusing and un-focusing on her face.

"Yes, but I will be back, OK?" she soothed. "Be a good soldier for me."

"OK, Nurse," he said, closing his eyes.

Going to the sink, she splashed water on her face and dried it with a worn-out towel. Her flask beckoned, and she caved, taking another sip. She could use all the liquid courage she could get.

THE SUN HAD GONE DOWN ABOUT twenty minutes ago. The cool air was still moist. The planet's two moons shed some pale light over the city, which was dense with palm trees and other tropical foliage but empty due to the rebellion. Deja squeezed the grip of her blaster again, reassuring herself, as she crept down the street close to the walls of the buildings on the right side. So far, she hadn't spotted any rebels. But they were bound to show up somewhere before she made it to the rendezvous location.

She was passing a deserted shoe shop when she heard a low rattling. The sound of a vehicle of some type. She had just made it to a street that ended in a T-shaped intersection. She peered around the corner and glimpsed a truck loaded with five or six figures, and they weren't police. *Crap!*

The courthouse was in the direction they were going. She'd have to try following them while staying out of sight. Good thing she was excellent at sneaking around. She waited for the truck to move far enough away so the shadows of the evening would hide her. Then she stalked forward, blaster ready just in case.

"*Pssst,*" said a voice from somewhere to her left. She stopped, seeking out the source. There, in a doorway, stood a small figure with bluish skin. The personage motioned for her to come closer. Cautiously, she advanced until she could see better. It was a young, Be'Voyan boy.

"Rip?" she asked in a hushed voice. "What are you doing out here?"

"Yep, that's me. I'm just tryin' to find more water and stuff. What are you doing, Missus?"

Deja saw no reason not to trust the little fella. "I'm heading to the courthouse to meet someone. I need medicine and food. Wanna come along?"

"Nah. I have other kids I need to get back to once I find some water." He pointed down to an empty plastic water jug.

"OK, well, if you want more creds or if you wanna trade for something I've got, you can always look me up later. I'm at the hostel on Fifth and Seventy."

"I know the place," Rip said.

"Good," Deja replied, then thought of something. "Remember the man who bought you all that food?"

"Sure, I remember him. Real nice for an outsider type."

"Well, he was kinda blown up and shot in the attack on the marketplace. I'm tending to him while we wait for the area to be stabilized. So if you want a job finding stuff for me and him, come on over to the hostel, OK?"

"Sounds good," said the child, nodding his head.

"Excellent. I'd be especially thankful if you could find a crutch or bedpan, some disinfectant...and maybe some alcohol." She had found it difficult to help Geoff to the toilet because of his wounds, his broken leg in particular. It would be good if she could locate a crutch or bedpan. And, well, the disinfectant and alcohol went without saying. She felt a pang rattling around in her heart. Perhaps she ought to be able to get by without drinking, but everything was so stressful right now. Wasn't she entitled to a little something to help dull the fear and worry?

Rip smiled. "Got it. See ya 'round." With that, he hefted the empty water jug and walked back the way she had come.

Parting ways with him, she kept to the shadows and advanced toward the courthouse. The pavement beneath her feet was cracked in places, so she picked her way with precision in the moonlight. She was wearing her boots now instead of sandals, so her feet were well protected. But she couldn't risk falling and getting injured or alerting the insurgents of her presence. The truck with the rebels had thankfully turned down a side street, so the path to the courthouse appeared open at the moment. Still, she remained alert.

Somewhere in front of her, she heard a noise like a door shutting. Instantly, she crouched down and hugged the wall of the building to her left. She focused her eyes in the direction of the sound. A pair of armed hostiles emerged from a building with loaded sacks over their shoulders. They were facing away from her, which was fortunate. But they were also going toward the courthouse, which was most *un*fortunate. Debating what to do, Deja decided to sneak up on them and ambush them if possible. Who knew what they could be carrying? She might just find some useful booty.

Quiet as a cat, she advanced toward the duo, one short and stocky Be'Voyan and the other tall and muscular. Both appeared to be males, though she couldn't quite tell from behind in the dim light of the moons. She pulled a throwing knife from her left boot so she had a weapon in each hand.

Once she was quite close, she whispered into the still air, "Halt. Don't make a sound or one of you is dead and the other is hobbled for life."

The two figures stopped, then both tried to look back.

"No. Don't turn around. Freeze," she ordered, creeping closer to the pair. "Good. Now, slowly put down your guns."

"Lady, you are messing with the wrong people. We are the chosen ones," said the stocky male.

"Well, I beg to differ. And *I'm* the one with the knife and the blaster ready to take you out. So don't try anything." Her voice was hard like plasticrete but low in volume. She didn't want anyone else hearing something and sounding an alarm.

Her captives leaned forward, lowering their rifles to the ground, and then straightened up. "Good," Deja said. "Now walk backward two steps. Then down on your knees with your hands behind your head."

They complied. Both of them were wearing black garb—pants and short-sleeved shirts. She slipped up behind them and placed her knife at the base of a major artery in the thickset Be'Voyan's neck. Then she spoke to the other one. "Tall guy, you tie up your friend with those zip ties you're carrying. In front of yourselves is fine. Then zip tie yourself."

"Lady—" the shorter one started to say, until she pressed her knife harder against his skin.

"Don't call me 'lady.' Just do as I say. Or you'll be martyrs for your cause in no time, trust me." She wasn't sure she *would* kill them. But they didn't need to know that. If she had to choose between them or her, she would choose herself. Just like she had during the attack on the marketplace. She gritted her teeth at the memory.

When her captives' hands were zip tied, she holstered her blaster but kept the knife where it was. Although the other guy was bigger, the smaller one was more hotheaded. She pulled a scarf out of the side pocket of her backpack. It would make a perfect gag. In short order, she had stuffed it into the mouth of the more troublesome hostile. That done, she pulled out her blaster again and sheathed the knife, pointing the blaster at the ungagged rebel.

"Big Guy, here's another scarf. Open up." She crammed the scarf into the second one's mouth. Then she ordered the two of them to get to their feet and walk into the nearest open doorway without turning around. She needed to put them in a good hiding spot—and she didn't want them to see her face in the process.

They hadn't gone far into the building before Deja could see what it was: a travel agency of some sort. There were pictures of different locales and various earthbound vehicles, seagoing ships, and spaceships on the walls. She wasn't wearing her LinguaLenses at the moment, but the Be'Voyan writing on the main wall had a character that meant "Go" and another that meant "anywhere" or something to that effect. Without much ado, she found a narrow door to what was probably a supply closet. "Open the door, Big Guy," she ordered. He pulled open the door and, voila, a supply closet. Perfect. It had a tall shelving unit filled with office supplies at the back and a rolling caddy with cleaning supplies against another wall. "Both of you get in there and *do not* attempt to look at my face."

"*Mmphooo,*" the shorter one mumbled in protest.

"Quiet," she barked. When they were standing side by side in the small closet, she said, "Now kneel again." Once they'd done so, she adjusted her blaster to stun and shot both of them. They flopped forward, unconscious. "Sorry, fellas. Can't have you freeing yourselves *too* quickly." Then she stepped back and closed and locked the door. For good measure, she wedged a chair underneath the doorknob. *There. That oughta do it.*

Adjusting her backpack over her shoulder, she proceeded to the entrance on quiet feet, then peered out. Nobody there. And the sacks of loot and the guns were still lying on the ground.

With no further time to spare, she scooped up the bags and guns and hurried on her way. The courthouse was just seven minutes away. She arrived and, to her great relief, found Kanicha waiting inside the front doors. "Hey, Kanicha!"

"Deja," she replied, relieved. They embraced. The slender Be'Voyan woman tried to smile, just barely showing the gap between her teeth. "Here are the meds you needed. And here is some food, including some broth cubes and gelled fruit. Might be easier for the Coalition officer to eat."

"Thanks," Deja said, her heart brimming with gratitude. "Tell Maizie I said hello."

"Of course," Kanicha promised. "What do you have in those bags you're carrying?"

"Good question. I, uh, 'liberated' them from their liberators," Deja said with a laugh. "Let's take a look."

Together, they searched through the bags for useful items. They found more food, some pre-loaded CredChips, some sterling-silver and gold jewelry, some data pads, some ammo, and various other items.

"Nice," Deja observed. "Here you take this stuff. I'll take the rest. Oh, has Sef managed to contact the GJC?"

"Yes. But they say they cannot do an exfil until the rebellion is put down. Could be a few days."

Deja cursed but attempted to smile again. "OK, I better get going. Be careful."

"Will do," the other woman said, adding, "What you did to save that man was brave. He's lucky you were here."

Deja managed a real smile. "Thanks. Goodbye for now." She turned and left the way she came. She made quick work of sneaking home, keeping to the shadows of buildings. She encountered a platoon of city police officers, who asked her a few questions. They let her go after she showed them her correspondence with Officer Doljang on her PalmStar. Anyhow, she didn't come across anymore rebels. *Whew,* she thought, entering the hostel. *Now let's just hope these meds kick that infection in the butt.*

GEOFF STARTLED AWAKE. Panic gripped him when he looked around and could not find Nurse.

Unable to move much, he couldn't tell if she'd taken all her stuff. He knew she'd had to venture out before to secure extra food and supplies. Maybe that's what she was up to. His whole body was drenched in sweat. And his head was still throbbing and his body felt floaty and sluggish at the same time.

Still, he forced himself to remain awake, despite the pain. Finally, about thirty minutes later, his rescuer trudged back in, a worn pack on her back, two guns over one shoulder, and a bulging sack over the other.

"You should be asleep," she scolded, putting down her load and kneeling by the makeshift bed.

"Nurse," he sighed. "You came back. You stayed."

"Whoa, don't get teary eyed. Heavens, I didn't know Coats were so weepy." She winked at him.

He gave her a goofy smile. He hadn't known his eyes were misting up. Must be the drugs.

"Sorry. I'm just glad you came back, Nurse." He had uttered the last word with a light caress, then closed his eyes.

"Actually, it's Deja. My name's Deja Ortega," she said softly.

"Deja," he repeated, opening his eyes. "Why did you save me?" he wondered aloud. "And how did you know I'm with the Coalition?"

"Well, I saw you buy that boy, Rip, a bunch of meat pies and stuff."

"Oh."

"Yeah. I knew you had to be a good man," she said in a quiet voice.

"I try." He swallowed painfully. His face was already flushed, which was good because he would've blushed a little.

"More than try. You *do*," she declared. "As for the Coalition, you rattled off your serial number and rank while in the grips of this fever, which is why I had to go out in the first place."

"Oh?" he said again.

"Yep. Got some antibiotics with the help of a mutual friend, Officer Doljang. I'm afraid the GJC won't be extracting you for another few days, though. So you're stuck with me."

"Somehow that doesn't seem like a terrible thing," he said, smiling.

"Haha," she replied. "Just remember that when I try to start your IV. I haven't practiced this in a long, long time."

"Don't worry, I can take it."

"I'm sure you can, soldier. But I'll try to make it as painless as possible." It took her three tries, but she got a line in. Geoff didn't flinch; he was used to needles. Then she started him on the antibiotics. He found he was amused as she created a holder for the IV bag from a metal hanger she found in the closet. She pulled the hanger out of shape until the wires were more-or-less parallel and then bent one end. Hammering the bent end into the wall, Deja hooked the bag to the other end. That would let gravity do the work. She also injected more pain meds. *Now* that's *nice*, he thought, trying to figure out how to keep her talking. He wanted to know more about her. So far she seemed...brave and kind, not to mention feisty and funny. All qualities he admired in someone.

"Deja...tell me more about you. You know what I do. What's your occupation?"

He almost cursed when he saw her grow pale. *Crud! What did I say wrong?*

"Let's just say I'm a...Jane of All Trades, yes?"

"Don't worry," he said before she could protest further. "If you think I'd rat you out after what you did for me, you can think again."

"You say that now, but—"

"No, I mean it. Just level with me. Please?" Geoff asked, forehead crinkling.

"OK, then, if it means that much to you." She sighed. "I used to be part of a traveling troupe of space carnies. But then an explosion on our ship killed most of my troupe, including my mother. It wasn't an accident." A shadow seemed to fall over her face as she said this, and he cursed himself.

"I'm sorry. What a wretched thing to happen," he said.

"Anyhow, without a ship or a troupe, I was kind of lost for a while. Until I landed on being an oddsbreaker. Yep, that's right. I'm a crazy, lowly oddsbreaker."

Geoff raised his eyebrows, thinking something else entirely. "Not lowly at all," he scoffed. "You have more guts than some of the soldiers I've worked with. And crazy, well, who isn't these days?" He smirked, trying to make her grin.

She stifled a chuckle. "There now, enough talking for today. You need some rest."

"Yes, Nurse." Geoff let his feverish eyes close at last. He had been saved by an oddsbreaker of all things while on vacation during a local holy war! *It sure beats Mom and Dad's origin story*, he mused. In no time, he drifted off to sleep, thinking of a time when he might introduce a girl like Deja to his parents.

LATER THAT NIGHT, Geoff was roused from sleep by a knock on the door. He forced his eyes open and saw Deja sitting on a chair to the side of the door. She didn't look alarmed at the sound, which was a good sign. Still, his hand reached for his blaster, which Deja had given back to him. He leveled it at the door. Deja also got out her blaster and held it ready.

"Who's there?" she called.

"Just me. Rip," came the answer.

Deja stood and eased the door open. The small Be'Voyan boy stood outside the door, holding a bulging pillowcase in his hands.

"Come on in, Rip," Deja invited. The child trundled in with his sack and put it down on the floor.

"Gotcha some good stuff," he said.

"Show us what you found," Deja invited.

Geoff, still too weak from the infection and his wounds, didn't try to rise from the cot, but he turned his head so he could watch.

Rip started unpacking the bag. He took out some protein bars, jerky, bread, icewine, disinfectant, blankets, a bedpan, and other assorted items. Heat flushed over Geoff's neck and face when he saw the bedpan. True, he'd been having some trouble getting to the toilet. But he was darned if he was going to resort to a bedpan! He decided to hold his peace until the kid left.

"Well done, Rip," Deja said. "What do you want for all of it?"

"I figure Đ120 should be good," the youngster said. "And I'll take some of that fruit you've got."

"It's a deal," Deja said, before Geoff could offer to pay. She took out her wallet and fished around for some CredChips. Handing them over, she said, "Pick out what you want."

"Thanks, missus," said the youngster, who took the CredChip then busied himself with choosing some fruit.

"Good job," Geoff told him.

Rip looked up. "No problem," he said. "Now you listen to the missus here and get better quick, yeah?"

Geoff chuckled. "Consider it done." He saluted the boy.

"Well, I'll be off now." Rip stood and left, shutting the door behind him.

Geoff said, "It's a shame that kid is on the streets. I'll have to see what I can do about that once I get back on my feet."

Deja focused her green eyes on his face, then brushed back a lock of black hair. "You know, I bet you will do something about that. It's admirable."

"Thank you, Nurse. Is that why you like me?" Geoff asked with a subtle grin.

"Oh, I didn't say I liked you," Deja corrected, cocking her head playfully.

"Ah. I stand corrected. Or I lay corrected, to be precise," he joked. "On a serious matter, though, I have to say that I am *not* using that bedpan."

The young woman pursed her lips. "Really? Then you best be using *these*." At that, she opened the door, leaned out, and retrieved something he couldn't see. Turning around, she presented him with a pair of actual crutches.

"Nice," he said, laughing. "Courtesy of Rip, I take it?"

"Yes. He left them outside the door as instructed. I just wanted to see your face when we presented you with the bedpan."

"Well, you've had your fun," he said. "Now please give me those crutches and go outside for a bit. I've gotta attend to some business."

"Aye, aye, sir," she replied, handing him the items and turning to leave. He did so like to watch her going—and coming.

THREE DAYS LATER, Deja kneeled by Geoff as he lay on the cot. "Now let me look at those sutures again," she said. With care, she raised his shirt and removed the bandage. "Excellent. No redness or puffiness anymore. Looks like you're healing just fine. It's a good thing I scored those antibiotics for you. Otherwise I would've had to force feed you some moldy bread."

"Ugh," he said, and meant it. He knew she had done him a great service, not just by saving his life in the first place, but by keeping him alive. But he would take IV antibiotics any day over moldy bread, having had to eat some of that to survive on one of his many missions.

"Let me check your arm now," she said. She looked at it carefully, and he remained quiet, wondering what else to say. He had seen her sneaking drinks from her flask all too often. But he didn't want to pry. *Besides, nobody's perfect.*

"Your bullet wound looks quite good, too," she announced. Moving the blanket, she revealed his bare legs and pressed down on his injured leg gently. He felt proud that he didn't wince. "The bone is mending nicely as well. Now for dinner and a nap. And don't give me any trouble," she cautioned, wagging her finger at him.

"Never, Nurse. I promise. Only, answer me this, what's it gonna take for me to see you again after this is all over?"

Deja paused, pressing her lips together. "How's this," she said. "Exciting dare. Slim odds. Good food."

"Oh, is that all?" he asked. "Whew. Here I thought I might need to get myself blown up again."

She laughed. "No, I would advise against that. Strongly."

"Very well, if you insist."

"I do. Now, how about we have some dinner before your buddies show up to take you off this rock?" Deja said.

"Sounds good. I'm famished." Geoff grinned widely and sat up slowly, swinging his legs carefully over the edge of the cot. "What are we having?"

"I'm thinking we break out the good stuff: jerky, yogurt, and nuts I've been saving."

"*That's* the good stuff?"

"Hey, what do you expect? A six-course meal?" she asked, pretending to be miffed.

"I'm teasing, of course. I've eaten more freeze-dried food than you can imagine. So it's all good."

"Well then, I'll get it set up," she replied.

"Now," he said conspiratorially, "there's just the matter of when you'll let me take you out for a *real* dinner."

"Right," she said, heat flushing her face. "We'll just have to see when the odds are in your favor."

Geoff smiled. With any luck, this would *not* be their last supper.

Eight months later...

Standing in her room aboard the Blythrian Space Station, Deja moved over to her favorite spot—the large viewing pane. Outside and far away, a nebula's molten colors bathed Deja Ortega in ripples of green, gold, and scarlet light. The swirls of beauty in space lulled her like the beating of a heart—or an excellent box of cherry cordials. Either way, the brilliant nebula made her want to stand there forever, forehead pillowed on the arm she'd pressed above the viewing pane.

But the nebula didn't need to make a living; she most definitely *did.* For all the time she had been crisscrossing the galaxy, taking dares and breaking the odds, she had never been this close to raising the money she needed to buy her father's freedom. She didn't often spend time in this luxurious cabin that an old carnie friend had set aside for her. That was fortunate, really. Too much of this would turn her into a gurzzlefop, soft and lazy. Sighing, she wriggled her toes in the plush, indigo carpet and straightened, ending her quiet vigil.

"Lights to eighty percent intensity," she ordered.

"Right away," responded Theodian, the cabin's automated butler. "Would you care for refreshment?"

"No, Theo."

"Perhaps a cup of hot rubarlo nectar?" asked the smooth, synthesized male voice.

"Just lights for now."

"So noted." Theo's tone was sulky for a computer. But she ignored it.

Settling into an armchair that conformed to her body, she took her time choosing which dare she would accept out of the many that were jamming up her PalmStar's inbox.

Let's see...

Hitchhiking from the Old Earth all the way to the Roxatorn System in just ten galactic weeks. Been there, done that. (And, yes, she'd always kept a trusty towel nearby during that trip.) Compete in a staring contest with a six-eyed Mawthraadite without dozing off—or worse, being hypnotized into acting like a spastic paruboru monkey or something. Interesting, but nothing she was in the mood for. If memory served, the first ambassadors of the Earth-Mars Alliance to visit the Mawthraadite home world returned to their ship on all fours, convinced they were domesticated buzlas. Deja shook her head and kept skimming.

Oh, how about streaking at a *live* match of Yukalorian wrestling—during mating season? For a mere ten thousand dorems? Not bloody likely. Might as well inscribe herself with a bunch of dotted lines, showing the Yukalorians how best to carve her up into hors d'oeuvres for the spectators. She'd need more than a paltry Đ10,000 to make it worth her while. And, well, public nudity wasn't her style. No doubt somebody wanted to get a gander at Deja in her birthday suit. This somebody underestimated just how hungry and inhospitable the Yukalorians were at a wrestling match, never mind during mating season.

Rolling her eyes, Deja raked the fingers of her other hand through her short hair. Wait a second. Now here was something interesting. The darebacker must have read her dossier.

Dear LuckGoddess,

I'm a galactic food writer with a dream. A magnificent, glorious dream—to dupe the galaxy's snootiest foodies in one of the choicest cooking contests anywhere. I dare you to enter the 30th Ultimate Chef of the Galaxy Contest on Vinadro.

Masquerading as a master chef may not sound all that disagreeable or difficult to one as talented as yourself. But—here's the rub—you'll have to use a very... unfortunate ingredient in all of your dishes. If this has failed to stir your competitive juices, how does Đ500,000 strike you?

In addition, Đ2,000,000 is yours if your concoctions outwit the gourmands to survive the elimination round wherein 5,000 chefs are reduced to a mere 50. Place in the top 15 at this gastric gala and win my undying worship—as well as another Đ2,000,000. Yours truly will cover the entry fee, travel, fake ID, and wardrobe.

If you blow your cover—or the judges' digestive systems—don't expect a second payday. That will be the least of your concerns, I think. Perhaps you've heard the rumors of how the Vinadroans treat those who violate the sanctity of food? Well, maybe it's best you didn't. Besides, don't oddsbreakers like yourself crave danger like Orooguphs crave blubber-and-seaweed casseroles?

As a longtime fan of yours, I dare to hope that you'll help me achieve my worthy aspirations. If interested, message me within seven Standard Galactic Days.

Yours Truly,

Famous Foodie

Deja read through the dare twice before looking up from the ice-blue screen of her PalmStar. She stared across the cabin, trying to compute the thought of 4.5 million dorems let alone half a million just for entering the contest. Moreover, Đ500,000 combined with what she already had would *almost* be enough to free her papá. In comparison, the total amount could also serve as down payment on a decent condo on Mars or another agreeable planet in the Milky Way. Thoughts of settling down were, ironically, unsettling. Deja shuddered and let her hands fall into her lap.

With 4.5 million dorems and the money she already had, she could buy her papá's freedom and then some. After well over two years of brutal living in debtors' prison, her father could be his own man again, for better or worse. (Probably worse, her mother would have argued if she were still alive.) Deja felt a tingle in her heart, imagining her father emerging from prison.

And thanks to him, she just might have a shot at winning. Her dad was an amazing chef. While Deja was growing up, her dad had learned new recipes in every port, teaching his daughter along the way. Naturally, Deja's mother didn't always approve of these cooking lessons. After all, the ship and troupe earned their keep by performing, not cooking.

Taking a deep breath, Deja realized she'd been grinding her teeth. She didn't like thinking of her mamá much, not after Esmira and the others died in the explosion onboard their ship. Hands fisted, she remembered how (of all things) her sweet tooth had saved her. "Papá, let's go out for a late-night snack, pleeeeease?"

Of course, Esmira *had* left her daughter some things that were tough to forget: the same startling green eyes, a similar talent for performances, and a stellar streak of bull-headedness. Despite such parallels, everyone in the troupe knew she was a daddy's girl, and her mother hadn't ever been keen on sharing the spotlight. And whenever Esmira caught Deja or Patricio playing games of chance, the fights were almost fierce enough to power a nuclear reactor.

For a moment, nothing roused Deja from her memories. Then she happened to glance at her phantom reflection in the powered-down holopanel. Some of her curls were sticking out at absurd angles.

With an effort, Deja shoved the uncomfortable thoughts about her future out of the proverbial airlock. Hungering for the bigger payoff too much could make her overeager—weak. So, enough of this lolling about in luxury. She had some research to do on this "Famous Foodie." But first she'd take a long bath.

"Theo, run me a bath at one-hundred-five degrees Fahrenheit. Five percent sassaflower scent; fifteen percent kallum milk; and eighty percent filtered water."

"My pleasure," drawled the resonant male voice.

"Tell me, how long until the next hyper-space ship is due to dock?" she asked, bringing her thoughts back to business.

"Long enough," Theo assured, "to give yourself a suitable soak and reconsider the ill-advised decision upon which you seem determined."

"Right. And that bad decision would be...?" A flicker of wariness flashed through her. Her computerized butler better not have tried hacking into her PalmStar. Artificial intelligence was over-rated. It was, after all, artificial—even more so when applied to the male mindset. Alas.

"Why, ending your stay prematurely, of course," Theodian said in doleful tones. "We here on the Blythrian Space Station live to pamper our clients, whether they think they deserve it or not. So we do what we must, else we fail to make the stars a friendlier place to visit. Surely you deserve to stay the two remaining days of your booking?"

During this appeal, Deja made no reply. Instead, she padded over to the sunken tub in the deluxe, in-cabin lavatory and removed her clothes. The floor panel over the tub slid back as the hot, pearlescent liquid began to flow. The steam's inviting fragrance hinted at captured sunbeams on a tropical beach. She slid into the bath with delight, intending to stay only a half hour.

An hour or so later, Deja emerged from her bath and wrapped her body in a self-heating robe. She took a seat and scooped up her PalmStar. Now to see if this Famous Foodie fellow checked out. She'd heard a lot of rumors, of course. But now she needed more information.

After prowling the G-Net and its counterpart, the Sub-Net, for some time, Deja was rather confident that this Famous Foodie persona had existed about two decades prior to contacting her and, supposedly, had no orange or red flags. Quite an accumulation of silver and black ones, though. Many of them for some rather amusing infractions. For instance, inciting the Frank Fracas, a food fight over imported Frankfurters on some planet in the Beta System. Or producing evidence that precipitated YeastCease, an explosive audit of the InterGalactic Yeast Farm Guild. Undercover reporting on an omelet racketeering ring for the illegal poaching of jumbo pegoruu eggs. Supposed financial support of the illegal strike among Tri-Solar Cheese workers. Alleged orchestration of the Rubarlo Riot, a simultaneous, illegal jettison of overpriced rubarlo nectar from space cruisers in six solar systems. And that was just a smattering of his run-ins with the law. Interestingly, his colorful rap sheet was posted for all to see on his Spicenet blog. That is, if the blogger was, indeed, the real Famous Foodie.

Deja sighed. The Ultimate Chef of the Galaxy Contest was a huge affair. She had to be sure the exposure would be worth the risk. And that meant she needed more reliable information from an unimpeachable source. And if she was being honest with herself, her best source was an officer in the Galactic Justice Coalition itself.

Ah, Lieutenant Colonel Geoff Thorne. What a valiant officer. Handsome, gutsy but prudent, and above all, a reputable man. True, she had other sources. But none were as...enticing as he was. It was a pity he was too good for her. Her past was littered with all sorts of illegal deeds. And, well, she had other flaws that didn't bear dwelling on too closely. Her eyes strayed over to the mini bar on the other side of her room. As usual, the bar never stayed stocked for long when she was on board. And she could use the drink dispenser whenever she wanted.

Just four months ago, she had agreed to meet Geoff and go on a real date. Actually, a series of dates over the period of five days. It went well. Too well. He even gave her a gift—a brand new pair of

LinguaLenses. But when he hinted at a more committed relationship on their final night, she had demurred and changed the subject.

Clearing her throat, Deja fidgeted with the tie on her robe and straightened in her chair. It just wouldn't do to dwell on Geoff as a love interest. She needed to contact him as a business associate. She'd already learned that Famous Foodie was voraciously active in galactic food affairs. And yet he didn't strike her as a malevolent troublemaker. No, more like a mischievous crusader who sported a ridiculous fascination with food. His exploits stirred a mirthful, if wary, admiration in Deja.

Sure, she might blow this dare and wind up washing dishes in one of Vinadro's infamous citywide kitchens. And *that's* if they went easy on her. But what she stood to lose outweighed what she just *might* win. Last she knew, her father was still okay. Although his sanity and health had dwindled somewhat, his liberty wouldn't ever be a lost cause if she had anything to say about it. One day she'd buy his way out and set him up to live somewhere in peace. Then maybe she'd think about what other things might be waiting for her.

Opening a message window to Lt. Col. Geoff Thorne, she typed out a quick message.

Deja: Hi Geoff. I need a little help on a dare. Care to help me with your extensive knowledge of the galaxy's criminal underbelly? Come on, you know you want to!

Okay, so maybe that wasn't the most businesslike message. But it would catch Geoff's attention. Deja put down her PalmStar and went to her closet. After some thought, she picked out a soft, yellow dress with a blue sash around the middle.

Ding. Deja jumped a little. She hadn't expected such a quick reply. And she tried to convince herself that the rapid beating of her heart had nothing to do with the prospect of talking to Geoff again. She tied the sash and then hurried over to her bed. Picking up the PalmStar, she read his reply and answered with her own.

Geoff: Deja! And here I thought that I might not ever hear from you again. And now you need my help, huh?

Deja: Sorry not to be in touch. My last dare was quite...preparation intensive. But I have a new dare that has me worried. I know you'll be able to help. Please?

Geoff: Well, you used the magic word. Brief me.

Deja: I've got a potential dare backer named Famous Foodie. I've learned all I can about his past, but I sense that something is missing. I hoped you could fill in the blanks.

Geoff: Sure. I'll see what I can do. I should be able to dig up his full rap sheet for you.

Deja: Perfect. You always know how to treat a lady.

Geoff: Yes, and I could treat her even better if she'd actually agree to go out with me again.

Deja paused, trying not to fidget with her sash. *What to say, what to say!*

Deja: I suppose I can't argue with that.

Geoff: Brilliant. I'll get to work and contact you when I've got what you need. And then you and I will set a date for that date, yes?

Deja: Agreed. Now run along and get me that rap sheet.

Geoff: Ha. Very well. As you command.

Sighing, Deja put down her PalmStar, a wave of nausea threatening to engulf her stomach. She had just agreed to another date. How could she do that to Geoff? She would never be good enough for him, and yet she couldn't help that she wanted him, too. Oh, what a mess. She needed some chocolate and a fair amount of gehut.

Retying her sash for no reason, Deja left her room in search of her favorite indulgences.

Patricio Ortega dipped a long wooden spoon into a huge pot of simmering soup in the galley of the prison where he had been incarcerated for bad debts. He hadn't prepared the soup himself, because he'd just started his kitchen shift. Thus, he was about to taste the concoction to see how much help it needed. It was a poultry-and-noodle soup with dumplings. By the fragrance alone, he could tell it needed more veggies and additional seasoning.

Patricio, a human in his mid-fifties, wore a black apron over his brown prison jumpsuit. The jumpsuit sort of blended into his brown skin. He had black hair that was getting long and a scruffy beard because it was no easy feat to get shaving or haircutting supplies in prison. He had a wide nose set off with brown eyes and a broad forehead. He'd never been much of a "looker" as some might say. But his daughter sure had turned out pretty. That was Esmira's doing, of course.

He resisted the urge to pull out the small photo of his wife that he kept in his pocket. Staring at it would do him no good, especially when he was trying to focus on cooking. She'd been gone almost four years now—murdered by an unknown bomber who killed most of the carnie troupe in one horrific explosion. He had Deja to thank for avoiding that fate. But he hadn't done his daughter any favors by devolving into a degenerate gambler after Esmira's death.

Enough of such thoughts, he scolded himself.

After stirring the soup a bit more, he pulled the wooden spoon out to get a taste of the dish. What he saw startled him. There, on the spoon, was an entire chicken foot—with a plastic ring still attached around the leg!

"Gross! *Eso es malo*," he exclaimed aloud. When most of the kitchen crew looked in his direction, he plucked the chicken foot from the spoon and held up the offending ingredient so they could get a glimpse.

Then he tossed it in the bin. The sad thing was that he'd seen *much* worse in his time here at the prison on Gredlar. How long had he been here? Hmm. About two years. Too long.

"Stempe," Patricio called out, "who prepared this *sopa horrible*?"

Looking up from his station, the human male said, "Who knows. Not me, though. I'm just pitting these torran peaches for the warden's dessert." Over time, the kitchen crew had become accustomed to Patricio's leadership. Some were somewhat resentful that he had risen to the top so quickly, like cream on fresh milk. But hey, when you've got it, you've got it. On the positive side, a few of the kitchen crew liked him and were eager to learn. Stempe was not one of those, however. No matter; Patricio loved to teach his craft. It reminded him of precious moments with his daughter onboard their spaceship.

Before he turned his attention back to the soup, he noticed Stempe stashing some peach pits in his jumpsuit's pockets. "What are you doing, Stempe? Why aren't you tossing those peach stones?"

The sandy-haired man looked at him and narrowed his brown eyes. "What's it to you?"

"Just answer the question, *por favor*." He couldn't let this slide or who knew what else the guy might try.

Stempe shrugged, pocketing another peach pit. "Just gonna sell 'em. They'll be ground up and used in a body scrub for those that likes to be extra clean."

Well, that was a little odd. After all, most inmates didn't care too much about hygiene. But certain prisoners *did* have some strange proclivities. So, really, he wasn't too concerned. "*Todo bien*," he said simply, then called out to the Orinkk at the end of the counter: "Jamm, what you got cooking?"

The porcine alien looked up. "Oh, just some cornbread to go with the soup. *Bien?*"

"*Sí. Gracias.*" At least someone here had a little good taste. Of course, they had to use pre-ground cornmeal. And it wasn't that high in quality. But they were lucky to have anything besides wheat flour.

"*De nada*," said Jamm, who went back to mixing the batter. His pinkish skin and piggish features lent him a disarming demeanor. His hands had four fingers and one opposable thumb, each with thick, almost hoof-like nails. His legs were constructed a lot like the back legs on swine from Old Earth. Unlike such pigs, though, he had no tail of any sort. Like most of his kind, he refused to eat pork at all. Some Orinkks still had the unfortunate tradition of dining on their deceased loved ones. *Blah, cannibalism!* Of course, food and the act of eating were fraught with all sorts of ramifications, as Patricio knew better than most: politics; religion, identity, sexuality, psychology, physiology, and so on.

He went over to the spice rack and grabbed a few jars. Then he picked up the salt grinder as well and headed back to the stove. Just as he reached the pot, another prisoner came through the swinging door pushing a trolley of supplies.

"*Hola*, Patricio," said Gisgor the Pintrel. He had black fur all over, except on his hands, and a bearish face, with short claws on his paw-like hands and bare feet. "I come bearing gifts from the warden who wants something special, *pronto*, for him and his guards."

"Another special order for *el jefe*? Why am I not surprised?" Patricio answered.

Gisgor chuckled and came to a stop in front of Patricio. "Here are the goodies. Hopefully, you'll be able to find something to satisfy the boss."

With practiced ease, Patricio began to catalog the contents of the shipment. *Let's see*...fresh garlic and cilantro, tomatillos, tomatoes, onions, various peppers, cheese, eggs, ortoo steak, and so on. Then he saw the bag of *masa harina*.

Excelente. Now he could make semi-fresh corn tortillas. A simple but delicious recipe came to mind: *chiliaquiles rojos*.

He shook his head, wishing he had enough ingredients for the inmates, too. But that would never happen. This prison didn't coddle its incarcerated individuals. No, they were put to work on all sorts of projects outside and inside the prison. They were supposed to be working off their debt. But that was practically impossible given how little they were paid. Hence, he was lucky he had someone on the outside who was saving up bribe money on his behalf. A prickle of guilt settled in his throat, however, when he thought of Deja working as an oddsbreaker because of him. She had only 'fessed up to her new line of work just recently when he asked her how she was making so much money.

He coughed, trying to clear the prickling sensation, then looked back up at Gisgor. "*Muy bien.* Help me with the soup, yes? Then I'll work on the special order." If he prepared some stellar *chiliaquiles rojos*, the warden *might* just let him send another letter to Deja this week instead of several months from now.

"They want *chiliaquiles* again?" Patricio asked Jamm. The Orinkk nodded then pointed to the loaded cart he'd just brought in.

"Here's everything they ordered in special. Should be what you need. Can I help?"

"*Bueno.* Sure, you can *ayudame,*" he replied.

"Us too," piped up Gisgor and his buddy, a reedy-looking, highly tattooed human named Jase. Stempe was there also, but he didn't even bother looking over at everyone else. Just as well. The guy was surly and hard to manage. So was the amphibious Zoox named Ribell who liked to hang out with Stempe. The two of them were talking to each other in the corner of the kitchen. Plotting something to make more money, no doubt. Oh, well.

"Okay," Patricio said. "Gisgor and Jase, make enough chicken stock for the warden and the guards, then start on the salsa. Jamm and I will begin making the corn tortillas."

"Right on," said Gisgor. He and Jase started preparations for making some nice broth. He trusted them enough not to screw it up. Patricio grabbed the *masa harina* from the cart while Jamm took out some large bowls and measuring cups. Patricio didn't need to measure anymore, but Jamm still needed some assistance in that area.

Patricio poured part of the cornmeal into his bowl and then went to get some warm water to mix it with. Jamm did likewise, only he used the measuring cups to pour out a specific amount of flour and to collect some water.

"*Recuerda*, let your fingers decide if the mix is too dry or too wet, *sí?*" Patricio prompted.

"*Sí, señor*," his kitchen mate answered.

So they both worked the water into the flour until they had dough. Then they began kneading it. The texture was grainy at first but became smoother as time progressed. Patricio decided to add a touch more water to his. He tested Jamm's batch, and it was fine. In no time, the dough was ready to be rolled into balls and pressed into tortillas.

"Start rolling the dough into balls," Patricio ordered. "I'll get the tortilla press and parchment paper."

"Okey dokey," said Jamm, humming to himself.

Just as Patricio reached the equipment cabinet, he heard a loud grinding, buzzing sound.

"*¡Ay, caramba!*" he exclaimed, turning around to look for the source of the sound. Stempe stood by the blender trying to grind something *extremely* hard in Patricio's *extremely* nice blender. "What are you doing?" he demanded. Jamm, Gisgor, and Jase all turned to watch the argument unfold.

"None of your business," replied Ribell, puffing out his throat in challenge.

"Oh, I say it is. That blender is *nuevo*. Stempe, what are you chopping up?"

Stempe glared at him, as did his friend. "Just some peach stones."

"Peach stones? Heavens! *¿Por qué razón?*"

"If you must know, I'm crushing them to make some face cream. *¿Recuerdo?* Now beat it," Stempe growled.

"Yeah, mind your own business," Ribell chimed in.

Patricio ground his teeth. "*Esta es mi cocina.* What you are doing *is* my business," Patricio yelled over the horrific sound of the blender. "Stop!"

Stempe punched the off button then turned to face Patricio fully.

"OK, but you'll have to explain to Yeltzin why I don't have his product ready for him." Yeltzin, the lead huckster and smuggler in the prison for over a decade, was a major player. Crossing him wouldn't be too smart. Patricio clenched his fists. Did he want to have to explain to the warden why a new piece of equipment might be ruined? Or did he want to explain to the violent smuggler that he couldn't have his crushed peach pits? All things considered, he had a stronger rapport with Warden Tock than he did with Yeltzin.

"Fine," he relented. "Just don't make it a habit. And next time, *ask first.*"

Stempe nodded tersely, but a smile played on his lips. He knew he'd won without really even trying.

"*Harumph.*" Patricio turned back to the equipment cabinet to grab the wooden tortilla press. The loud grinding resumed. One of these days, Patricio was going to have to stand up to Yeltzin. It was strange that anyone in the prison wanted an exfoliating cream, of all things. It made him wonder... Bah. He just hoped they weren't up to something stupider than what they'd admitted to doing.

$\wp$

Patricio returned from the bathroom to find Stempe hovering over the tomato bisque he'd been preparing for Warden Tock and his crew.

"Hey, what are you doing?" he asked, his tone sharp. He glimpsed Stempe stuffing something into his jumpsuit pocket before the other man stepped back, away from the pot.

"Just stirring your stupid soup so it wouldn't burn," Stempe retorted, turning away.

"Wait," Patricio commanded. "What's that in your pocket?"

"Nothing," said the other man. "Right, Ribell?" The Zoox stood behind Stempe.

"Yeah, it's nothing," said the Zoox, voice low and hostile.

"I'll be the judge of that in *mi cocina*," Patricio said.

"Fine, big man," said Stempe, taking out a paper envelope. "It was just some thickening agent I bought. I thought the soup was a little thin."

Yeah, right. Patricio never made his bisque too thin. "That sounds a little *thin* to me, Stempe. Let me see the envelope."

"Sure, knock yourself out." Stempe walked forward and handed over the item.

At that moment, Patricio noticed that none of "his" people were in the kitchen. Where had they gone? Cautiously, he brought the envelope up to his nose and took a whiff. Immediately, he smelled a bitter odor, almost like almonds. The smell was odd.

He stepped over to the pot of bisque and sniffed it too. He could sense the same aroma, only stronger. Oh, dear. Not good. Something stirred in his memory.

"¡*Veneno!*" he declared, shaking the envelope in Stempe's face.

"What's that even mean?" Stempe yelled back.

"It's poison! You poisoned the soup with cyanide from those peach pits you wanted so much!"

"*Estas loco,*" Stempe laughed.

"Really? Well, we have plenty of soup to test for poison, don't we?"

The other inmate, who had forty pounds on him, took a swing at Patricio. The blow connected with his face, and pain exploded in his jaw. He brought up his arm to fend off another blow and tried to yell "guard!" but the Zoox beared down on him, landing a blow to his stomach. All the air whooshed out of him, and he doubled over. He'd been in some brawls in his day, but he was outmatched, and he knew it. He danced backward, preparing to yell again when something hit his head from behind. And that was all he remembered.

THE MUSCULAR, six-foot-three Lieutenant Colonel Geoff Thorne continued waiting to speak with his CO. He resisted the nervous urge to run fingers over his brown hair, which was cropped in a short, military style. His eyes focused on his Coalition field-op data unit, looking through various bulletins.

"Lt. Col. Thorne, he's ready for you," chimed the receptionist, brushing back a few strands of—what would you call them?—hair feathers.

It's not like she can fly with those feathers, he thought. *And they're on her head. So they're hair. Sort of.* The sleek orange feathers sprouting from her head marked her as a Ractyl from the Gunth System.

Geoff Thorne was already standing, but he took a moment to straighten his dress uniform and slide his Coalition data pad into his pocket. His body chose this moment to remember that even he, a trained black-ops officer, ought to be nervous. Super slaggin' nervous. His heart surged into high gear. If this meeting didn't go well, he could be facing citations, demotions, a hundred laps around the training compound, and then, oh, wrestling with a poisonous beast or two.

"Thanks," he told the feathery woman, striding toward the office of his CO. She smiled and preened as he passed, but he gave her only a quick nod. A different woman was on his mind and, well, in his heart. Deja Ortega. Her future, and maybe even *their* future together, was in jeopardy here.

You will *win this one*, he told himself.

Simple, right? All he had to do was sell his CO on a covert mission to catch one of the galaxy's most violent food activists by letting Geoff enter a ridiculously expensive cooking contest as the sous chef for a non-combatant who just happened to be an oddsbreaker on the wrong side of the law—and who just happened to be *the* one that his heart desired. He'd known his heart was hers not long after she, a stranger, had rescued him following an explosion and gunfire. Now, Geoff hoped to make sure Deja would survive this dare —and that Famous Foodie wouldn't get away.

As Geoff opened the wooden office door, he saw his CO, General

Rex Trikk, behind his desk, standing, as always. General Trikk rarely sat or laid down. He did most everything standing up, including sleeping. His desk had, in fact, been special ordered to accommodate this.

If he were human, this would all be quite fantastical. Yet Trikk was Rekloran, so he was more like a saber-toothed, bipedal reptile than a human. No one could forget Trikk's favorite mantra: *Live standing or die sitting.* That is, no *soldier* on active duty could ever forget it after Trikk had caught him or her sitting on the job. Hence the reason Geoff had been standing, not sitting, in the reception area.

General Trikk looked up and flicked out his long, greenish tongue, casting for pheromone cues to Geoff's state of mind. Combat training kicking in, Geoff's heart slowed and his body relaxed. Hopefully, he hadn't just lit up an "I AM BLOODY NERVOUS" sign for his CO. He stood at attention and waited for the general to address him. The Rekloran blinked and the tip of his forked tongue traced all two inches of his right fang.

Uh, oh. Right fang action. Not good, not good.

Geoff stood unmoving, though, refusing to react.

"At eassse, lieutenant colonel. For now," hissed Trikk, who always hissed at random times; you just never knew whether he was mildly pleased or downright angry. Hissing and intimidating: two things Reklorans did well. And Trikk was marvelous at both. Geoff moved his legs out a bit and clasped his hands behind his back, still keeping his mouth shut.

"I have read your proposal, Thhhorne. Tell me, is this Deja Ortega your lovemate?"

Crap. A trick question really. He wasn't sure. The answer depended on whether Deja was even communicating with him and if she was feeling only somewhat scared of commitment or holy-heck-we-can't-ever-meet-again scared of commitment. So Geoff went for a compromise: "Yes, when she feels like it, we are, sir."

His CO nodded, the light playing over his copper-scaled skin. "I thought so. And how sure are you that this oddsbreaker will cooperate? What if we do not help her father?"

"Sir, if we don't help her father, her only motivation will be to avoid angering the GJC. And, to be honest, she's not too afraid of doing so, as you can see by her record. She'd just cut and run." He resisted the urge to add that extracting her wounded parent from that barbaric prison was the most ethical thing to do. Results, not ethics, mattered more at the moment.

Trikk flicked his tongue, then nodded. "And you would stake your future on her cooking skills? You would stake your *career* on the chance that Famous Foodie is truly the backer for this dare?"

"Yes and yes, sir. Ms. Ortega's cooking is beyond delicious. And it is likely that Famous Foodie won't be able to resist the chance to personally witness Ms. Ortega wreaking havoc at the largest and most pompous cooking contest in the known galaxy." Geoff swallowed and waited, squeezing his hands behind his back.

"And what did you tell your...when-she-feels-like-it lovemate about the foodie's killings?"

"Nothing, sir. She knows only the rumors and the Class B and C infractions." And Geoff sorely regretted not telling her the whole truth. But, well, the Class A information was classified. Famous Foodie was far and away more lethal (and unstable) than he had told Deja. He felt itchy just thinking about what he hadn't told her.

Yet, if he *had* told her, she might have passed on the dare, which meant he would once again be waiting for *her* to contact *him*. If she ever did again. And her father would most likely die in the prison's shoddy medical bay. Oh, and Geoff would also lose his chance to catch a vicious, food-crazed criminal. Yeah, he couldn't exactly forget *that* astronomical, career-enhancing opportunity. Still, he'd rather "catch" Deja once and for all than catch the bad guy. If only she would let... Geoff cursed himself. *Stay focused.*

"Very well," Trikk said, picking up his own Coalition data unit, tapping the onscreen keyboard with one black claw. "I will discuss your plan with Marshal Hart and the high council. If they approve it but you *fail*, you will become a missserable cadet. I will see to that." The alien's vertical pupils expanded, punctuating the seriousness of that last promise.

"Yes, sir. Thank you, sir." Geoff waited to be dismissed.

"But, Lieutenant Colonel Thorne," the general added softly, "spend your time writing, not waiting. Tell me exactly *how* you met this woman and *why* you failed to mention her until now."

Gulp.

"Yes, of course, sir."

Trikk nodded sharply. At that, Geoff turned on his heel and strode from the room, a fierce hope tugging at the corners of his mouth. This time when his heartbeat picked up, it was with the anticipation of seeing Deja once more. Maybe this time she'd finally and truly stop running; maybe she'd let him love her. If, that is, she didn't strangle him when he butted into her dare. And if Famous Foodie didn't kill them both. Ah, so much to look forward to!

♀

BACK IN HIS OFFICE, Geoff let his thoughts drift to when he first met Deja Ortega. Okay, not "met." That wasn't the right word.

There Geoff was, on a vacation, not a mission, and he almost got turned into hamburger. The galaxy must have a sense of humor. And, clearly, the intel about that planet's governmental stability was woefully flawed. He *harrumphed*, mostly out of habit. After all, if he hadn't made such an unlucky choice, he wouldn't have become so lucky in love.

He thought again about the circumstances of their meeting. Several days had passed before the police had contained the citywide rebellion. All the while, this woman had tended to him, cleaning and stitching his shrapnel and bullet wounds, setting his broken bone, giving him painkillers and antibiotics, feeding him, and helping him get to the toilet. If he'd been any less injured, he would've felt as embarrassed as could be. As it was, this woman became his lifeline.

He knew she thought herself beneath him, but that made him sad. To him, she was feisty and funny, brave and beautiful.

With as much objectivity as he could muster, Geoff got down to typing up the whole experience on Be'Voya as well as his and Deja's reunion a few months later. He strove to write the Be'Voya incident like a militaristic report—as if an op had gone bad and he was describing the fallout. Hence, he tried and failed to make the entire report devoid of subjective feelings and thoughts. *Argh. This is tough.*

But it didn't matter. What happened had happened, and he wouldn't change it for the world or even the galaxy. However, he did leave out a few tidbits that were rather personal and, well, weren't anybody's business but his and Deja's. When he finished, night had already come and gone. He stood up from his desk and stretched. He went to the drink dispenser and ordered some coffee, black. He itched to contact Deja, but he had to wait until he got the final word from his commanders. Patience was key. He was patient. Usually.

Sitting at his desk again, he sipped his coffee and reviewed his report once more. The statement was sound. Ready. He held his breath a moment and said a prayer as his parents had taught him. Then he sent the missive off to General Trikk. He knew he wouldn't be able to rest until he received his orders on this matter.

So once he had donned a fresh uniform, off he went to the mess hall. Even this early, it was busy with officers and enlisted members. A few people waved hello or voiced greetings. He almost didn't notice, though. He was thinking of the last time he'd seen Deja.

In the early evening, they'd been sitting outdoor at a café in Paris, France, on New Earth. She sipped at some rubarlo nectar spiked with gehut while he enjoyed black coffee.

"Tell me, Deja, have you given thought to my question?" Geoff asked at the time. He'd asked if she would date him exclusively, but she had demurred and refused to give him an answer. This was their last night in Paris, and he hoped to coax her into agreeing to his request once and for all.

"Oh, Geoff." She frowned. "I...you don't know what you're

asking. I am—I'm not ready. There are...things about me that you don't know," she finished, looking down at her drink. He reached out and tried to take her hand, but she pulled back.

He sighed, placing his hands around his coffee mug again. "Deja, you're right that I don't know everything about you. But I *want to*. Is that really so astounding to you?"

"I'm sorry, Geoff. Truly." She licked her lips, then took another drink.

"Okay," Geoff said heavily. "Just know that I will never stop asking, *mi corazón*."

Deja blinked her green eyes at him, then said, "My dear, you are too sweet, as usual. Why don't we go take a stroll by the river?" So that's what they had done.

Geoff snapped back to the present, brooding. As he ate some scrambled eggs and a side of plimber porridge, Geoff wondered what Deja was doing at this exact moment. He wished her well. And he wished her his.

O pening a message window to Famous Foodie on her PalmStar, Deja tapped out a quick greeting on the keyboard. "Considering your dare," she typed. "Let's chat." With any luck, he would be online. She was about to go find some lunch when she heard the beep.

Famous_Foodie: Excellent. How soon can you arrive in the Wannavak System?

LuckGoddess: Depends. As they say—all talk and no creds can't keep an oddsbreaker fed.

Famous_Foodie: Check your CredChum account. I think you'll find the funds awaiting your acceptance as of this moment.

Pausing, Deja toggled over to her CredChum account and logged in to find that Famous Foodie was as good as his word. All Ð500,000 had been dumped into her virtual holding account. Her blood surged a little faster as she punched in her acceptance code. Later, she'd be sure to transfer it to one of her permanent accounts.

LuckGoddess: Creds check out. I'm in. How about we get cooking?

Famous_Foodie: My pleasure. Catch a flight to Vinadro's capital, Remla. At The Atomic Meatball in the lower east side, order a batch of their signature

dish and a side of fried oyuchen with extra sauce and a lemotte twister.

LuckGoddess: No problem. Just don't expect me to eat it too.

Famous_Foodie: Indeed. That would require an entirely new dare, wouldn't it?

Chuckling, Deja pushed back some of her damp, black hair. This guy, she could work with. Whether she could actually pull off the dare itself was something that remained to be seen. Still, she hadn't nosed around her father's galley for years without learning some serious culinary skills.

LuckGoddess: Will I be creating my own recipes?

Famous_Foodie: Yes; anything you like. But keep in mind that the special ingredient is non-negotiable and will require some…creativity to disguise.

LuckGoddess: Done. And what is this ingredient?

Famous_Foodie: Never fear, it will be included in your "care package" at the diner.

LuckGoddess: And my alias?

Famous_Foodie: Also awaiting you at the diner. You will be a middle-aged chef. That's all you need to know for now. I just need your measurements for some chef jackets.

Nodding to herself, Deja spoke aloud to Theo without looking up from her PalmStar. "Theo, I'll have that nectar now. Double strength with a shot of gehut."

"Excellent choice, Ms. Ortega. Allow me fifteen seconds to prepare your beverage."

Meanwhile, Deja speculated to herself. What could this ingredient be? Something weird, maybe disgusting. The bile or snot of an alien perhaps? The larvae of an odious insect? Some sort of pungent, fermented meat? Well, whatever it might be, she would just have to blast her way through that obstacle when she came to it.

LuckGoddess: Not giving me much prep time, I see.

Famous_Foodie: Didn't think you'd want to compromise that thinks-on-her-feet rep of yours. Besides, Vinadro's food markets are second to none.

LuckGoddess: Fair enough. I plan to be second to none in this little cookoff. I'll contact you when I arrive. I'll send my measurements shortly.

"Your nectar is ready," Theo announced.

Flinging down her nigh-indestructible PalmStar, Deja walked over to the beverage bay to get her drink. "Excellent." She lifted the cup of chilled liquid then took a sip and found it satisfactory. Tilting her head, she downed the remainder in two gulps. The drink scorched an icy path from her throat to her stomach. Deja Ortega never started a dare without a stiff drink and a warm bath. Now she'd done both, and it was time to get on the trail of a new adventure with all its blazing promise and atomic meatballs.

TURNING toward the wardrobe to gather her possessions, Deja said, "Theo, notify me when the ship is on final approach to the hyper-travel hub."

"But, Ms. Ortega," he protested, "you have a full day and a half more aboard our station. This time is non-transferable, and it would be a pity for—"

"Enough," she said, retrieving her black duffel bag and setting it on her cushy bed. "If you want to be useful, you can confirm my flight to Vinadro. First class. Under Rolina Hoffler."

The cabin's automated butler paused longer than was necessary. She didn't take the bait. Theo could pout as long as he obeyed her; and he would. One just had to know how to deal with AI personalities. Opening the duffel, Deja rummaged around. Hmm. She wanted a preppy-punk tourist look. In a few seconds, she'd selected several items: a rectangular, silver-toned box of cosmetics, a plastic pouch filled with tiny, colored pills; comfortable, stay-put underthings; a wig of curly blue tresses; a loose, long-sleeved, scarlet blouse; black knee trousers; calf-hugging black boots; and, most importantly, her lucky vest.

"Searching for your flight, Miss Ortega," Theo replied at last.

"Thank you," she said reflexively, her long fingers opening the pack of colorful pills. Selecting one the color of cinnamon, she popped it in her mouth. Swallowing it, Deja soon felt a familiar pressure behind her eyes. She counted to sixty. There, now she was brown-eyed. Disrobing, she began to dress. For a flitting moment, she worried that her workouts hadn't offset all the indulgent dining she'd done on board the station. When her trousers buttoned with just a tad more effort than usual, Deja exhaled in relief. Then she picked up the wig and cosmetic kit and went to the full-length mirror.

Theo spoke up just as she began adjusting the wig. "Miss Ortega, your first-class flight itinerary has been confirmed. Departure in four Standard Galactic Hours. The *Comet Chaser LV* will dock at Outer Ring Station in one SGH."

"Excellent, Theo," Deja said, opening her cosmetics case. Now it was time to indulge in one of her favorite pursuits: the art of disguise. Within moments, she'd applied a fake but convincing tattoo on her cheek: an emblem depicting a turquoise planet speared by a plume of orange-red flame. Most everyone would recognize it as the logo for the Afterburners, a popular, though dead, space punk band. Then she obscured her eyebrows altogether, as was the space-punker style, using two self-adhesive strips of simulated skin. Yet more custom prosthetics reshaped her unique nose and rounded the square of her chin. Foundation went on after that. Still in the groove, she mixed some color into her mascara, painting her long eyelashes turquoise. Her eyelids she painted light gold. A rosy blush and plum-tinted lipstick finished off her makeup. Her earlobes and wrists she adorned with matching ovals of polished blue stones set in gold. She nodded at her transformed self in the mirror and walked back to the bed where her lucky vest awaited. She put it on and fastened it, feeling more secure and confident.

Several hours later, she sat in an upholstered chair aboard a lighted cabin on a hyper-jump space cruiser. The climate for this particular cabin was calibrated to fit Class H life forms, so she didn't even need an oxygen mask or enviro-suit. And, rather than sleep the trip away in stasis, she would use the time to become an expert about the Ultimate Chef of the Galaxy Contest, past and present. A longtime fan, she had seen many of the competitions. But to prepare more fully, she would need to study everything: previous judges, competitors, critics, scandals, grudges, and, of course, the gastronomical conquests and catastrophes.

Well, she *would* just as soon as she did something about the oh-so-ingratiating fellow sitting next to her, intent on drawing her into conversation. Lukas Inciardi was a human and about thirty-five or forty years older than she. His skin was light and his features aristocratic in their own way. His short brown hair was carefully cut and combed. A trimmed moustache perched on his upper lip. And she was sure that his dark-blue suit had been tailored just for him.

Currently, the man was eating a rather elaborate dinner that consisted of several courses. She shuddered to think how much it had cost, especially on a space cruiser. He often commented on each component as if he were judging for a rapt audience. Sure, it made her hungry. But she had opted for the much more affordable meal—a hot sandwich, fried trists, and (of course) some icewine.

For the second time, her seatmate offered to share his meal with her, and she politely declined. When Inciardi finished, he wiped his mouth and smoothed his moustache. Then he tried to strike up a conversation. Again.

"Ever seen one of these," he asked, showing her a length of golden metal in his hand. It twinkled with a few gems of varying colors. At one end it narrowed into a point, but it didn't seem to be a writing implement. Despite herself, Deja was curious.

"Nope," she said.

"Well, it's a toothpick equipped with these delightful nanobots that scour one's mouth clean. It leaves one's mouth fresh without the hassle of brushing or flossing. This gadget leaves me quite ready for anything." He smiled and glanced down at her lips suggestively.

"Right. How wonderful for you," she said flatly. This guy didn't need much encouragement.

The man merely started using the toothpick. When he finished, he put the implement in a pocket and remarked lazily, "Well, I do suppose that I pamper myself too much these days. But I like to share when I can. In fact, I have a sleeping compartment onboard ship that you are welcome to share with me if you haven't one of your own."

At this, Deja was ready to stab the guy with his precious toothpick. Restraining herself, she thought up a plan. Turning to meet his gaze, she said, a bit too loud, "Really? You'd share your sleeping compartment with a total stranger?"

"Of course," he replied, smiling again. "I will always strive to help any ladies in distress."

"How very kind," she said a little more loudly and winked at him. People were already looking in their direction. Perfect. Then she summoned an android steward who was walking by.

"Yes, Miss Hoffler?" asked the flight attendant, all chrome and efficiency.

"Ah, there you are. You heard Inciardi here. My fellow passenger noticed a frail, elderly human female in cargo class—row 820A—and he would very much like to share his sleeping compartment with her. Can you make the arrangements, please?"

Nearby, passengers were now alert, watching with interest. This dashing traveler wanted to share his first-class digs with an even older lady? Her suave seatmate began to redden as he realized what slim choices lay before him. Ultimately, he chose wisely, and Deja had a much quieter seatmate for the rest of the journey. Besides, she had her own small sleeping compartment, thank you very much. And she could study in there just as well as she could study out in the seating area.

At one point, Deja paused to consider why she had been so annoyed by the man. After all, he hadn't been excessively rude or tried to manhandle her in any way. An image of Geoff popped into her head. Maybe, just maybe she reacted as she had because she thought of herself as, well, taken. But that couldn't be. Not really. As much as she wanted to be the woman Geoff deserved, she knew she would always fall short.

With a yawn, Deja went back to studying, then eating, then sleeping until the ship reached its destination. She already knew most of the contest's rules. For instance, if you had four arms, you'd have less time to cook than someone with two. And you couldn't cook any animal with an intelligence rating higher than a four—so no eating of fellow contestants, of course. This was a *civilized* spectacle after all.

Before the space cruiser docked in Remla, the industrious Deja had a workable idea of what to expect at the gastric gala. As she left the black-hulled spacecraft, Deja caught the eye of her talkative seatmate. He certainly looked more tired than he ought to, what with his own personal sleeping compartment. She giggled a little inwardly. As she passed by, he just raised one slender hand and gave her a little salute.

The open-air vehicle in which Deja rode allowed her every opportunity to enjoy the city, its people, and the oxygen-rich atmosphere. Twenty-five percent oxygen. What a treat. Breathing in another lungful, Deja appreciated the buzz of wellbeing it brought. But, at some point, she ought to use nose filters to limit her oxygen intake. Otherwise she'd wreck all the excruciating days she'd spent conditioning her lungs to survive on the barest amounts of the precious gas.

Playing the part for which she'd dressed—a naive tourist—Deja let her gaze roam with obvious enthusiasm. Before long, she decided this planet was more fanatical about food and eating than any other place she'd been. She'd watched quite a few seasons of Ultimate Chef of the Galaxy. But the little vignettes they showed about the planet just didn't do it justice. All things epicurean held sway as the planet's favorite pastime and religion all blended into one. The architecture alone testified as much.

All along the route she traveled, edifices bore food-inspired moldings, murals, and signs. To her amusement, she soon saw that many of the structures were shaped like food itself. Here, a bakery impersonating a three-tiered cake of some sort. There, a church resembling a gigantic, gilded egg. Across the street, a cheese monger shop modeled after a tremendous wheel of aged cheese. And over yonder what seemed to be a school masquerading as some sort of pomegranate-like fruit.

Her stomach gurgled as she sniffed the air, catching scents so enticing she almost stopped the cab right then to find some grub. Scores of pushcarts beckoned, the peddlers' tasty wares ranging from soups of unknowable origins and skewered edibles she'd never seen before to flatbreads stuffed with curious combinations and frozen sweets she longed to try. Of course, Deja couldn't read the ideographic language on the pushcarts or the shop windows, but the prominent displays of edibles spoke quite well enough. Other street vendors peddled non-food items: synthetic and hand-woven fabrics and showy trinkets; sculpted figurines and games, many of them edible; holographic paintings and maps; and one-of-a-kind dinnerware that, strangely, looked just like the dishes being sold by another hustler on the next corner.

Lofty of height and solid in girth, the locals themselves also drew her attention, though the city had its fair share of non-natives, too. All the photos and videos she'd viewed in her research hadn't quite captured their complexions of dusky blue, bright yellow, soft green, and many other shades. A downy layer of fur the same hue as their respective skin tones covered their powerful legs. Weight balanced chiefly on the balls of their feet, they seemed to trot rather than walk, swinging their long arms as they went. The Vinadroans' knees were complex condyloid synovial joints like hers. Yet their ankles, formed by hock joints, were hinged the opposite way. None of the locals wore shoes; their taloned feet had no use for such protection. Somewhat less-intimidating talons tipped the three fingers and opposable thumb on each hand. Thank heavens handshakes weren't a normal mode of greeting here.

The females couldn't be called dainty by any means, but they didn't carry the same bulk and height as their male counterparts. However, the women had distinct assets of their own, what with having breasts in triplicate. Both genders, though, had a crest of hair that traveled from their heads, down the sides of their necks. Similar hair graced each eyebrow. Broad foreheads and elongated faces seemed to radiate an alertness and genial warmth. Of course, the fangs protruding at the corners of their bluish lips negated that geniality somewhat. And their noses, resplendent in their bigness, left no doubt as to why they were renowned for their olfactory aptitude.

With a sideways glance, she studied the shock of graying white hair atop her driver's head. Would it feel more on the wooly side or the silky side? The driver swiveled his large, oval-shaped ears in her direction, expecting her to say something perhaps. The outer edges of his ears looked crimped like the crust of a pie. Small hoops pierced the entire length of his left ear, like many of the adult males she saw. For women, large jeweled hoops were popular as earrings in both ears.

Deja wasn't surprised in the least to see that their clothes often bore stylized images of burgeoning orchards, fields, flocks, and so forth. Women favored wraparound skirts cut just above the knee, flaunting their plump lower legs. Men were more inclined towards snug ankle trousers. Male youngsters scuffled about in knee breaches, and the girls wore ruffled petal skirts for the most part. Only the children, incidentally, took all that much notice of Deja as she passed by on her way to the Atomic Meatball. Her driver, she realized, had been humming to himself the entire time but had made no attempt to talk with her.

But she didn't have more time to study him because the vehicle slowed to a halt in front of the most enormous meatball she had ever seen. Or, at least, a restaurant that *looked* like a gargantuan sphere of meaty goodness with a lighted sign flashing THE ATOMIC MEATBALL: DINER AND MUSEUM. Delicious smells of spiced meatballs, battered edibles, and other enticing but unfamiliar fare wafted to her from where she was positioned outside the restaurant.

"Here we are, lass. Lovely, isn't it?" her driver asked.

The translator chip behind her ear made his words intelligible. Staring at the absurdly realistic meatball, she almost didn't avoid a bout of laughter. "Oh, yes," she breathed, "and a more breathtaking meatball I have yet to see."

The Vinadroan paused as his own translator chip converted her words. "It's a start," he said. "Just be sure you don't miss the Old Quarter. My little ones is always pestering me to take them over there. You'd think they'd never had a dish of iced belasino in their lives."

Handing him her CredChip, she thanked him. He held it up to the payscanner then returned it to her. She slid the door open and stepped out onto the walkway, studying the remarkable texture of the diner's exterior. It had to have been molded and then painted by airbrush. The craftsmanship involved sobered her—but only a little. After all, it *was* a giant *meatball*.

Her driver hefted her bag from the trunk then handed it over. In response to her thanks, he scratched at one of his eyebrows and bid her farewell. "Bounteous table to you," he said, striding back to his vehicle and zooming off. Strolling into the eatery, Deja wasted no time placing her "order" as directed by Famous Foodie. The cashier, somewhat short for his race, eyed her and called his manager over. The manager, a white-haired beauty with a slight limp, wore a dark-green apron emblazoned with the restaurant's name in scarlet thread.

"Come along then," the woman instructed, her voice husky and deep yet feminine all the same. She took Deja up several floors to a back room—a storage area for the museum, the oddsbreaker decided. Water dripped with a steady rhythm into a sink with a mottled copper basin. Strange contraptions, stacks of old holophotos, and a dusty scale model of the restaurant occupied the room. Ragtag tables, legless chairs, and faded décor peaked out from beneath retired tablecloths. But she focused on a sizable crate covered with a green tarp. That must be what she'd come for. Her instincts proved true when her guide pulled off the heavy tarp with one fluid yank.

"Do as you will, my dear," said the middle-aged Vinadroan, gesturing toward a crowbar leaning against the crate. Deja thanked her. The woman blinked and smiled, showing more of her fangs, and pointed to a comm button near the door. "Press this when you're finished. I'll have your supplies delivered to your destination of choice."

"Got it," she replied, and the manager left.

Stashing her duffel beneath the sink, Deja shoved her sleeves past her elbows. What she found in this crate might give her the means to buy her father's freedom. *If* she knew how to make the judges like eating whatever dreadful thing Famous Foodie had seen fit to inflict upon them. Deja got to work loosening the crate's lid. With a creaking sound, the lid popped off at last. Peering inside, Deja surveyed the containers and parcels and a small data pad all stacked with precision. Regrettably, the contents lay nestled amidst a multitude of spongy packing nuggets. The bothersome nuggets would be sure to scatter all over the place. Oh, well, she'd just have to slip the restaurant's owner a pre-loaded CredChip to compensate for the mess.

Retrieving the data pad, she slid the power button to the on position. The gadget, about the size of her PalmStar and only a few millimeters thick, blinked to life.

Dear Oddsbreaker,

Before you are the makings of a challenging dare. Among the items within this package are custom-made chef uniforms, and, yes, the all-important mystery ingredient. Observe the see-through plastic containers. Care to guess the contents?

Deja did just that, taking a few seconds to clear away some of the blasted packing nuggets to get a glimpse of the plastic containers. The box on top had a greenish, wet-looking material inside. The one below that contained a brown powder. Several others were buried deeper down where she couldn't see them. No vile insects or atrocious bodily fluids. So far. *What in the galaxy....?* Picking up the featherlight data pad again, she scrolled down to the next few lines.

What you have here are some lovely samples of calcium bentonite and calcium montmorillonite from some of my favorite planets. Put more simply: I have given you dirt. And your task is to make the judges eat dirt and *like* it. One judge in particular deserves it, believe me. Should you run out of soil, I'll have your supply restocked within the day. Luck be with you.

Yours,

F.F.

Laughter escaped Deja's lips before she'd had half a second to consider her situation. Chuckling to herself and shaking her head, Deja couldn't help but admire Famous Foodie's taste in public humiliation. Sure, a few cultures adored eating various types of soil. On Old Earth, this practice was called geophagy. But most people did *not* like eating dirt. And in most cases, telling someone to "eat dirt" was still an insult.

Opening one of the square boxes, Deja pinched off a bit of what she now knew to be a damp, greenish clay. The soft clay felt smooth beneath her fingers, and it had the fragrance of a forest after a rain with a hint of tang. Popping it in her mouth, she had the instant reflex to spit the stuff back out. It coated her entire mouth all at once. A woody chalkiness enveloped her tongue, and she found it somewhat challenging to swallow. But, hey, at least it wasn't alien poop, right?

Still... her stomach grumbled with more than simple indignation at the odd snack. Why would her backer be willing to ante up such a huge sum just for the chance to embarrass all the foodies lording over this cooking event? Why hadn't he decided to muddy the culinary waters himself? Then again, this guy seemed to operate from the shadows, orchestrating food fights from the sidelines.

She shrugged. Perhaps this was Famous Foodie's way to avoid becoming too famous for his own good. Besides, the odds *were* still against her, as always. Even without the stupid dirt, she might not even make it past the first round. For her father's sake, though, Deja Ortega hoped to break the odds once more.

With that goal in mind, she began to unpack and open all the other cases of dirt. No sense in avoiding a complete taste test. Either she tasted them now or she wouldn't know what other ingredients to buy that could disguise the distinctive soil types. After sampling six other pinches of soil, both moist and powdered, Deja took another few swallows of water from the sink. Rinsing out her mouth again, she spit into the discolored copper basin. Okay, so she could've been stuck with much worse. Still, she found herself wishing for a few weeks, not a few days, to create suitable dishes. The chefs against whom she'd be competing had spent months, if not years, perfecting their own dishes. Never mind; she couldn't change that. And so, after locating one of her chef smocks and her contestant badge, she repacked the crate, already busy concocting recipes in her head.

Moments later, she'd set up her travel mirror on the ledge above the freestanding sink. First, she stripped down to her underwear, then she removed the synthetic skin and scrubbed off all her makeup. The bio stats linked to her fake contestant ID indicated she would be impersonating a human female in her early fifties. Although anti-aging treatments were rather effective these days, she decided to create a more un-tampered look.

Rifling through her duffel, she pulled out a kit with some scissors and tubes of red and gray hair dye. With quick snips of the scissors and a careful highlighting job, Deja created a hairdo that swept back from her face in controlled waves of silver-kissed auburn. Tweezing her eyebrows into suitable arches, she dyed them to match her hair.

Then she set to work on rounding out her features, even sculpting in more padding beneath her chin and jaw line. After some debate, she decided to change the shape of her nose. Adding age lines to her skin proved simple enough thanks to the marvelous weathering balm she'd picked up several months ago. (Well, not so much "picked up" as absconded with. But, hey, if a backer reneged on a bet, she found other ways to recoup her losses.) Then she inked in some moles, including a smallish one above her left eyebrow. Searching through various capsules and powders, she took a two-toned pill that would turn one eye violet and the other blue. A subtle fashion statement for a respectable chef like herself.

When the pressure let up behind her eyeballs and her vision cleared, she swallowed something else: tiny biocircuitry discs and the pain blockers she would need to tolerate what they would do to her larynx. Deja studied herself in the mirror. No sense in wasting good pain blockers on just one major alteration. On this planet, the females had three breasts apiece. The least she could do was magnify her twosome a cup size or so. She'd already planned on this when she sent Famous her measurements anyway.

Holding her hand steady, she administered several injections in her breast tissue. Injections that normally had some dreaded side effects. But aren't side effects always dreadful? For the most part, she escaped the body aches that made decompression sickness seem blissful. But she felt nauseous enough that she had to lay unmoving on the carpeted floor long enough to make her impatient. The worst pain and dizziness gone, Deja used collagen stimulants on her hands, feet, and face to help give the appearance of a little extra weight. Then, because every bit of disguise helped, she created dimples in her cheeks with a different subcutaneous formula.

When she was able to stand on her own power again, she got dressed. Donning a pair of pleated black pants with upturned white cuffs, she wrestled with the clasp. Great. She'd have to watch how much sampling she did while experimenting in the kitchen. After pulling on a breathable camisole, she reached for her vest, pleased that the chef's jacket would easily conceal it. No bra yet; the tenderness in her mammary tissues made her wince at the thought. The expandable fabric of her vest would do well enough for now. A pair of no-fuss shoes with square toes completed her ensemble; they were roomier than her other shoes anyway, so they fit her plumped feet. The makeup she applied was restrained, except for the luscious shade of coral lip tint.

Packing up her supplies, she made a mental note to buy more role-appropriate clothes and restock her supply of pain blockers. As she reached to close her bag, though, her hand went instead to a padded, inner pocket. Hesitating a moment, she opened it anyway. Thoughts of Geoff ignited as she slid out the pair of slim LinguaLenses he had given her. Why shouldn't she wear them? Her old ones wouldn't do; too scruffy looking to suit the sleek chef she played. Besides, her translator chip only worked with vocalized language, and she had no idea how to read Vinadroan, which was more prevalent here than Common.

Slender and gold-rimmed, the glasses seemed fragile, which was deceptive. The shatterproof lenses were a somewhat rounded, rectangular shape, just right for her facial structure. Adjustable in color and tint, the lenses would give her an advantage that she couldn't pass up. Faint scrollwork ran along the outside of the temple pieces, which contained the small power supply and wiring. A smile reached her lips as she read the inscription Geoff had chosen for inside the left temple piece: "Exciting dare. Slim odds. Good food."

A few months after Deja's daring rescue of the unconscious lieutenant colonel, Geoff had surprised her with this pair of high-end LinguaLenses. She remembered the kiss she had given him in return and flushed. Naturally, he hadn't needed a translation for *that*. Yet even now, Deja cursed herself for getting involved with a man who was not only out of her league but also most certainly out of his mind for pursuing her. Scowling to herself, she put the lenses on anyhow. Such thoughts would just distract her. And right now, Deja, or rather, Chef EvaLynn Dubois, needed to do a little grocery shopping. Grabbing her flask, she took a few drinks and put it inside her vest. She'd refill it at the market.

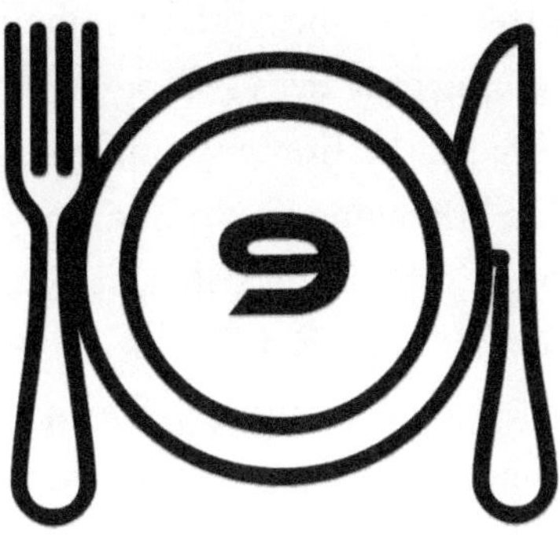

Deja's spirits lightened a little as she prowled the expansive marketplace. Rented hovercart in tow, she selected all manner of foodstuffs and seasonings, some of which she had only heard about. One section of the marketplace housed a collection of brightly colored, striped pavilions; another section included stalls with permanent roofs; yet another area seemed dedicated to pushcarts with shaded awnings. The proprietors were of many races and sexes, including a good number of Vinadroans of course. The beings with whom she did business noted her chef's attire and contestant badge and did all they could to be of service. This they did whether they had two eyes apiece or eight, two legs or eight tentacles, and any mixture of skin, fur, scales, spikes, and whatnot. The merchandise itself was as fresh and plentiful as she could have wanted. They had everything from the choicest of meats to the purest of spices and ripest of fruits and vegetables—and other things in between.

At ease in this crowded environment, she kept a sharp eye out for fellow competitors. She wasn't the sole contender doing some shopping. Not by a long shot. But they ignored her, and she pretended to do likewise. An oddsbreaker never knew what details about her foes could tip the odds in her favor.

The unspoken code of non-fraternization among contestants held true—up until the moment she set her sights upon a lone basket of red hixote peppers, possibly her favorite peppers of all time. As she made haste to claim the prize, she noted a female competitor with a rounded face and piercing gray eyes sidling up to the same pushcart. In her mid-sixties perhaps, the human female bore all the marks of a serious chef. The main one being that of irritating arrogance—or so it seemed to Deja anyway. The impeccable, starched chef's jacket she wore identified her rival as Chef R. Glass.

Each of the women placed a possessive hand on the basket of coveted vegetables, though Deja's reached it first. Years of preparing food had left Chef Glass's hands and forearms with scars from burns and cuts that, pointedly, hadn't been erased with derma-regeneration. Thinning, silver-blonde hair slicked back into a tight bun, Chef Glass raised her eyebrows at Deja with a disapproving glare. Naturally, Deja stared right back.

The other woman's sous chef, a thin fellow with long, black hair and a sun-like birthmark on his cheek, said nothing. With the creases on his face and hints of salt-and-pepper in his hair, Chef T. Rin was older than Deja by quite a bit, yet younger than his boss.

The pushcart's owner, a bald, male Vinadroan who had his back to them, whirled around after the two women had converged on the ill-fated produce. He rumbled a laugh, showing considerable fangs as he smiled over the rivalry. The mottled green of his skin reminded her of striped watermelons back home.

Deja spoke first. "My apologies, Chef Glass, but I seem to have beaten you to them."

"How much for these?" the woman demanded of the vendor, ignoring Deja's remark.

"Seems like your translator chip isn't working, chef. These are mine."

Straightening and tugging at the cuffs of her immaculate jacket, Chef Glass sniffed with disdain. "I see," she said, looking Deja up and down like an inferior cut of meat. "I suppose you think your culinary credentials outclass mine then, Chef Dubois?"

Now *that* wasn't anything like Deja had anticipated. Clearly, she should've read up on the city's marketplace customs a bit more. But, in full bluff mode, she answered back. "Credentials? I thought we were shopping for peppers. And as it so happens, I laid first claim to them." Shifting her attention to the hulking form of the proprietor standing behind the cart, Deja held out her CredChip. But he didn't move to take it. Not good. Behind Chef Glass, her sous chef just shook his head. What was Deja missing?

"Respected chef," the green-skinned Vinadroan said to Deja, "I believe your colleague here is correct. In matters such as this, we sellers are obliged to award the most honored chef with the disputed merchandise." As his words were translated by her chip, Deja forced her expression to remain impassive.

But Chef Glass nodded in approval and unclipped her badge, which she handed to the produce monger. "Excellent. I cannot stand this woman's prattling much longer."

A passing urge to engage in some colorful "prattling" seized Deja. After a pause, she offered her ID. "Fine. Compare our credentials, by all means. I don't intend to quarrel endlessly about this bloke's *peppers*." She quirked her lips at the owner in a suggestive smile.

"Not that I wouldn't enjoy your continued presence, but I do have to abide by the code," he said. If she was reading Vinadroan body language right, the way he tugged at his ear suggested a little ribald amusement. Running their IDs through his computer, he said, "It's no mystery we love our food. So naturally we make a mystery out of everything else. No reason to be embarrassed, Chef Dubois. One moment here." He paused, studying the digital readout behind the counter. His eyes flickered in her direction but then settled on the other woman. "Looks like Chef Glass is entitled to this produce."

"Indeed," agreed the woman, snatching her ID back from the seller.

"Thank you," mustered Chef Rin, who had the same gray eyes as his employer. He lowered his gaze when Chef Glass frowned at him.

"Must you always try to get involved in everything?" she asked him.

Sheesh. What a "fun" boss, Deja thought.

Then the vendor spoke. "Naturally, I'll have to add a surcharge for running your ID, Chef Glass. New regulation. Ninety-five kips."

"Ah, a pity," Deja observed, accepting her own ID.

"You needn't worry so," the other woman retorted. "A few kips are nothing." Turning to the Vinadroan, she handed him her CredChip and said, "Please use the premium thermawrap to keep them chilled."

The vendor processed the payment and began wrapping up the purchase. He wasn't about to give up on another sale, however. "Chef Dubois, I have these other, sweeter-tasting peppers here, if you please. Yellow xintabelles," he said, tapping the produce in question. "Or I can send over some hixotes from my shipment in the morning."

Deja opened her mouth to accept the latter option...

"Thanks, friend, but that won't be necessary," said a voice on the deep end of sexy. The newcomer spoke in Common, so she didn't have to wait for her translator to kick in.

Geoff? Pivoting on her heel to face the speaker, Deja attempted to block out the disbelief that hit her stomach like a pint of malted yeegerwomp. Attempted and failed. She *never* should've contacted the officer about Famous Foodie's run-ins with the law.

"Didn't you get my message, Chef Dubois?" he continued. "I already picked out some hixotes for you myself."

If it weren't for the subtle hand signal he'd flashed as she turned around, she wouldn't have been sure of his identity. Voices could be duplicated, as she well knew. Yet both of them had learned a standard form of sign language—him as a Coalition officer and her in all her travels.

But how could Lieutenant Colonel Geoff Thorne be *here?* And looking so different that only the voice was unmistakably his. He stood there smiling in a sous chef jacket, sporting a number of uncharacteristic features, like not being human.

Somehow, he'd morphed into an albino-skinned, Evuutan male. As such, his head, devoid of his thick brown hair, now boasted row after row of raised bone running perpendicular to his face. Intricate tattoos detailing the history of his (newfound) birth clan laid claim to the areas between these crests of bone and down the sides of his head past where his ears should have been. His ears of course, had been "relocated" according to Evuutan physiology: marquis-shaped apertures near his left and right temples. His eyes were still blue, but, my, how large they seemed.

The lower half of his face was more muzzle than anything else; nose rather flat and nostrils sitting almost flush against his skin. Other narrow crests of bone encircled his neck and arms like fearsome bracelets, the skin between decorated with yet more tattoos. Oh, and this incarnation of Geoff had developed a slight paunch, unheard of for a man who kept his body battle-ready.

The wannabe Evuutan held aloft the sack of fine hixote peppers. "See, the pick of the bunch. Bought them just as this fellow opened shop. I've also acquired all the items you sent me for." He indicated the lumpy tote bags hanging from both shoulders. As he spoke, she glimpsed his strong, ivory-colored teeth—both rows of them—and a somewhat forked, purple tongue.

Although her mind (and pulse) raced, Deja didn't stumble. Reading his alias from his chef coat, she said, "Message? I suspect you meant to surprise me, Ian, dear. As usual." As she dropped the word "surprise," she shot him a glance of weapons-grade fury.

Deja turned so she could see both Geoff and her snobbish competitor. "Sous Chef Ian Blackleaf, meet one of our worthy opponents, Chef Glass." The two newly introduced individuals blinked at each other. Geoff (or Ian) was the first to feign a polite greeting. The rival chef inclined her head. "Enjoy your hard-won purchase," Deja said. "If you'll excuse us, we have to transport *our* goods back to the test kitchen."

This time, Deja was sure the other woman had to suppress a scowl. Geoff would be getting thanked for that. After she walloped him for messing about in her dare, of course. The two of them left the scene of disputed peppers with Geoff following behind, towing the hovercart. She'd just have to send him back for the other items she needed. Right now, she wanted to get him somewhere private. So she could pummel him. When they reached the transport platform with waiting taxis, she relished ordering him about.

Despite that, she chaffed at the necessity of holding her questions—and her rage—until they were in private. How in the name of all wormholes had he found her? If only she hadn't contacted him to verify Famous Foodie's alleged criminal acts. What was the lieutenant colonel trying to do, anyway? Execute an elaborate practical joke? Perhaps. Yet his makeover was heavy duty and made to last. Why? Could he be hoping to recoup the life debt he owed to her? She paused in her inward ranting to consider another possibility. Maybe he liked her enough that—no, she knew better than that. And anyway, this life, this dare, was *her* livelihood, and maybe her father's too. Famous Foodie could very well disqualify her when he found out about her supposed partner. *Gravgummit!*

As she and Geoff rode together in the transport's back seat, she crossed her arms and refused to look at him. Somehow, it helped contain the anger and fear twisting inside her gut like rifterworms. Also, she felt a little flustered about her augmented bosom. Despite avoiding his gaze, however, she couldn't keep her nose from appreciating his distinct scent. Laser rifle oil, boot polish, and cardamom.

♪

THE COMM-SHIELDING DEVICE LIT UP: *Area Secure.* And Deja lit into Geoff.

A swarm of curses came first (in five languages). Breathing came second. Questions, last. "What did I save your butt for? So you could toss mine into a blazing reactor the first chance you got? What am I supposed to do now? How'd you even find me here, you—" and here she reverted to cussing again. The heels of her shoes clacked as she paced. Geoff, leaning against the textured wall in her assigned quarters, said nothing. One muscular shoulder remained pressed against the carved ebony doors covering a triangular alcove—a shrine reserved for offering food to the Vinadroan gods. All six of them. Or maybe it was seven? Ugh. Geoff was shorting out her neurons.

When she paused for a breather, he pushed off from the wall. Though his features were now unfamiliar, he *seemed* concerned, his white lips turned down at the corners.

"Deja, please, hold up for one nanosecond, would you?" He held out a hand, not quite touching her. For response, she flashed an impolite hand signal. The lieutenant colonel dropped his arm, and she considered throwing a punch. But the Coalition trained its officers well. Besides, he'd be expecting something like that and just dodge his sneaky self out of the way.

Deja's PalmStar took the opportunity to rumble in a pocket of her vest. Glaring at the lieutenant, she turned away and unfastened her wraparound chef smock to get to the device. He kept talking as she read the communication.

"I'm sorry, Deja. I'm not here as a joke. I'm here on official business. I wanted to send you a warning but I was afraid you wouldn't see the...benefits of Coalition involvement." Her head snapped up when he mentioned the Coalition.

"You mean to say that you've brought the *law* into my dare?" she roared, whirling around.

"I—yes. But let me explain. And, if it's any comfort," he added, "I almost didn't spot you. I figured your patron might send you into action on your lonesome. Still, I watched scads of contestants register, looked at scores of profiles, cross-referenced registration dates against the date you contacted me, etcetera. Only when I spotted you wearing those LinguaLenses I gave you was I sure I'd found you. Speaking of your disguise," he finished smoothly, "I can't say I mind being in the service of an older woman."

With a groan, she ignored that and raised her PalmStar to get his attention. "Well, Geoff, can you guess who just contacted me? It's Famous, and he wants to know whom my new partner is. And he'd like to know what's to stop him from backing out right now. Flatter me all you want, but this *older woman* is dang close to boiling your eyeballs into a mint jelly and shoving the rest of you into the nearest rubbish compactor shoot."

He paused. "Uh, I suppose my peepers would make good eating... But, *think.* Aren't you a little worried about this sponsor of yours?"

"Should I be?" she taunted. He fixed his blue eyes on her as she continued speaking. "I think I'm brilliant at taking care of myself. And you, too, Geoff, if you care to remember how we met." There, let his ego try to sop that up.

"Unfortunately, Famous is much more dangerous than I could let on, trust me," he explained, sidestepping her ego jab. "The big leaguers at the GJC haven't been able to touch him. Or even ID him. Yet. But *we* could catch—"

"Riiiight. The evil fiend who orchestrated YeastCease must be stopped!"

Geoff crossed his arms, fingers tucked against his sides as he often did when trying to keep his cool. "Yes," he said flatly. "But only because he's masterminded much more than that."

She cocked an eyebrow at him. "Seems like that newly forked tongue of yours suits you perfectly, lieutenant." She left off the "colonel" part on purpose.

"Now, now," he half groaned, and she could see the deep purple of the tongue in question. He looked down as if afraid to brave her gaze any longer. "I wanted to tell you everything I knew, but I couldn't at the time. It was classified information. Anyhow, I figured this food freak might've dared you to enter this galactic food fest. I told my CO that I wanted to bring the culinary brat to heel, and"—his eyes darted up to meet hers—"that I had an insider who would make a brilliant informant and partner."

Perfect, he just wanted to use *her*, a middling lowlife, to catch *Famous*, an exceptional lowlife. Of course that's why he'd come. Gritting her teeth, she tensed, looking for an opening to land a solid punch. Yet his next words flowed with a satin and fire that paralyzed her.

"Sure, I'd love to collar that fanatic. But, to be honest, he's mainly my excuse to see *you*, Deja. Are you such a horrid thing for me to want? Or is it that I'm not enough for you?"

That wasn't the problem. He was *too* much for her. But he wouldn't believe it if she said so. Unless she told him about... *No.*

His steady stare made her clench her jaw and look down. Gazing at the tiny tiles in the floor, Deja's mouth felt dryer than the powdered dirt she'd eaten that morning. No one should be able to make her insides twist with fear and shudder with hope all at the same time. This mess was her fault. It started *after* she had saved his life, really—when she stuck around long enough for him to remember her and vice versa. And then meeting up with him a few months later. Blast it. She couldn't let him screw up her dare, not when failing could mean it would take her a whole lot longer to get her father out of prison.

Geoff had a passing fascination with her, that's all. Could she picture him ever introducing someone like her to his fellow officers? Hah. That would be a riot. Literally. Or inviting her to dine with his family? Not in a hundred lifetimes. Clutching her PalmStar, she pondered throwing it at him. The man was delusional. Putting a dent in his head might reboot his common sense.

When she still hadn't answered his question, he spoke again. "Deja, I know this isn't anything you expected. I know this isn't the best—"

Turning away, she cut him off. "I don't—I *can't* think about this other stuff right now, *lieutenant colonel*. Now's not the time to squabble over whatever you think we might be to each other. Oddsbreaking is my work. It's not any more civilized than I am. I know it, even if you pretend not to. But it's what I do."

To that, Geoff stepped closer. "I'm in *your* world now," he agreed. "Yes, you have an 'unorthodox' job. But I prefer to think we define our work, not the other way around. Trust me, bullying you isn't what

I set out to do. What's more, I'm not some kind of unwavering 'Justice Man.'" She turned her head, delivering a sidelong glare. "Okay, not all the time," his lips gained a rueful dimension. "Deja, listen, I know things that will make you glad of my interference. Thanks to the Coalition—"

That did it. "Thanks to them, what?" she demanded, facing him once more. "Geoff, you had no right. You have *no idea* what I stand to lose here. For all you know, my sister could be dying somewhere and I need this money to cure her." Okay, so that was as close to the truth as she wanted to get. But perhaps the dolt would give up on his nutty mission to corner Famous Foodie. I mean, who knew if Famous would even attend the contest in person.

Letting his arms drop, Geoff shook his head. "And if you *did* have such a reason for living this life, then what? Don't you think the two of us stand a better chance?" He came closer, breathing faster. "Or do you think I'm such a bumscuffle idiot that I wouldn't have a plan? That I wouldn't make sure you benefited from this?"

"Oh, so I stand to gain something, huh? It had better be stellar, mister. Otherwise, you're looking at the defendant in your murder trial." Most likely, if she and Geoff succeeded, the Coalition would pat her on the head for her trouble and be magnanimous in forgoing an arrest. At least until she jumped into some other, not-quite-legal pursuit.

Instead of replying, Geoff brushed past her, reaching the beverage bay in three fluid steps. "Chilled rubarlo nectar with two shots of chocolate," he ordered. Her second-favorite drink, as if that would soften her up. The machinery whirred with activity. He gestured towards the nearest couch, a pastel green settee modeled after a delicate leaf. "Think what you will of me right now. But you might want to sit. I have more information—information that should prove I've got your best interests at heart."

Exasperated, Deja rubbed her temples with her fingertips. His voice had a storm-cloud heaviness to it suddenly. A tone she rarely heard from him, and it chilled her. Still, she stood. Geoff held the drink out to her. Well, why not? Space knew she needed it. Screw the extra calories.

"Just talk," she said, leveling her tone and plucking the nectar-filled plastimug from his hand.

"Fine," he replied. His gaze now held something she would recognize no matter what disguise he wore. Pity. "Deja, I know about your father. And I just learned that he's been injured. Badly."

"My..." she trailed off. *No!* Before another thought could flash through her mind, she drew back her arm and hurled the plastimug of nectar at Geoff.

Only the lieutenant's training saved him from a contusion. "Deja, your father is—" But she was already moving at him, her muscles burning with the need for action, her heart aching with a need for Geoff to be wrong.

Although she angled her body as if to tackle him, she bent sideways at the last moment. Landing a satisfying punch to his midsection. He grunted. Deja dived in the direction of her blow. As soon as her opposite hand and one knee touched the floor, she kicked backwards with her free leg. Her shoe flew off and her foot didn't connect. *Blast it.*

Reacting, she used her momentum to spin around. Crouching and facing Geoff again, she panted, more from anger than exertion. To her surprise, the man didn't even look mad. He held his long-limbed body in a fighting stance, yes, but his features weren't contorted in anger. In that instant, she knew he could've caught and restrained her if he wanted to. His reach was much better than hers. Besides which, her blazing emotions had never improved her brawling reflexes.

Swallowing, she stood up as worry, shock, rage, and a lot of other annoying emotions burned up and down her spine. How had he found out about her father? Was her papá dying? "Everything, Geoff. Tell me everything. *Now.*"

"Of course," he said, rubbing his stomach where she'd jabbed him.

"Is my father dying?"

"No, but it was a close thing. Please, sit down?" he ventured.

A retort came to mind, but all she cared about was learning what Geoff knew. Anyhow, now that her adrenaline had ebbed and she stood there wearing only one shoe, finding a seat seemed prudent. Kicking off her remaining shoe, she plodded over to the odd-looking couch.

"For some time, I've been curious about your family, Deja," he began as she sank into the plush, green cushions. Though she knew her face must be pale, she smoothed her expression and waited for him to continue. Goosebumps prickled her skin, so she bent her legs and tucked them against her chest, wrapping her arms around her knees.

At her silence, the officer placed his hands behind his back. "I just wanted to know all I could about you. But you always guard your past with more zeal than a Felxian cat guards her litter. I don't blame you. Most of us don't get to choose who our family members are. Maybe I shouldn't have snooped." He tilted his head at her. "If I hadn't, though, I wouldn't have discovered that your father had been injured recently. In fact, I wouldn't have thought to negotiate his treatment and release as your reward for helping me apprehend our foodie friend."

Gratitude flushed her cheeks pink. Almost choking, she asked, "His release? But what happened? How did he get hurt?"

"Well, you and your father are far too spirited for your own good." Geoff smiled, encouraged by the relief in her voice. "Seems that he didn't like the idea of poisoning the warden and the guards as part of a planned breakout. Some inmates showed your father how much they disliked his decision. They started with a beat down and ended with a frame job, saying *he* was the ringleader of the escape plot." Geoff paused, clearing his throat, a sign he was nervous.

"Go ahead. Give me details," she said, rubbing her sweaty palms against her slacks.

"OK. Broken kneecaps and legs. One hand...smashed. Tongue,

almost severed. Various lacerations and bruises. Bad concussion and cracked skull. Nerve damage here and there. Some memory loss. And a bruised liver and kidney."

Dazed and queasy, she closed her eyes. Determined not to appear as weak as she felt, Deja resisted putting her head between her knees. She kept her eyes squeezed tight against the tears and the images of her battered father. She was tough. An oddsbreaker had to be.

"Security barely had enough time to deploy some detention bots to quell the violence. Once that was under control, the prison boss had your father transferred to the medical ward. But I expect you know that their personnel and equipment aren't so great."

"So you," she said, looking up at him, "got him out of there and placed him in a better facility?"

"Of course."

A bothersome number of tears slid down her cheeks. Geoff must have called in a whole slew of favors to make that happen. "Thank you," she said, swiping at her tears. "But why didn't they notify me?"

"Oh, this happened right before I contacted them about your father. I asked them if I could break the news to you."

"Ah."

Silence reigned until she heard Geoff punch in an order at the beverage bay. She watched him approach with another plastimug. "Here," he said. "Just don't fling this one at me, okay?"

"No promises," she answered, unable to smile yet. After draining the entire glass, she set it down in slow motion on the end table masquerading as a polished tree nut. "Can I talk to him, Geoff? Please?" The prison had only allowed written correspondence and, oh, how she wanted to speak to her papá now.

But Geoff shook his head. "I wish you could, but his injuries are just too severe. The doctors have him sedated. The healing process is tricky enough without waking him up. I'm sorry, Deja."

"Yeah, I understand," she sighed.

"But he is getting the care he needs. I told my superiors it would go a long way in gaining your cooperation. Yet... I would've done whatever I could to help him once I found out."

"Mission or no mission?" she challenged.

"Exactly." His eyes never left her face.

She believed him, and her throat didn't hurt so much. A brief smile, she found, felt good. "And your plan is...?"

"Why not break the odds *and* help me break my case? Who knows what dangers I'd be willing to risk with *you* as my partner?" He waggled his eyebrows at her. Or tried to, but the alien face he wore couldn't quite translate the movement. So instead his forehead suffered an undignified seizure.

Allowing herself an honest reaction, Deja snorted. However, she couldn't help but tighten her arms around her knees. "And as for Famous?"

Geoff rubbed his traumatized forehead as he spoke, "Did Famous Foodie ever tell you that you *couldn't* have a sous chef?"

Twin jolts of mischief and hope blazed through her, and she grinned. "Nope." She paused. "In fact, wouldn't Famous *want* me to do as the Vinadroans do?"

Interlacing his inked, albino hands, he cracked his knuckles in a familiar gesture.

"What's more," she pressed, "I'll have a useful accomplice in what I'll be making them eat."

"Right," he said, failing to balk at the "accomplice" jab. "Something barbaric?"

She paused with prim unconcern, leaning back against the couch where she perched. "Just the finest dirt this side of the Gutha Quadrant."

"Crap," he said, tugging at his collar.

"No. Dirt," she replied, laughing.

"Pfft," Geoff grunted. "That means I'll definitely be getting my hands dirty, won't I?" he quipped, plopping himself down beside her.

"No way to escape that once you've thrown in your lot with the likes of me."

"Who said I wanted to escape?" He tilted his oh-so-altered-looking cranium at her, the paleness of his skin at odds with the dark, tribal etchings. Dang, even dressed as an Evuutan kitchen warrior, Geoff had a knack for burning through her atmosphere.

She narrowed her eyes. "Just be sure to remember that when I put you to work. The dirt won't just camouflage itself."

"Guess we'll just have to do a lot of...experimenting, won't we?" He leaned closer, his breath subtle and warm on her neck. "And, with me as your co-conspirator, our dirty work will be sanctioned by the Coalition."

"Hmm. Fancy that," she said, resting her chin on her knees. And when he put his arm around her, she reached up to touch the back of his hand, tracing the tattoo that curled around a knuckle.

Then, just because he deserved it, she clamped down on his wrist and slid off the couch, unfolding and turning her body so she had his arm in a painful, locked position. Or, she would have, if the jerk hadn't expected it. Close combat wasn't her strong suit. Now he had both arms tightened around her, and her knees were pressed against the heated tile floor, thighs flush with the padded furniture. For a few seconds, his scent—the waxy hint of boot polish, the oily scent of a laser rifle, the musk of his sweat, and the fiery freshness of peppers—was all she could smell. In that moment, she wondered what tricks his modified tongue might have in store.

Yet almost as soon as such thoughts bloomed and her body softened at his touch, Deja inhaled a deep breath and wrested control back. This would not do. Although she had other means by which to extricate herself, she just leaned away as best she could when he bent to kiss her. "*That* will be quite enough, lieutenant colonel," she said. Slowly, he pulled back and loosened his arms. A little. But it was enough. Pushing against the couch's edge, she rose to her feet, out of his warmth.

"I'm *working*." She stared him down until he straightened in his seat, passion ebbing from his posture. "As grateful as I am about what you did for my papá, Famous needs a response because of your meddling. And the judges will be announced soon. Then I've got a few measly days to make dirt taste yummy." She breathed out and in once more, steadying herself. "So, the only kind of all-nighters you can expect will involve slaving away in the kitchen. *My* kitchen."

He nodded. "I suppose I'm just lucky you've decided against boiling my eyeballs into jelly."

"Oh, that option's still on the table," she said with a stealth smile. "Some ground rules: Before you go chasing after any leads on Famous, you clear it with me. In the kitchen and at the contest, you are my employee, that's it. Not my boss. Not my partner. Certainly not my—not a, uh—" Gravgummit, why couldn't she just say it?

"Not the love of your life, you mean? So noted," Geoff conceded with a playful smile.

Dang.

"It's about time I briefed you on Famous," he said briskly, getting to his feet in that limber yet controlled manner he possessed. In that brief movement, he was once again the hardworking, efficient officer she knew him to be.

"Yes, about time," she echoed. Her father needed her, and she would use whatever tools the galaxy sent her way.

"Wait, so you're saying that Famous is a *murderer* many times over?" Deja demanded.

"Yes. That's what I wasn't allowed to tell you before; it was classified. I'm sorry. But this activist is a dangerous felon. He's orchestrated and perhaps even carried out many food-motivated killings. That said, we have to expect something more sinister than giving the judges dirt to eat. Any ideas?"

"None come to mind," she admitted. "Why couldn't this have just been a simple dare for once?" Her thoughts returned to her wounded father, and she gritted her teeth. She *had* to make this dare work for his sake. If the GJC took him back to the shoddy infirmary at the prison, well... She couldn't bear to think of what might happen then.

As if sensing her thoughts, Geoff moved closer to her. "Deja, it's okay to be upset. I know I've made this even harder on you, and I apologize. I just want what's best for you. And I feared for your safety with Famous as your backer. I hope—"

She cut in, softly. "It's okay. I'll survive. And what you did was save my father. I won't ever forget that, not ever. But I need to... I just need to take a shower and think, okay?"

"Sure, sweet—" he stopped himself. "Of course," he finished.

As she showered, she cried. A lot. The water drowned out her cries and warmed her cold heart. Fear threatened to crystalize around her heart, but she wouldn't let it. The crying helped. She just hoped Geoff couldn't hear.

Before she went to sleep that night, she responded to Famous Foodie.

Luck_Goddess: I have enlisted the help of an associate who is well versed in food prep. You never said I *couldn't* have a sous chef. So I don't see how this negates the dare. Besides, I still have my work cut out for me. If you end the dare now, you'll simply be missing out on a lot of fun, I promise. So what will it be?

A few moments later, Famous replied with "So be it. Good luck."

Relieved, Deja logged on to some local fashion websites and ordered some new clothes that would suit her persona. She also let herself have a few drinks. That done, she went to bed where she tossed and turned, thinking of her father.

The next day, Deja and Geoff found themselves sitting in oversized wooden ladles—er, chairs—amidst thousands of spectators and competitors packed inside the cooking coliseum. Could this planet be any more enthralled by food? She felt so ridiculous. Or edible, to be more exact. The clamor and odor—yes, odor—of countless languages swirled through the bowl-shaped amphitheater like flour at a bakery. Some of the "seating" consisted of large water tanks to accommodate amphibious guests or specialized enclosures for those who couldn't breathe the planet's air. Untethered holocams zoomed around; the proverbial flies at a picnic. Some would be for security, others for entertainment coverage.

Geoff nudged her and raised his eyes upwards. Near the domed ceiling, a six-sided holopanel hung. Pre-recorded and live-action ads from sponsors played out in 3-D. Culinary wares and gastronomical adventures literally jumped off the screen. It didn't surprise her much that Geoff was fixated on the big-screen holopanel. A fascination with large screens seemed to be encoded into male DNA.

Deja turned her attention back to the setup down below. Engaging the handy zoom feature on her LinguaLenses, she went in for a closer survey. One central platform, vast and circular, stood draped in crimson fabric. Standing higher than the rest, it was devoid of any furnishings whatsoever. Around it, several shorter, teardrop-shaped platforms clustered like petals on a flower, each cloaked in luscious fabrics of solid colors. Linked by staircases and ramps to the main platform, the nine smaller stages were also decked out with various tables, chairs, tanks, and other equipment, all to accommodate the motley cabal of as-yet-anonymous judges. Speaking of which, how much longer before the gurus of gastronomy made their appearance?

Surveying the crowd around her, she noticed her nemesis, Chef Glass, sitting just two rows down from her. Her slender sous chef sat on her left. Deja elbowed Geoff. "There's our mutual 'friend,'" she said. With a casual movement, Geoff spared a second to follow her gaze. There, indeed, was their fellow contestant, looking just as severe as ever. This despite sitting silently and straight-backed in a cutaway version of a metal sieve while other spectators around her were chatting and carrying on.

"Quite the model of rigid professionalism," Geoff observed.

"Yeah. Maybe she didn't eat enough of those peppers to 'loosen up' her inner reserves."

"You never know," Geoff agreed with a chuckle.

The seat in front of Deja was still empty, and just as she wondered if it would remain so, she saw a tall Vinadroan with navy-blue fur making his way up the steps. He wasn't moving very fast due to a throng of people around him. A distinct scar marked his forehead above his right eyebrow. His mouth curled back in a broad smile, showing off his bright fangs. The alien wore a white chef smock with short sleeves and tailored white slacks. His dark fur stood out against his pristine clothing. As he progressed up the stairs, Deja could hear the people around him clamoring for his autograph. In an instant, she recognized the contestant before she could read the name on his chef jacket.

"Look," she told Geoff, "that's Chef Bastian Boyar! He nearly won the contest five years ago. Quite the celebrity still."

"Interesting," her partner said.

Boyar finally reached the end of the row where he intended to sit, it seemed, because he shooed away his admirers. "Go on, now.

Everyone, please skedaddle. The presentation is about to begin!" he said in a deep but jolly voice. The people in question turned reluctantly and moved away from him down the stairs.

When Boyar had made his way to the seat right in front of her, Deja couldn't stop herself from standing up and greeting him with a small bow. "Chef Boyar, what a pleasure to meet you. I'm quite the fan," she said, smiling. Geoff sprang up from his seat, following her lead.

"Are you now," Boyar said, flashing his fangs at her with a debonair smile. "Always a pleasure to meet another fan. You may call me Bastian. What is your name?"

"I am Chef EvaLynn Dubois, sir. And this," Deja said, pointing to Geoff, "is Sous Chef Ian Blackleaf. I can't wait to watch you in action."

"Charmed," Boyar said, nodding at them both. "Now if you'll pardon me...?"

"Oh, of course," she said, feeling foolish. "Please sit. I'm sure you've had enough attention from admirers to last quite a while."

"Ah, 'tis but the price of fame," said the Vinadroan, smoothing back his blue hair, which had golden highlights. He bowed and then turned around, sitting in the empty seat right in front of Deja. And just in time, too.

In a flood of dancing lights and up-tempo string and percussion music, the program began. Orange and red flames leaped from the holopanel above. A voice, speaking Common and then Vinadroan, rumbled from speakers everywhere. "Welcome, one and all, to the thirtieth Ultimate Chef of the Galaxy Contest! Thank you for coming out to the show! Shall we present our tasteful judges?"

Deja joined in the cheers, eager to see the beings who held her father's fate in their hands—or claws or, well, whatever. Just as the shouts and applause seemed close to bursting her eardrums, something began to rise up *beneath* the red covering on the central stage. The object was a smooth dome-shape and topped with a small squarish lump of some kind. Suddenly, several heavy-duty robots appeared, tugging the dark cloth until it puddled to one side of the stage. And there stood the judges, presented on a carved marble platter and enclosed in a transparent dome, much like a host of tempting pastries.

Deja stifled a jovial noise at the back of her throat. Geoff coughed to cover his own chuckle. A previously undetected panel slid open. One by one, the disembodied announcer introduced the judges, who exited the see-through cloche and took their places on the smaller stages. Five of the eighteen were Vinadroans, which made sense. Four were humans. Two males and two females. But her magnified view of one of the human males made her curse aloud. The man from the transport! The one she condemned to sharing his sleeping compartment with an old lady. He was a sodding *judge?* Now she remembered him saying something about how his private ship had been decommissioned, resulting in his being forced to use public transport.

"Gravgummit, not him! Not that Inciardi guy!" she burst out. Oh, stars and suns. Her new disguise had better be good enough. She hadn't realized how loud her outburst was until Chef Boyar turned and stared at her with brow furrowed and a hint of calculated interest in his large eyes. A few others turned their heads to gaze at her with varying levels of curiosity and annoyance.

Geoff, who'd been keeping an eye on the crowd rather than the judges, cleared his throat. Great, now he was nervous, too. "Who?" he asked, still not looking at her.

"Sorry," she told the chef in front of her. Chef Boyar cocked his head and swiveled his ears forward, but turned back around to face the stage. The other once-interested spectators turned around, too. In a quieter voice, she answered Geoff's question, "That judge, Lukas Inciardi. The jerk sat next to me on my flight here. Tried to persuade me to engage in some...extracurricular activities."

"Hmm," Geoff said. "And?"

"Uh." She wetted her lips. "I tricked him into sharing his sleeping compartment with a *much* older woman."

"Slag me, you're good!" he said in a cheerful tone. Not what she expected him to say. He didn't often cuss, for one thing. He didn't even say anything about how this might jam things up.

Deja exhaled forcefully. Still speaking under her breath, she said, "Good enough that he doesn't recognize me now, I hope."

"Indeed. Even Chef Glass heard you," Geoff said.

Did I really speak that loudly? she wondered. Vinadroans had great hearing, so she wasn't surprised that Chef Boyar had heard her. But Chef Glass was only human—at least, she *appeared* to be only human. Suspicion sprouted about the female chef, and Deja's belly soured a little. For the second time, she felt grateful to have Geoff there to back her up.

Turning her attention back to the grand stage and the other judges being presented, Deja noted two porcine Orinkks, two bearish Pintrels, and one each of the following: a blue-skinned Be'Voyan, a one-eyed Tondwian, an amphibious Zoox, a reptilian Rekloran, and a birdlike Ractyl. She recognized a few of the judges' names and knew that she and Geoff were in for a big fight. The rest of the presentation was rather instructive, though somewhat mind numbing. The announcer regaled the crowd—for six hours—with details of the judges' credentials and outtakes from their various shows, writings, and adventures. By the end, Deja's PalmStar was filled with pages of notes about the humans and aliens who would decide not only her fate but also Geoff's and her father's.

⚲

Once Deja and Geoff had returned to her quarters, she reactivated her comm-shielding gadget. From his rucksack, Geoff retrieved an ultra-sensitive bug detector. Nicer than her own, she had to admit, though she kept that to herself. Naturally, Deja had already done a sweep of everything Famous had shipped to her. Everything had been clean. Or so she'd thought.

"What makes you think Glass could hear us at the ceremony?"

"Remember when you recognized your prior seatmate as a judge?" Geoff replied, still working.

"Of course."

"Well, our mutual 'friend' suddenly whipped her head around and stared straight at you. I noticed from the corner of my eye. I was keeping her in my field of vision just out of curiosity."

"Wow. Okay, that does seem suspicious," Deja said. "Chef Boyar heard me also. But he was sitting right in front of us. Chef Glass wasn't."

"Exactly. But your exclamation was kind of loud, to be fair. A few others noticed your outburst as well. So maybe Glass just happened to hear you," Geoff said. "Heck, maybe her hearing has been enhanced. But we might as well make sure we don't have any bugs."

"Sure," she sighed. Grudgingly, she said, "I already tested what Famous Foodie sent me. Maybe my scanner didn't catch something, though." Geoff's bug scanner remained silent until he reached her chef jacket, which she had removed and placed near a pile of stuff from the original crate Famous had sent. Geoff's device beeped as it passed over the front of the chef smock. Deja leaned in as he fiddled with the offending item—a button.

"Do you have something I can pry this open with? I think it's hollow."

"Yeah. One second," she answered. She retrieved some tools from her vest and handed them over.

"Now *this* is genius." Geoff held up the button he'd popped open with one of her delicate tools. The button itself was of no consequence. The opalescent blob embedded with circuitry and hidden inside, however, did not belong there. And the only way it could be there is if it was planted *before* she received the chef jacket.

When Geoff exposed the strange glob, he and Deja watched it tremble and begin to ooze itself away from the light. The bug moved as an amoeba would, by stretching half its goopy mass forward and pulling the rest behind. Despite what this discovery might mean,

Deja couldn't help marveling for a moment. "I heard rumors about a new, organic-based bug. Never seen one."

"Yeah, even the Coalition doesn't quite have these in the field right now. Yet our new scanners *can* pick them up."

Deja grinned, and Geoff did likewise. They both now knew that Famous Foodie might have tipped his—or her—hand. Chef Boyar and Chef Glass could very well be the culinary activist. And yet... something still didn't sit right.

"This little guy can just transmit," Geoff remarked. "No data storage, either, unlike normal tech."

"So," Deja said, "the comm shield is blocking the transmission, and the bug won't have any stored record of our discovery."

"Exactly. Let's seal the blob back where we found it, shall we?" he proposed.

"We'll give Famous—or his or her lackey—a good show," she agreed, rocking back on her heels from where she crouched next to him. His long-fingered hands put the button halves back together. The tattoos on his pale skin seemed to weave and shift as he worked.

"I just wish we knew which one of the contestants was Famous," Deja said, trying not to fret. "At least we have some suspects now. Chef Boyar was reportedly quite bitter when he didn't win the contest five years ago. Said there was corruption among the judges and a cover up. So he might be looking for revenge or at least vindication. Don't know what Chef Glass has against Inciardi in particular or the judges in general, though."

"Hmm. Interesting," Geoff said.

"Yeah," Deja agreed, "guess we'll just have to be on the lookout for odd behavior."

"We can use sign to communicate private messages for the most part," he said.

"I agree. However," she butted in, "if either of us needs to jam the transmission again, use a signal like this." She flattened her hand and made a small slashing motion. "After all, Famous knows what I am.

But we wouldn't want him or her knowing that you're not exactly the disreputable type."

"Disreputable rogue at your service," he avowed, and she caught a fiendish set to his expression. But then he sobered. "Trouble is, Famous shouldn't need you if he or she is here to compete, right?"

As if Deja didn't know that. With a shrug, she locked up her worry. Her dad was worth seeing this through.

"I expect," Geoff said, "that the activist wants you to take the fall for something besides what he or she dared you to do. Which is why I'm here. To make sure you don't."

"Don't go all protective on me. I just wanted to make sure we're in the same orbit, is all," she said, feeling the cold chill of anxiety fade just a little.

"We are. Though some might say I'd rather just orbit *around* you." He smiled so wide she could see his unusual number of teeth and the odd tongue within.

Scowling, she snatched her chef jacket from the floor and stood up. She pointed toward his eyes with two fingers. "You, eyeballs, jelly," she reminded him. "I'm going to freshen up. Then we'll hit the test kitchen."

"Yes, chef." He saluted, touching his fist to his forehead and then his chest like a true Evuutan warrior. Pivoting on her heel, Deja tromped off to the lavatory with her duffle.

A TEST KITCHEN? No, this was paradise. Of a culinary caliber. Deja, standing at the west-facing counter, paused from kneading a third (and hopefully final) test batch of clay-based sweetbread. She could hear Geoff shuffling things around in the temp-controlled locker in the southeast corner. Again, she thought how her papá would revel in such a setup. He would have been thrilled by the ovens, which could be powered by wood, gas, electricity, or even kowtons depending on what sort of flavor you were going for. Two of the marvelous ovens were set into the south wall; the third, an oven-and-stovetop combo, was built at ground level, on the east side. It was right beside the walk-in food locker Geoff was rummaging around in.

Also present was an arsenal of knives and other scary-looking implements, along with assorted pots, pans, molds, and such. Certain buttons would open wall panels or drawers with gleaming machinery. The sort of machinery that could blend, grate, chop, and perform many other complicated culinary tasks. Like getting washed lettuce leaves well and truly dry.

At the kitchen's heart stood an island workspace complete with heating elements, a grill, and another sink. All of it was easy to reach from any side of the kitchen. "A kitchen's gotta have work *triangles*," her papá always told her. Well, this place had enough so-called triangles to enchant any mathematician. If the mathematician liked to cook. Stainless oshondrite sinks with two basins apiece were positioned on each wall except the north one, which was reserved as the plating area. The kitchen had storage space galore, too. Another smaller, temp-controlled locker stood diagonally across the room from the one Geoff seemed to be ransacking.

Someday, she would build her father a kitchen like this. One for herself, too. She sighed.

"Something wrong?" Geoff asked, voice muffled.

"Not really. I just wish I had a kitchen like this—and I wish we didn't have to cook in a communal kitchen with other chefs during the competition. That's gonna be rough."

"True," Geoff said, walking out of the fridge with a sausage in one hand. "But you've worked in a busy kitchen before. And so have I, as you know." Here, he was speaking of his cover story. Finished with his pep talk, he bit into the sausage and hummed approvingly.

Blowing out a large breath, Deja shelved thoughts of having to share a kitchen with lots of contestants. "Blackleaf," she said commandingly, using the tone she'd adopted for her character, "I needed that swephorra compote *yesterday*. No time for snacks, apprentice!" Of course, that wasn't all he had been doing. They had come back from a break, and Geoff had been sweeping the kitchen again for any hidden comm or imaging devices. Her voice boomed impressively, bouncing against vaulted ceilings high enough for taller competitors.

"Just keepin' my strength up," he rumbled back. Turning around, he gave her the all-clear signal. And a wink. The small, telescoping black wand in his hand hadn't lit up to indicate anything suspicious. That didn't count the biobug Famous Foodie had concealed in Deja's chef jacket. Thus, Deja and Geoff always had an audience of one, and they'd put up a good front thus far. Famous had every reason to think his or her pawns were engrossed in the contest and unsuspecting of the culinary crusader's true identity. Tucking the device away, Geoff snagged the bowl of compote.

"Got the compote right here." He walked across the tiles of darkest purple and deepest green that weaved a lazy pattern on the floor. Most of the walls flowed with a mural of prickly, green vines heavy with blue-black fruit and golden blossoms. Geoff, with his pale, tattooed skin and white chef jacket, looked like a ghost amidst a tropical jungle.

"About time. Now I can finish these lovely fruit-and-dirt rolls," she joked. Deja moved to wash her hands in the sink to her immediate right. Waving a hand over one particular sensor, she added, "I need those bevsnips peeled and sliced. I want to do another run-through of those toasted clay-and-bevsnip chips. Then get a reduction going for the flatbread filling. And don't forget to baste the ortoo roast again." Warm, sudsy water misted over her hands as Geoff skirted the island, heading for her side of the kitchen.

"Oh, have some pity, will you?" he huffed as if tortured by the thought.

"You heard me," she said.

He put the dish of compote on the black countertop beside the ball of dough she'd been kneading. "Can't I cut up another ortoo beast or do something interesting?" he asked, affecting peevishness.

"Come off it," she said, flicking soapy water at him. "You take to butchering too easily."

"You know, that's what all my targets thought, too. Right before I finished them off. Like I always say, the—"

"Yeah, I know," Deja said, cutting in. "The higher the body count, the fatter your cred account. All fine and good, since you're on my side. Now get to it." In reality, Geoff loved to hunt and fish, hence his amazing skills at butchering animals. But he always followed the laws of the land, wherever that land happened to be. And he never, ever let the meat go to waste. True, sometimes his black ops job did lead to his protecting innocents by killing bad guys. But Deja couldn't believe he took lives with any real pleasure.

"Okay, boss." The officer exuded counterfeit sulkiness as he tromped off to get the starchy vegetables and a peeler. Ah, it was a perfect time to "beef up" his cover story for Famous.

Removing her hands from the sink, she activated the blower to squeegee the water from her hands with sanitized air. "Just think," she encouraged, "you won't owe me any more favors when this is done. Stop griping and start reliving your glory days of culinary servitude."

Geoff, peeler in hand, snorted. "Some glory. I never did make chef at The Wormhole. Even after the three years I slaved at the place." The Wormhole, as anyone in the inner galaxy would know, was a restaurant distinguished by its nefarious criminal clientele. Her partner reached up and selected a pot from an overhead equipment rack.

"Yeah, that's what happens when a best customer's son is found with *your* knife in his gut," she shot back.

"Ah, well. Right. Sloppy of me. Didn't have time to take the knife back after I relieved him of the gratuities he owed me. And the woman he stole from me." Both of them hooted with laughter.

How odd it still felt, though, to have him there. Her partner in all this. Someone she could strategize with. Someone who wanted to share the risk. Why not see the positive side of something she couldn't change? Besides, he'd already found out about her incarcerated father. Geoff knew all about her papá and somehow thought more of her, not less. However, there was that nagging thought that he didn't know all her faults, like the one she herself couldn't quite think about.

She sighed, pushing those thoughts away. Gliding one hand along the jet-black countertop, Deja walked toward a blinking control panel. To her delight, she had discovered she could control the height of the counters. Even better, the countertops could maintain a range of temperatures. Reaching out, she lowered the temperature for the space she was using to make the rolls. A chilled surface would keep the dough from getting sticky and soft. Too cold, though, and it would go hard, especially with the high clay content.

Rolling out the dough, Deja ran through all their menu items in her head. She'd had to come up with three main dishes and sides. Dish one: Ortoo steak empanadas with a clay-and-flour crust, mole poblano, and rice resting on juniper ash flatbread rounds made from yet more dirt and flour. All accompanied by a rustic salad of nuts, seaweed, riverberries, and toasted croutons infused with garlic and clay and served with twizzle dressing. Next dish: Triple-bean soup with clay-and-flour pierogis stuffed with several kinds of dark meat, all served in a bread bowl made of flour-and-clay dough. It would be complimented by a side of popped kernels of sweet, juicy ziphers dusted in a fiery pepper sauce. Last dish: Pounded breasts of kurrocco bird stuffed with a paste of duxelle mushrooms, wutoo nuts, and, yes, dirt. Served, of course, with a side of toasted bevsnip chips tossed in balsamic vinegar powder and parmesan cheese.

Three deserts. Desert one: truffle-flavored, iced belasino featuring chunks of sweetened dough infused with lemony mud, presented beneath a globe of dark chocolate that would separate into little petals once some hot caramel was drizzled over it. Next desert: Two cheesecakes made from three kinds of chocolate and two types of mud, cut into disks then topped with a creamy marmooka whipped cream. Final desert: Fruit-and-dirt sweet rolls with fiery cinnamon-

and-guanchu glaze served with tivel sticks garnished in chocolate and nuts. When she presented her entries to the judges, of course, they would hear nothing about the "earthy" contents.

Finished rolling the sweetbread dough into a rectangle, she looked over at Geoff. His back to her, he was half-humming, half-warbling a smutty tune about a freighter pilot and a hoverbike racer. A song the real Geoff wouldn't have even *admitted* to knowing. The lieutenant sure was taking his role as a scoundrel in stride. Deja shook her head and picked up a pastry brush. With expert strokes, she painted the dough with cinnamon butter and then the orange-red compote. Finally, she sprinkled cinnamon, raisins, and sliced almonds over it.

Six days, six dishes. But before she could even present her dishes, she and Geoff would have to perform well in a number of intimidating contests. She'd watched many such contests before as a mere spectator and marveled at the creative and harebrained nature of those competitions. How long would Deja and Geoff last? How long before Famous did whatever it was the old foodie activist had been plotting? As Deja began rolling the dough into a tube shape, she mulled over the nastier crimes attributed to Famous Foodie. Murder conspiracy charges. Oodles of them. According to Geoff, the victims —all guilty of some food-related offense—suffered poetic, and therefore unpleasant, deaths. Not that Deja hadn't dealt with murderers before, but this time she had more on her "plate" than ever. Her father's freedom. Her livelihood. Geoff's livelihood.

Knife in hand, Deja sliced the dough into plump disks. *This,* she thought, *this is what I'll do to any rotten person who dares to endanger me or mine.*

After the session in the test kitchen, Geoff went off to communicate with his superiors. Deja waited for him in her room, anxiety dripping through her veins.

"Okay, so what do we know?" Deja asked as soon as he entered her quarters.

"Well, whoever Famous is, he or she might just have an unhealthy interest in Inciardi."

"Oh, really?" Deja asked. "Well, Chef Glass is annoying enough that I wouldn't mind if she turns out to be the bad guy. What about the backgrounds of Chef Boyar and Chef Glass? And does the Coalition have any new info on Inciardi?"

"My CO says that both contestants have impeccable credentials. But they weren't always famous and not much is known about their earlier years. As for Inciardi, that probably isn't his real name. General Trikk found evidence that the judge's past is a bit murky in details, too."

"I figured as much," Deja admitted. "It seems like Famous must've run afoul of at least one of the judges in his or her past, maybe even Inciardi himself. Has Trikk spoken to Judge Inciardi directly, just in case?" Deja asked.

"Yes. And, get this," he added, "it turns out that the judge signed on as a CI for someone even more high-ranking than the general!"

"Whoa," Deja exclaimed, thoughts churning. "You should've led with that. So...did his handler already tell him about our undercover op here?"

"Yep. We're only just finding out now because Trikk himself didn't have clearance."

"*Really!* The GJC sure has lots of red tape." Disapproval coated her words despite an attempt to hide it.

Geoff cleared his throat, looking down. "I know, I know."

"No wonder Inciardi hasn't called me out as an imposter. He's on our side," Deja concluded.

"Precisely," Geoff smiled. "Trouble is, he won't say much about his past. But he reports that he's gotten plenty of hate mail."

"Why? Because he's a ladies' man?" she wondered, frowning.

"No, apparently that's just his way of looking more flawed and open to being on the take."

"Oh. Well, we still don't know if Famous intends to simply humiliate all the judges or just Inciardi or if Famous plans on doing something worse, like the chef's rap sheet suggests. Feeding dirt to a judge isn't a crime, just embarrassing—for the judge."

"Unfortunately, yes," he agreed. "We'll just have to stay on high alert until the activist decides to make another move."

"Indeed," she said. "We don't have enough to catch him or her red-handed yet." Deja sighed.

"Well, the next event is in under an hour," Geoff reminded her. "You'd better get ready."

"Sure. I just hope we stay in the contest long enough to figure out who Famous is and what he or she is up to."

⚬

BLINDFOLDED, Deja prayed she'd be able to figure out what the contest official was going to put into her mouth. This was the eighth mini challenge she'd experienced so far.

First, he let her sniff the food. Then she opened her mouth, and he put the spoon in.

"What will she guess, folks?" asked the jubilant announcer, Chub Dornack, a chubby Vinadroan with teal fur and matching eyes. "Will she fail once again or will she beat the odds?"

Odds, huh? Funny.

Deja chewed the silky-smooth food, testing it with her tongue. She tasted a hint of fire but, most of all, a tangy sweetness and a hint of tropical flavors. She smiled.

"This is rashaneeda pudding," she said.

"That is *correct!*" shouted the host, and the audience cheered. Well, most of them did. She seemed to be a popular entrant already.

The next food item was hard and crunchy and, well, nasty. She asked for water and washed it down.

"Tick tock, Chef Dubois. Ten seconds to identify the ingredient," admonished the speaker.

Deja tried not to grit her teeth. She had two ideas but could offer just one. If she missed another item, she'd be eliminated from this round and maybe the entire contest.

"My guess is roasted shar beetles," she ventured, clenching her fists.

"That, too, is correct!" said Chub. "One more food item to go!"

Deja licked her lips, relieved. Then she prepared herself for the last taste test. This time she recognized something nutty and a little burnt. She smiled.

"Oh, we have a smile. But will we get the right answer?"

"Guntle nuts," she said.

"That is right, Chef Dubois! And you have survived to compete further in the Ultimate Chef of the Galaxy Contest. Let's hear it for her, folks!"

People cheered as the tester took off her blindfold. She stood and took a bow.

Walking toward the exit, she saw the porcine Orinkk named Chef Louis Gaskón emerge from the soundproofed rooms backstage. She gave him a little nod, which he returned.

Once she passed through the exit, Geoff swept her into a big hug.

"Ian!" she protested.

"Sorry, had to do it, old gal." He set her down. "I thought we were out of the contest for a minute there."

"Yeah, I missed too many. But, heavens, they had some hard stuff," Deja said.

"Yet you pulled through. Nice work, boss."

"Yes," Chef Boyar interjected. "You did a fine job, Chef Dubois. Tell me, how did you become so well versed in food?"

"Oh, just a lot of traveling as a kid," she answered, trying to keep her cover intact.

"Ah, that explains it," the Vinadroan said, nodding. "Well, I'd love to discuss things over dinner sometime before the contest is over. I'm particularly curious about your run-in with that judge, Lukas Inciardi."

Deja perked up. So Chef Boyar wanted to know more about Inciardi, did he? Perhaps he would slip up and reveal himself as Famous Foodie if she accepted his invitation. "Why, how kind of you to offer, Chef Boyar," she said, brushing her hair back from her face. "As it happens, I'll be free two days from now."

"Brilliant," said the blue-furred chef, giving her a quick bow, his sapphire hair ruffling with the motion. "And call me Bastian, please."

"Okay, Bastian. Now if you'll excuse me, I'm going to take a nap before the next event. I'm almost out of steam."

"Of course," the Vinadroan said. She and Geoff turned and walked toward the exit.

"No rest for you, though," she told Geoff. "I need you to practice our sauces again—all except the mole."

"Oh, okay. No problem," he said.

"Perfect. Now get going," she told him. He nodded and turned left when she turned right. As soon as he was gone, she smiled, thinking of the hug he'd given her and the date she had secured with Chef Boyar. She would have pleasant dreams. She was sure of it. In celebration, she took a few sips from her flask before lying down in bed.

WITH GREAT EFFORT, Patricio opened his eyes. He blinked, even though the light he detected was dim. He looked around, trying to figure out what was happening—or what had happened. He felt... disembodied. With sudden fear rising like bile, he tried to move but couldn't budge even a finger. He couldn't even tell if he still *had* fingers. His eyes took in his surroundings and he started to feel a sense of...confusion. The last thing he remembered was being in a fight with Stempe and Ribell. And he had a vague recollection of being smacked on the back of his head.

Yet he wasn't in his prison cell. He wasn't even in the prison's medical ward. Instead, he was in some kind of high-tech hospital room. Also, he was by himself—which was quite the luxury. Machines were hooked up to him, displaying blood pressure, heart rate, temperature, and other things. He also managed to determine that he was wrapped in a yellow blanket on a hospital bed with metal rails on the sides. There were lights lining two sides of the room, all on a low illumination level. He also saw a wooden door, closed, with a holopanel that displayed his name and some other things he couldn't quite decipher.

He sighed, then tried to make a noise. "Hhellp," he croaked, feeling something strange going on with his tongue, which felt too big or something. He hadn't spoken very loudly. Would anyone hear him?

To his relief, the handle of the door turned. Someone was coming! The door swung open without a sound, and a figure entered. Yellow feathers fluttered from its head and large black eyes blinked above a small, beaked mouth. A Ractyl. And it looked male. Yes. And he was wearing a long, white lab coat and holding a medical device of some kind in one taloned hand.

"Hello," said the doctor. "I see you are awake. That's very good. My name is Doctor Chipton. Can you tell me how you feel on a scale of one to ten with one being 'terrible' and ten being 'terrific,' Patricio?"

"I...I don't r-really f-feel anything," he managed.

"Ah, okay." The doctor nodded, hair feathers moving up and down. "You have been on painkillers and paralytics for quite some time while you were healing. You should start to get feeling back soon. But we will monitor you closely for pain, all right?"

Patricio heaved a sigh. No wonder he couldn't feel his own body. "O-okay. What...what's w-wrong withhh my t-tongue?"

The Ractyl walked forward and looked down at him with gentle eyes. "I'm afraid that some inmates severed most of your tongue. We had to reattach and repair it. So you will struggle with speech for a little while. But the fact that you can speak at all is very good. You have other injuries, but I don't want to overwhelm you."

"Oh. *G-gracias.* Wh-where am I?"

The birdlike man smiled. "You are at a Coalition hospital. Your daughter's friend arranged for you to be transferred here after the attack on your life. I have to say, you have friends in high places, Patricio."

A friend of Deja's? Could he mean a boyfriend? Patricio opened his mouth to ask, but the doctor followed up with another question. "Are you thirsty?"

"Y-yes, *muy.*"

"Nurse?" called the doctor, turning his head toward the open door. Someone else hustled into the room.

"Yes?" answered a tall, human male with light skin, a tidy beard, and thin lips. He wore purple scrubs with blue stripes, which made Patricio's eyes feel a little swirly.

"Sterling, please bring in some ice chips for Mr. Ortega and feed them to him over the next hour."

"Right away," Sterling said, leaving.

Dr. Chipton patted Patricio on the shoulder, then said, "Don't worry, we'll get you on the mend. And I'll let your daughter know you're awake."

"D-Deja? Is sh-she here?" he mumbled, excited.

"No, I'm sorry. But we know how to get in touch with her."

"Okay." He tried not to sound disappointed. It had been so long since he had seen his own daughter in person. How had his daughter's "friend" managed to get him out of that nasty prison? He just hoped he wouldn't be returning there when his hospital stay was up. That thought made his throat tight.

"M-must I g-go back to prison?" he asked, just as Sterling came back in with a cup of ice chips.

"Oh," said Dr. Chipton, "I doubt that very much. Don't worry yourself over it. I believe your freedom is guaranteed thanks to your daughter and her friend. Now, let Sterling help you, and I'll be back to check on you later."

"*G-gracias, doctor.*"

"*De nada*," said the Ractyl, surprising Patricio with Spanish. Then the physician turned and left the room. The male nurse sat down on a stool by the bed and waited for Patricio to open his mouth.

The first ice chip tasted like heaven wrapped in sunshine. He could get used to this treatment. He just hoped he could handle the recuperation. The doctor had been careful not to say anything about his overall injuries. Who knew what the next days and weeks and months had in store for him? But, well, he was alive. And out of prison. He could live with that.

S omething beeped in Deja's ears. Images of dancing vegetables disappeared from her brain. She groaned, awakening. Dancing vegetables? Why not something Geoff related? Oh, well. The nap had been welcome anyway.

She threw back the covers and stood up, stretching her back and limbs. Then she showered. She stepped from the shower and almost dropped the towel when a knock sounded on the door.

"Deja. It's just Geoff."

"Good grief. You scared me. What is it?" She secured the towel around herself and stepped in front of the mirror.

"It's about your dad."

She had the door open in two seconds.

"What happened? Is he okay?" she asked, steam drifting around her.

"Uh," Geoff took in her state of undress for a second before speaking again. "Yes, he's doing quite well. He's even been talking again! The doctors think his tongue will heal all the way in just a day or so. At first, they weren't sure it—"

Deja let out a whoop and cut him off with a very wet hug. And then she did what she'd been wanting to do ever since he'd told her he had saved her father from the prison's medical ward. She reached around his neck and pulled his face down to her level. When she kissed him, she let herself go. Stunned, he responded with a hand at the base of her back, pressing her closer. She tasted his makeup, but she didn't care. After a few precious moments, she pulled away.

"Deja," he breathed.

"I'm sorry. I shouldn't have done that." She blushed, remembering she was in just a towel. "I can't—we can't—" She stopped, taking a big breath.

"It's okay. I understand. But for what it's worth, I don't regret it at all."

Her heart pounded. "I just wanted to thank you, Geoff. For what you did for my father."

"Well, you know how I love it when you thank me." He grinned.

"Oh, stuff it," she said, smacking his arm and turning around. "Now get out of here. I need to finish getting ready."

"Of course. You're on in ninety minutes."

Talking. Her father was talking again. She smiled as she closed the bathroom door and shed her towel.

⚬

"Chef Dubois, you're up," said the stage assistant who was holding the door for her.

"I'm ready," she said, walking up to him.

"Let's test your mic." He reached over and pressed a button on the mic attached to the front of her chef smock. She also had an earpiece in case someone needed to give her instructions for her ears only.

"One, two," she said.

The Vinadroan gave her a nod and motioned to the entrance. "Just wait for your cue and head on stage. Good luck."

Standing by the entryway, Deja breathed in a few deep breaths. She could do this. Or rather, her tongue and palate could do this. Just a little while ago, she had managed to stay in the competition by identifying enough of the foods she had tasted while blindfolded.

Her father had often made a game of guessing all the ingredients in one dish. Now she'd do the same thing in front of trillions of people. No pressure.

"And back to show us how strong her palate is—Chef EvaLynn Dubois," Chub Dornack announced.

Deja walked onto the stage as the spectators cheered. Many more cheers than boos anyway. *Luck is still with me,* she thought. She kept walking and waved at the crowd, which responded with louder cheers.

"Here she is. Let's get her ready to taste!"

She had reached the staging area where a seat awaited her. A female Vinadroan with purplish coloring stood next to the chair holding a blindfold. "Please sit," she instructed.

Deja did. The blindfold went on, and the theatrical host said, "Okay, people. Chef Dubois can miss just five ingredients total or she'll be disqualified. Do we think she can do it?"

The crowd roared back, "Yes!"

"Conductor," Chub ordered, "bring out the first item."

"Sniff, please," instructed the female conductor to Deja.

Deja obeyed. A metallic fragrance hit her nose.

"Now open, please."

She did so, and her mouth was full of a soft pudding with a metallic tang and a hint of sweet smokiness. This was blood pudding. Not her favorite. But, more importantly, she *thought* she could tell what was in it. She started listing ingredients aloud.

"Tryfus blood, ortoo suet, cream, rice, onions, raisins, malt vinegar, salt, pepper, paprika, and a bit of sherry."

"Is that your final answer?" asked Chub.

"Let me have one more taste," she said. After eating the second bite, she mulled things over. There was one other spice. Aha! She had it.

"And powdered yurthin," she said, relieved.

"What do we think, folks? Did she get it right?" The crowd voiced their opinions. Deja curled her hands in anticipation. "Chef Dubois scored twelve out of twelve!"

Yes! Now to keep up her momentum.

"Tester, the next sample, please."

Deja sniffed then tasted the next bit of food, a creamy sauce. This would be tough.

"Yyrtle stock, butter, flour, cream, irix juice, egg yolks, salt, pepper, and... Can I taste it once more, please?"

"Certainly." The female gave her one more taste.

Deja resisted biting her lip. There were at least two more spices. Well, she'd just have to try her luck. "And I detect rithius and holante."

"I'm afraid you've missed some," replied the announcer. The crowd took a breath. So did Deja. "What you thought was holante was actually saffron. And..." They waited. "That's it! Your score is nine out of ten. You can miss another four ingredients before you're cut for good."

The next four samples of food were even tougher. She missed another three ingredients. The hunshian stew had been especially hard. Cursing inwardly, she tried to cheer herself by thinking there was just one more dish to taste. As long as she didn't miss more than one ingredient, she would rank as a winner in this task, which would boost her overall score.

"You may sniff," said the contest official.

The scent that hit her nostrils took her back to her father's galley. She smiled when she tasted the fiery sauce with a hint of chocolate. The concoction was a version of mole poblano, one of the very sauces she would be preparing for the judges—if she got that far. The ingredients tumbled out of her mouth like a word waterfall.

"Onion, garlic, hixote peppers, ancho chilies, pasilla chilies, chipotle chilies, tomatoes, tomatillos, ortoo lard, cloves, cinnamon, coriander, marjoram, anise seeds, raisins, almonds, pumpkin seeds, sesame seeds, flour tortillas, oil, tythrill chocolate, salt, black pepper, and sugar." Whew. She took a deep breath, waiting.

"Wow. What a quick recitation. Anyone care to guess if she missed anything?" the announcer asked. "Well, I can tell you, it's a close one. If she misses more than one item, she fails this task. Chef Dubois, do you think you got everything right?"

"Well, I'm still in the dark," she indicated her blindfold, inciting some laughter. "But I think I stayed within my cutoff range."

"We'll see about that. Conductor, please remove the contestant's blindfold. Chef Dubois, look at the main screen. We will reveal if you missed or mistook anything in that sauce."

Deja blinked against the lights as the blindfold came off. She and everyone else looked up at one of the main screens. Then, in bold letters, the word "Thyme" appeared. Deja's heart stuttered. Slag it. She'd almost added that one. Would the screen reveal another ingredient she'd missed? The screen blanked out and then "Congratulations" flashed across it in 3D. Deja smiled and blew kisses at the onlookers as they went wild.

"As the screen says, congratulations, chef. You've mastered this task. And here's your ranking for today." The screen showed her ranking and the six chefs below and above her. Deja wanted to grit her teeth when she saw Chef Glass ranked above her. But she kept a smile on her face until she reached the exit.

DEJA WAITED with little patience for her PalmStar screen to light up. "Papá! I'm so glad to talk to you at last." On her PalmStar's screen, she could see her father lying in his hospital bed; but she had turned on just her mic, not the camera. "Sorry you can't see me. But I'm undercover right now."

"D-don't worry about th-that," he said, his words still slurred a little. "I'm s-so lucky th-that I get to h-hear your voice, although it s-sounds different to me. I must've gotten bumped on the head h-harder than I th-thought."

She laughed. "No. That's part of my disguise, Papá."

"Oh. *Gracias.* I th-thought I was l-losing my mind again."

"No. But you could have *died*. Why didn't you keep your mouth shut?"

"Because."

"Of course. Because it was the right thing to do. I know, I know. But I wish you'd been more careful about it. If it weren't for Geoff, you might still be unconscious. You might never have woken up again."

"Yes. I was t-truly fortunate. *Tu novio* is most kind. When will I f-finally get to m-meet him?"

"Oh, he is not my boyfriend. Not really."

"Ahh, we'll see about that." He grinned at her.

Ugh. She rubbed her forehead. "So...tell me what happened? Geoff gave me the basics."

"Well, I f-found out that some of the inmates w-were hoarding torran p-peach pits for the arsenic in them. Th-they planned to poison the w-warden and s-some g-guards in an escape attempt."

"Peach pits. Huh."

"*Sí*. And s-so I tried to blow the whistle. But n-not before the bad guys stomped on me."

"I see. Well, I'm glad the detention bot found you when it did. How are you feeling?"

"*Muy mal*. About as you'd expect," he added. "I'm up for double knee replacements in a few days. Sh-should be q-quite the adventure."

"Oh, Papá. I'm so sorry. I'm sure they'll do a splendid job, though. GJC doctors are the best in the biz. Even old Tina wouldn't be able to match them," she said, referring to the physician who used to be part of their troupe.

"N-no. I imagine n-not. *Mija*, don't worry. I'll be f-fine. You just concentrate on whatever you're d-doing. And...g-give your f-friend my thanks."

She smiled. "Oh, I already thanked him, don't worry."

"*Should* that worry me, Deja?" A sly smile settled on his face.

"Um," she stammered. "No. Of course not."

"If you say so." He yawned.

"Ah, I've kept you up too long. Get some more sleep, OK? *Te amo.*"

"*Te amo.*"

"Sleep well. I'll talk to you again as soon as I can."

"*B-bueno. Adios, mija.*"

B efore the sun had crested the horizon, Deja found herself wide awake with her head stuffed in a black sack. Yet her heart wasn't spasming in fear. Instead, she was just curious. This was all part of the competition. Sitting in some kind of moving vehicle alongside some other contestants, Deja tried to keep track of the turns and stops but soon gave up. All she could tell is that they had been traveling for about two hours.

At last, the vehicle halted, and someone opened the doors with a creak. A voice spoke in front of her. "Give me your hands, please, and step down." So she did. Someone gripped Deja's hands and helped her step out of the vehicle. She waited for the hood to come off, but no one removed it. Instead, she was prompted to place her hand on someone's shoulder and follow behind with slow steps. They wound this way and that, with Deja straining to hear anything that would clue her in on where they were. At last, her guide stopped and said, "Good. Stand right there and wait to take off the hood until we give the signal, okay?"

"Sure thing," she said, adrenaline revving up for whatever battle lay ahead. She soon heard others being given similar directions. *Must be a group challenge!* she thought.

"Welcome, one and all, to the first team trial of the Ultimate Chef of the Galaxy!" Deja recognized the voice; it belonged to the show's host, Chub Dornack. "Cheftestants," Chub continued, "please remove your head coverings! The fun is about to begin!"

Deja reached up and pulled off the sack, blinking in the bright light. She and several others stood in a huge factory of some kind. Holocams and spotlights were trained on the cluster of contestants, which included herself, Chefs Boyar, Glass, and Gaskón plus a Rekloran chef who was unknown to her.

Chub, the teal Vinadroan, stood next to a massive wooden box, which was hooked to a series of ropes that led to a large crane. *What's under there? It's gotta be something awesome!* Deja mused.

Chub gestured to the enormous container. "Under this crate, chefs, you will see your next culinary challenge! On three, we will reveal the food that you and your team must recreate as faithfully as possible. One, two, three..." The crane lifted the box, and Chub said, "Behold, I give you, guntlegracci!" As the crate rose up, Deja glimpsed a giant, sausage-shaped tube of meat that was over seven feet long and probably weighed in at one hundred pounds. *Whoa!*

"Yes, folks, it is the premium meat product known for its superb taste, high fat content, and challenging preparation that all originated right here in the Vinadroan town of Guntlegrella! And all of you together must make one guntlegracci sausage in just nine hours using some spectacular wild boar. In this round, we have the following chefs: Chef Bastian Boyar, Chef Riva Glass, Chef Louis Gaskón, Chef EvaLynn Dubois, and Chef Geckuano Skal. Will you all collaborate for culinary perfection? Or will you fight and then fail? For this challenge, you will choose a team captain. You have five minutes to decide!"

Deja and the others soon hustled into a tight little circle. Bastian spoke first. "I've made plenty of guntlegraccis in my day. Does anyone else have any experience with them?"

"Me," Deja said. "I've helped make the Italian version of the meat. It's known as 'mortadella' back on Old Earth. I know ratios and so on. I'm also good with machines."

"Great," Chef Boyar replied just as Chef Glass tried to interrupt him. "No, just listen. I want to be team leader. I have home court advantage here. We *will* succeed if I am captain."

Skal said, "Fine by me," while Gaskón just nodded. The porcine chef looked a bit off color, probably because they would be cooking with pork, which he didn't eat.

"Agreed," Deja said. Chef Glass opened her mouth then closed it again.

With that, they lined back up in front of Chub, who said, "Ahh, we have a decision. Who is the lucky leader?"

"I am," Chef Boyar said.

"Excellent. You now have nine hours starting...now!" Chub declared. He clapped and five mobile holocams buzzed around the group of contestants.

"OK," Bastian said as they huddled again, "I want Gaskón assembling the spice mixture. Dubois, you help him with the portions of each spice. Then carve out the belly and back fat—about twenty-seven pounds. You and Gaskón need to chop one-third of the fat into quarter-inch cubes for show pieces. Cut the rest into big bits for the grinder. Then stuff it in the blast chiller until we're ready to grind it."

Deja and Louis nodded. Bastian turned to the other two teammates. "Glass, measure out two pounds, nine ounces of guntle nuts and five ounces of whole peppercorns. Both ingredients need to be cleaned and blanched. When you're done with that, measure out nine cups each of red wine and water and put those fluids in the blast chiller.

"Skal and I will select about sixty-three pounds of choice lean meat and cut it into rough hunks for the grinder. Glass, you can help us with that when you're done with the other tasks. OK, everybody, let's get to it!"

"Yes, chef!" they all answered.

"You okay, Louis?" Deja asked when the other chef failed to move.

"I...I'll be fine," he said. "Just feeling a bit out of sorts."

"I understand." She placed a hand on his shoulder and squeezed, and he smiled a bit.

"Thanks. Now help me figure out what spices we want and in what quantity?"

"Yep," she said. "Let's go." She let her hand drop from his shoulder, and then they both turned to dash toward the large pantry. Inside, she saw huge jars of so many spices it made her breathe in sharply. The scents of all the spices caressed her like a long-lost lover. Brushing those feelings aside, she grabbed a data pad on a nearby table and started scribbling out measurements and figures while Gaskón commented over her shoulder, making a few additions and corrections.

"OK, since we are working with about ninety pounds of meat, I figure that we will want the following amount of spices: one pound, eleven ounces of salt; two-point-five ounces of curing agent; five ounces of white pepper; one-point-two-five ounces of coriander; three-point-eight ounces of garlic; two-point-five ounces of anise; two-point-five ounces of mace; one-point-two-five ounces of caraway; and two-point-five ounces of holante. Whew." She paused, tallying that up. "That's just over three pounds of spices!"

"Indeed!" said the other chef.

"Here, double check my figures and start assembling the mixture while I go butcher some fat."

"Will do." He took the data pad from her. She sprinted to the meat locker, red-and-silver hair billowing with her movement. There, Bastian and Geckuano were already hewing out hand-sized blocks of lean meat and shoveling the growing piles into metal wheelbarrows. For a moment, she marveled at the immense amount of meat and fat in the freezer. *How many wild boars died for this? I'd better not mess this up!*

The left side of the meat locker held row after row of fatty meat on hooks. She grabbed a nearby cleaver, sharpened it, and set to work, carving off fat with efficient yet artistic strokes—sort of like sculpting a marble statue in reverse because she wasn't discarding the pieces she carved off.

"How are you doing?" asked the cheerful Chub through the holocam flying near her shoulder.

"Just fine. Busy, though."

"OK, carry on!"

Before long, even in the cold air, sweat poured down her face and across her chest and back. She panted a bit as she labored, pausing only long enough to check the weight of the belly and back fat that she'd collected thus far. *OK, I need another five pounds, then I'm good.* At that point, Louis appeared, followed by a separate hovercam.

"Where do you need me?" he asked.

"Over there," she pointed to a nearby metal table piled with glistening fat. "Start chopping all that up into quarter-inch cubes and putting it in the bowl. We need nine pounds."

"Got it." Gaskón trotted over to the appointed station and selected a knife. Naturally, he first sharpened the knife with a few quick strokes. Then he began chopping up the show fat. Meanwhile, she finished hewing out enough belly fat and wiped her brow. Then she joined him, standing on the other side of the stainless-steel table.

"We can do this. *You* can do this," Deja told the chef, whose pink skin still looked a bit pale.

"I won't let you down," he said, eyes focused on his hands, which were busy mincing up the lard into lovely little chunks.

"It's looking great," she encouraged him, now also chopping up ounce after ounce of fat into quarter-inch pieces. Before too long, Deja stopped him. "Let's get this weighed," she said. Louis carried the bowl over to the scale.

"Nice," he said when the numbers flashed on the scale. "We're only off by less than a quarter of a pound."

"Yep. You finish dicing the rest that we need, and I'll start chopping up about eighteen pounds of fat into rough hunks for the grinder."

Just as they separated, Chef Glass appeared, running into the meat locker so fast she might as well have had a Felxian cat chasing her. The older chef ignored Deja and Louis, heading straight for Boyar and Skal's station. "Where are we at with the meat?" demanded the woman.

"Just need another thirty pounds or so," Boyar said.

Eyebrows arched, Chef Glass said, "That much? What have you two been doing all this time?"

Deja glanced over, somehow not surprised. *The gall of that woman!* Bastian straightened and glared at Chef Glass, his large ears folding back a little. "We've been working just as hard as you, chef. Don't start making trouble now."

"Oh, ho!" said Chub suddenly through one of the airborne cameras. "Do we have a fight brewing here?"

Bastian looked up at the device and frowned. "No, we are having an adult conversation. The only thing we'll be brewing is a victory."

Chef Glass harrumphed but didn't say anything further. Instead, she began carving up the remaining meat into grindable hunks and tossing them into one of two wheelbarrows.

"All right," the host's disembodied voice said. "Keep up the teamwork. Let's see what Dubois and Gaskón are up to!"

"We're hacking up the fat, sir!" she chimed in. Deja wiped away more sweat with the back of her sleeve as she and Louis worked.

"Mind your fingers!" advised Chub.

"Thanks," she and Gaskón said.

"Louis, can you throw the show fat in the blast chiller?"

"No problem. Be right back," he said.

After he returned, they spent a good ten minutes chopping the lard into rough pieces. As they were about to weigh it, Chub himself strolled in.

"Pray tell, how much fat did you reap?"

"Hopefully about eighteen pounds for grinding," Deja answered as Gaskón moved the wheelbarrow onto the scale.

"Well, you've done it! You've got just over eighteen pounds! Nice precision, folks!"

"Oh, yeah," Deja said joyfully, then high-fived her partner. Shifting her attention to their captain, she said, "Chef Boyar, shouldn't we blanch those pieces of show fat before they're incorporated into the ground meat?"

"Oh, yes, quite right," Bastian replied. "Good catch, Chef Dubois."

"Thanks," Deja replied, smiling. "Gaskón, that diced fat should be chilled enough. Put this batch of lard in the blast chiller. While you're there, grab the show fat and meet me at the stove!" she yelled, already headed out of the walk-in cooler to the area where she could find the water-boiling station. She found a few enormous, self-heating pitchers of water not far from the meat locker. The oddsbreaker pressed the buttons that would get the water boiling in under three minutes. Louis soon joined her, bowl of cubed lard in hand.

"Shall I get some ice water ready?" he asked, setting down the bowl.

"Well, well, well," Chub said as he strolled over with two holocams in tow, "what are you working on now?"

"Just going to blanch the fat so it is better incorporated into the meat emulsion," Deja replied. To her partner, she said, "Yes, get some ice water ready and a large colander."

Louis rummaged around the cabinets and found a bowl for the ice and a colander for the fat. "Be right back," he said. When he came back with the bowl partly full of ice, the boiling water was ready to go. He put some cold water in the bowl of ice and plunked it into the sink; they'd use that to quench the fat after blanching.

Wordlessly, while Chub chattered on, the two contestants worked to put the fat in the strainer, pour a cascade of the boiling water over the cubes of lard, and stir them around a little. Steam billowed up, making her and Louis sweat. After only about a minute or so, Deja plunged the colander down into the ice water. Steam erupted again, but not as much.

"Whew!" the host declared. "Looking hot!"

"Oh, always," Deja said with a smirk at one of the cameras. "Let's get this in the blast chiller with the rest of the fat," she told Gaskón. When they had done just that, they met up with the rest of their team to plan the next crucial few hours.

"OK," said Chef Boyar, "we've put the meat in the blast chiller. It will take a precious thirty minutes for the meat and fat to get cold enough to put it through the grinder the first time. I'm setting a timer. Dubois, I want you with me. We're going to do a maintenance check on all the equipment. Gaskón, you're going to get the spice mixture loaded in the food processing machine. Join Dubois and I as soon as you're through. Skal and Glass, I want you to clean up the mess we've left behind. And do it fast."

"Yes, chef," they all echoed, though Chef Glass didn't say it that loudly.

"Dubois, let's check the grinder first." So they did. After poking about a bit, Deja didn't see anything wrong with the machine's innards. Bastian flipped on the "chill" function for the grinder so that it, too, would be ice cold when grinding the meat and fat.

"Does everything look good?" asked the porcine chef as he approached.

"So far, so good," the oddsbreaker affirmed.

After that, Deja messed around with the sausage stuffer and food processor but found no issues. Those machines also had a chill feature, which Bastian activated. And, as far as Deja could tell, the sous vide machine—a giant, heated water bath—checked out, too. All the while, Chub kept narrating their actions and the holocams kept darting around them getting all the action from multiple angles to be edited and aired later. Deja swiped at the sweat on her face with an already-damp sleeve, and Bastian did the same.

Right then, the timer Chef Boyar had set went off, and they all rushed to get the meat and fat from the blast chiller. Geckuano and Bastian each hefted a large wheelbarrow and wheeled them out to the grinder while Louis, Riva, and Deja grabbed some special shovels and followed in their wake. Before long, the crew had shoveled about a quarter of the meat into the grinder, which was grinding away using a six-millimeter plate—until the contraption made a loud shriek and ground to a halt.

Everybody swore, but no one as loudly as Boyar. "Chef Dubois, didn't you say this equipment looked ready to go? What's wrong with it? Fix it. *Now!*"

Blood rushed to her face at the tone of his voice. She did *not* like being spoken to like that. But now wasn't the time to quibble about management style.

"Uh oh," said Chub. "It appears that the team has hit a rough patch. Will they be able to troubleshoot the machine in time?"

Flipping off the power to the grinder, Deja grabbed a nearby stepladder and pulled it over to the giant apparatus. If she didn't figure out what was wrong and fast, the whole challenge could be lost. "I'm going in," she said, then opened the main hatch to the motor.

"Oompf!" Deja gasped, pulling a belt back into place with her oily hands. "Yeah, that ought to do it," she said, then punched the power on. Besides the belt, she had found a few gears that had loosened during operation. She wiped her hands on a towel, praying inwardly. *Come on, come on. Work, gravgummit!*

In a cacophony of grinding metal, the grinder powered up and began extruding pulverized meat once again.

"Yessss!" she shouted as the others yelled, too.

It took only about thirty minutes to grind sixty-three pounds of the lean meat, which Louis then wheeled off to the blast chiller. The meat had best be refrozen a bit before they ground it up even finer.

"Now for the fat," Boyar instructed, and he, Deja, and Louis shoveled in the eighteen pounds of primo lard. It oozed out of the grinder in practically no time. "Skal, get that to the blast fridge," Boyar said. The copper-scaled Rekloran stepped in and wheeled away the extruded fat.

"Now what, Chef Boyar?" asked the ever-inquisitive Chub.

"Now we wait another, oh, fifteen minutes."

"And what are you waiting for?"

"We've gotta make sure that the meat and fat are nice and cold before we run them through the three-milimeter plate. After that, we'll mix the seasonings into the meat and then combine the ground meat and fat together. Once we've done that, it's time to toss in the diced show fat and fold it into the emulsion. Then we're off to the sausage stuffer!"

"Oh, excellent plan. You sound like you've made a lot of guntlegraccis in your day."

"Indeed I have," said Bastian, ears perking up in pride.

Once they'd waited long enough, a few team members brought out the ground fat and meat. Glass went off to fetch the chilled water and wine. "Now for the three-milimeter plate," Bastian said. Everyone pitched in to run the meat and then the fat through the smaller grinding plate.

"OK, now comes the fun part!" Chef Boyar announced. Under his direction, they slowly transferred the ground meat to the food processor. "Gaskón, start feeding in the spice mixture." The chilled metal blades roared to life, and the spices rained down on the meat, slowly becoming incorporated into the pinkish blobs of tissue. Skal and Boyar had to push the globs of meat down a few times back into the path of the blades while Glass systematically poured in some slushy wine and water.

"And why, dear chefs, are you adding some frozen liquids to the mixture?" asked Chub.

"Oh, just an old trick to add flavor and also keep the mixture cool and pliable," Bastian said. Finally, it was time to incorporate the ground fat. Fascinated, Deja watched as the processor whirred and started combining the fat and the meat, with Glass once again adding more chilled fluids. Now light pink, the emulsion was ready to receive the diced fat pieces, peppercorns, and guntle nuts. In they all went, and the concoction began to get a bit gummy. Bastian powered down the food processor and Gaskón whistled.

"Nicely done, chefs! Now we're off to the sausage stuffer." After transferring the goopy mass into an enormous, wheeled container, the males led the way to the next piece of equipment.

"Glass, get the casing into place," Boyar said. "Skal and Gaskón, you both help load the canister while Deja and I supervise the casing as it is filled. Keep the setting on medium or it will come out too fast."

"Yes, chef!" Louis and Geckuano shouted.

"You ready for this?" Bastian asked Deja with a warm smile.

"Never more ready," she agreed, smiling back, though she still smarted from his rebuke over the grinder malfunction.

Deja and Bastian stood on either side of the casing that was fitted snugly over the machine's tube. As the meat emulsion oozed into the casing, they focused on creating as few air pockets as possible. "Good, that's good," Bastian coached, his navy-blue fur damp with perspiration.

"Goodness me," Chub declared. "It's looking wonderful, cheftestants!"

As the team of five chefs worked, the tremendous sausage took shape and glided onto a slow-moving conveyor belt beneath the sausage stuffer. The belt allowed Deja and Bastian to supervise the steady filling of the casing with their expert fingers. At long last, the seven-feet-long, almost one-hundred-pound sausage was complete. "Let's tie her off," Bastian said. He and Deja twisted the end of the casing and then Glass put on a zip tie to cinch it closed.

"Whew! Well done, all. Now what?" Chub asked, holocams buzzing around them all.

"Now we pop a mesh sack over the sausage to keep it nice and tight. Then we'll slip the guntlegracci into the sous vide apparatus. It'll need to cook at a hundred-seventy degrees Fahrenheit for about, oh, five hours."

"Ah, I see. Will you have time, though?"

Everyone automatically glanced up at the digital clock on the wall. Deja winced. *It's gonna be close!*

"We can get her done, don't worry," Boyar asserted, who began to supervise the next step involving the mesh sack.

Trying to sound helpful, Deja glanced at Bastian and said, "Wait, don't we need to use meat combs to poke the little air pockets?"

"Oh, right," he answered. "I was just going to order that."

Sure you were, she thought, but didn't say anything. Each of them grabbed a meat comb and pricked any air bubbles they found. Then they guided the sausage into the mesh sack. At long last, they slipped the colossal guntlegracci into the sous vide cooker for a nice, long water bath.

"Whoa! Now *that* was intense," Gaskón said, patting his sweaty face and neck with a towel that he'd found somewhere. Bastian grinned at Deja then gave her a little bow. She bowed in return, still wary of his temperament.

Almost as one, they found places to sit. And wait.

"Astounding teamwork," Chub said, then proceeded to interview each of the chefs, starting with Chef Boyar. *Please let that sausage turn out well*, Deja thought. The meat would need to cook for five hours and then cure for at least two days before the judges could do a taste test. That was a *long* time to wait to see if they'd been successful. But Deja could be as patient as a pregnant elephant. It might *seem* like a year and a half, but the fruits of their labor would all come to pass in good time.

TWO DAYS LATER, Deja was cramming for the next culinary challenge. "Crap, got that one wrong. Ask me some more questions," she said. Her brain was verging on the edge of insanity, but she had to cram as much food trivia into her head as possible.

"OK, but don't be so hard on yourself," Geoff replied.

"Easy for you to say." She frowned. "I should've known that one about pegoruu eggs."

"Now you know it, though. OK, here's the next question: Red Vines was a popular type of what kind of candy on Old Earth?"

"Oh! Licorice. Red licorice," she proclaimed.

"Yep, that's right," Geoff said. "Now how about this one: Once processed, what food can remain good for thousands of years?"

"That would be honey," Deja said, confident.

"Right! What's a famous cocktail from Ryos that is served in a copper mug?"

"Ah, that's easy. A Ryos Rillzer," Deja said, having drunk plenty of those.

"Yep. And how about this one? What food do the Yukalorians consume during mating season?"

"Yikes. Um, I think that would be...creamed shewl?" Deja guessed.

"Exactly. Good job!" Geoff applauded. He then asked her about eighty more questions, some which she got right and some which she didn't. But at least now she knew the correct answers to all of them.

"Whew," Deja said, running a hand through her silver-kissed, red hair. "I think I'm trivia'd out for now."

"Yes, I agree," Geoff said, cracking his neck and then his knuckles. "How about we find lunch. Get you some brain food. By the time we're done, the game show portion of the contest will be just about ready to start."

"Great. I'm starved. Let's go try out someplace new."

"You got it, boss." Geoff stood and extended his hand to her. She took it and got up. Then off they went to find a place for some grub in the nearby area. Tonight, she was slated to go out to dinner with Chef Bastian Boyar. With any luck, she'd be able to find out if he was really Famous Foodie in disguise.

"HELLLLLLO CHEFTESTANTS AND AUDIENCE MEMBERS!" exclaimed Chub, his blue-green fur almost sparkling in the light. Deja stood behind a small pulpit-style game console and held a clicker/buzzer thing in her hand. The front of her console showed her name on a holopanel. She and seventeen other contestants stood behind identical consoles holding their own buzzers. They were all arranged in a semi-circle, with the host standing in front of the players. Chub whirled around in a circle, looking at all the contestants and then waving up at the audience in the colosseum.

"Today, we have a new batch of participants ready to test their knowledge of food trivia from across the galaxy. Who will be victorious?" the alien asked.

The crowd roared back an incomprehensible jumble of names. Deja forced herself to loosen her grip on the buzzer. *Don't let nerves get to you now!* she admonished herself.

"OK, friends. You know the rules. Whoever buzzes in first will get to answer. If that contestant is wrong, the next person to trigger their buzzer will get a shot. After the second guess, the question is dead. Whoever guesses the most questions right wins, with a first runner up and a second runner up. Everyone clear?"

"Yes, sir," Deja and the others echoed. She spared a quick glance at some of her competitors, including Chef Gaskón and Chef Glass. The others were a mixture of humans, Vinadroans, Pintrels, Ractyls, and various other races. Their respective names were displayed on the console for all to see. The host had conducted similar game shows for other participants throughout today and the previous few days. Now it was her turn, and she just hoped she had studied enough. Bastian had won first place in his game show session, which was unsurprising.

"Let's begin!" Chub said. "Question: In the country of Tortin on this planet of Vinadro, who is the God of Grain?"

Deja thumbed her buzzer just a fraction too late. A brainy human named Chef Aleksander beat her to it. "That would be Gyan," he said.

"Correct!" Chub announced. "Next, what city on Old Earth is known as the 'Big Apple'?"

Deja beat everyone to *that* question. "New York City."

"Right on, Chef Dubois." Chub tapped the data pad in his hand to pull up the next question. "OK, everyone. On the planet Navith in the Bejón province, which fruit is used during the annual food fight festival?"

Chef Skal got that one: "Rotten dripplesss!" he replied with a hiss.

Curses. I almost had that one!

"New question: Carmine, a red food coloring, is made from boiling what?"

This time, Deja pressed her clicker first. "Cochineal beetles," she answered.

"Perfect. But who knows this next one? What food is known as 'Gretchen's Hand'?"

Chef Glass, darn her, buzzed in first. "Yamallow fruit," she said. Deja frowned.

"That is right! Good work," Chub answered. "Next up is this: The Heathrún Scale is used for what purpose?"

Deja pounced on that one. "Rating the spicy heat of peppers!" she said. No way she would miss that question.

"Yes, nice job. Now, who can tell me this: What animal is used to create the delicacy called chemmak pie?"

Chef Gaskón buzzed in first. "That's the zithip lizard." *Dang it.* Deja—or even Skal—should've gotten that one.

"Precisely! Now on to another piece of trivia," said Chub, who proceeded to ask another forty-two questions, many of which Deja answered correctly.

Then the host asked another tough one: "On Old Earth, what is the Jewish term for dietary law?"

Chef Aleksander pressed his clicker first. "That would be kosher."

"No, I'm sorry. Anyone else want to try?"

Deja jabbed her buzzer and took a deep breath. "I believe the term is Kashrut," she answered.

"That's it! Well done. Now for the Lightning Round!" Silently, Deja thanked one of her old carnie mates for being able to guess the last one correctly.

"The top five of you are now going to throw down for a chance to win this entire match," Chub declared. "And the top five are as follows: Chef Glass, Chef Aleksander, Chef Gaskón, Chef Dubois, and Chef Trill. The rest of you are excused. Everybody, give them a round of applause!"

The crowd responded with the requested clapping, and when it died down, only the final five chefs stood on the stage. Deja wished for speedy reflexes and an even quicker mind. The other four chefs were major contenders.

"Time for the first question: On Vinadro throughout the main continent, what is the 'star' of the customary meal for a funeral?"

Chef Gaskón buzzed in, with Deja right behind him. *Shoot!* "Atomic meatballs," Gaskón said smugly. *Argh! So close!*

"Exactly! Second question: On Ractyl, who is in charge of serving tea at a wedding?"

This time, Chef Trill, the Ractyl, pressed her clicker first. "The bride's *opuscommin* or first aunt."

"Indeed, Chef Trill," praised the stout Vinadroan. "Third question: On Old Earth, what food would the cartoon character Popeye the Sailor Man consume in order to gain super strength?"

Deja buzzed in. "Kale?"

"Nope, that's incorrect. Anyone else?"

Chef Glass rang in next. "Spinach."

"Yes, that's the one!" Chub affirmed. Her opponent grinned widely. Deja cursed under her breath, readying herself for the next question. "All right," the host said, "second to last question: On New Earth, what flower is the herb rithius derived from?"

Chef Glass beat Deja—and everyone else—again. "Taccafolia," said the other chef.

"That's correct, Chef Glass. Now for the final question. Are we ready, cheftestants?" Chub asked, raising his arms to encourage applause.

"Yes!" shouted Deja and the other finalists.

"OK. Here is the final question: Name the first food eaten on planet Shair's second moon during the Discovery 13 mission."

Deja practically broke her buzzer because she pressed it so fast and hard. "Freeze-dried pegoruu eggs."

"Brilliant job!" Chub agreed. "Now for the final tally. The winner is...Chef Glass!" Deja groaned. Still, she smiled with bravado as the audience thundered their approval and the winning chef took several bows. "The first runner up is...Chef Dubois!" *Yes!* A rush of adrenaline surged to her heart like an incoming tide. She nodded and waved at the crowd.

More applause followed that announcement. If she was right, Chef Gaskón would be in third place. Chub opened his mouth and announced just that: "And second runner up is...Chef Gaskón! Let's hear it for all three of them!" Deja and Gaskón beamed at each other and joined hands, raising their arms up in victory. After all, second and third place weren't that bad.

"Contestants, thank you for the wonderful participation. We will post everyone's rankings when the final trivia game is given tomorrow. And with that, we will now take an intermission!" Chub finished, taking a series of dramatic bows himself, the teal hair ruffling atop his head. Deja released Gaskón's hand and they followed Chef Glass off the stage.

Backstage, their sous chefs were all waiting for them. Geoff reached Deja first and gave her a light punch on the arm. "Nice work, boss! You almost took the whole game."

"Oh, but she *didn't*, did she?" piped up Chef Glass with a gloating smirk.

"Yeah, yeah," Deja said. "Gaskón and I still gave you a run for your breakfast."

Chef Glass *harrumphed* and gestured for her lanky sous chef to follow her from the small room.

Chef Trill and Chef Aleksander came over to Deja and Gaskón, offering hands to shake in congratulations. After exchanging some pleasantries, the remaining participants and their sous chefs left the room, headed for their respective quarters. Deja was ready to celebrate. And that meant some top-shelf icewine. Or gehut. Maybe both! And with Bastian due to take her out in about three hours, she wouldn't even have to pay for it.

CHUB GESTURED to the huge array of guntlegraccis before him. Geoff counted twenty of them on an equal number of stainless-steel tables. "Here, you see a collection of guntlegracci sausages that were made several days ago. Now we will find out who flunked this tasty test and who aced it!" the host announced. The crowd roared in eagerness. Geoff squeezed Deja's arm in reassurance, then stepped back as the four other members of her guntlegracci team joined her and stepped forward onto a platform.

"First up, we have a guntlegracci made by Chef Bastian Boyar, team captain, along with Chef Riva Glass, Chef Louis Gaskón, Chef EvaLynn Dubois, and Chef Geckuano Skal. Will their creation please or displease the mighty judges?"

Chub raised a long cleaver up high over the sausage and then brought it down near the end of it. He began slicing with care, back and forth, back and forth until at last he had cut through the enormous tube of emulsified meat. A collective gasp sounded in the cooking coliseum. "Oh, my, this is a *lovely* sight! It is a beautiful, light pink, sprinkled evenly with peppercorns, guntle nuts, and cubed fat. Look at it glisten!"

Geoff clapped along with the others. *I knew she could do it!*

With great fanfare, Chub sliced off thin pieces of the guntlegracci for each of the famed judges. And, just twenty minutes later, the verdict was in: Team Boyar had earned ninety-one points out of a total one-hundred.

"Woot!" Geoff yelled, though he couldn't hear himself over the sound of the raucous crowd. *And* that *is how it's done!*

�♪

"Do you think I'll get Bastian to tell me some of his secrets?" Deja asked Geoff, who stood near the shared door between their suites. For her date with Chef Boyar, Deja had slipped into a black-and-red sheath dress with a V-neck and ruffled lace at the hemline. She'd ordered it, some gold jewelry, and some cute, red pumps just for tonight.

"Looking like that, I don't see how he could resist telling you *all* his secrets," Geoff said in an approving tone, cracking his knuckles absently.

Deja chuckled. "Good answer. Let's just hope I can determine if he's actually Famous Foodie or not."

"Yes. Good luck. Make sure you record the entire conversation so I can listen to it with you later."

"Of course," she said, then watched Geoff retreat to his room. Soon after that, three knocks sounded on the door. She opened the door and found Chef Bastian Boyar standing on the other side. He was wearing Vinadro's version of a tuxedo, a long-sleeved, red suit coat over a white, button-down shirt and a matching pair of red slacks with crisp pleats. *Good thing I dressed up*, she thought.

"Good evening, Chef EvaLynn Dubois. How are you tonight?" Bastian asked with a bow.

"Doing splendidly," she answered, bowing also.

"Wonderful. Let's be off, shall we?" He offered her his arm, which she took, and they walked to the elevator. Her quarters were, after all, on the 75th floor of the contestant housing.

"I saw that you only came in second in the gameshow portion of the contest," he said, turning his head and smiling at her.

"Yes, I was *this* close to winning. But that blasted Chef Glass beat me."

"Well, it was a close one. You did very well," he said in earnest.

"Thank you. My sous chef helped quiz me for hours on end. Given that and the contest itself, my brain is rather...mushy right now," she admitted. Showing a little vulnerability didn't hurt. In fact, doing so usually provided the wooer with an opening to offer assistance.

"Then I am glad I have the honor of taking you out for a night of fun." Bastian chuckled, placing one large, navy-blue hand over her small brown one and squeezing a little. Once they'd reached the lobby, Chef Boyar spoke to the concierge and ordered some transportation.

"So where are you taking me, Bastian?" she asked.

"Just to one of my old haunts, EvaLynn—may I call you EvaLynn?"

"I don't see why not," she answered in a flirtatious tone.

"Well, EvaLynn, I think you'll enjoy the place I am escorting you to. It made me into the chef I am today. Saved me from a misspent youth, in fact," he related in a confiding voice.

"Oh, really? Now I am intrigued," Deja said, pleased with the direction of the conversation. The more she could learn about Chef Boyar, the better.

"Ah, here is our chariot," Bastian said when a long, red limousine pulled up outside. *Wow. Splashy.*

First, the chef opened the lobby door for her. The limo's driver, a slender human blonde, held open the vehicle's door for both of them. Deja entered first and Bastian second.

Inside, the windows were heavily tinted, so she couldn't see outside too well. That was somewhat disconcerting; she liked to know where she was going. But she decided not to complain. Besides, the interior of the vehicle had a killer mini bar and some comfy, red leather seats. The ceiling of the limo was high enough that Bastian, when sitting, didn't need to duck his head.

Seeing the direction of her gaze, the Vinadroan grinned. "Up for a bit of refreshment, I see. Well, we do have a bit of a drive, so we might as well make the best of it. First, I'd better give our destination to the driver, though."

Deja expected the chef to speak to the chauffeur, who was already behind the wheel again. But instead, Bastian turned to a small console in the wall and tapped out some directions in Vinadroan. Deja wished she were wearing her LinguaLenses. Then she'd know what manner of place he was taking her to visit. But she'd just have to deal with the suspense for now.

"Now," Chef Boyar said, sliding over to the mini bar on the other side of the compartment, "would you care for some of your customary gehut or icewine? We have both."

Deja almost clenched her jaw. *How does he know that?* He must be spying on her—either for nefarious reasons or for romantic ones. Hmm. Maybe both.

"How about just some icewine for now. Green, if possible," she said in a tone she hoped sounded casual.

"Yes, green icewine coming up. A nice vintage, too, as it is fifty years old."

"Perfect. It's about as old as I am," she lied on purpose, wondering if he would miss a beat. He didn't.

He poured a glass for each of them with a steady hand and then gave her one. She sipped it. "This is top shelf. I'll give you points for that," she said, but resisted taking another drink. She needed to stay alert.

"Indeed. I think you deserve only the best," said the Vinadroan, his navy-blue eyes unwavering as he gazed at her. As he spoke, he toyed with one of the smaller gold hoops in his left ear.

"Why, thank you." She flashed a sassy smile although she actually felt more like his next meal than his date. His gaze had an amorous yet predatory edge to it. This man was more than a skilled chef. As he'd shown in his past competitions and in his interactions with her, he knew a thing or two about strategizing and outmaneuvering others. In truth, the Vinadroan could very well be Famous's right-hand operative or even Famous Foodie himself.

"So how did you come to enter the Ultimate Chef of the Galaxy Contest?" he asked, playing with his earring again.

She decided to give a mixture of truth and untruth. "Oh, my dad and I watched the show almost every year when I was growing up. He was a self-styled gourmand, you see, and we traveled many places because he was in the shipping industry."

"No wonder you have good taste," Bastian said with an appraising and cunning look.

"Thank you kindly," she said. "What about you? How did cooking steal your young heart?"

"That is a good question. My heart was rather set upon vices like thievery for quite a while. But I did that to survive. You see, I was orphaned at a young age. I didn't have any other talents. Or so I thought."

"Go on," she prompted when he paused.

"Well, I would like to show you rather than tell you. For now, let's just say that a talented individual took me under her wing. I'm taking you to meet her."

"Sounds like someone I'd definitely like to see," Deja said with genuine warmth.

Chef Boyar nodded. "And so you shall. Looks like we are here." The limo slowed and Deja handed her drink to Bastian who held out a hand for it. "Thanks. We'll leave our drinks here and get fresh ones inside."

"Perfect," she said. The female driver opened the door on Bastian's side of the vehicle. The tall chef stepped out onto the cracked pavement then held out his hand to her, which she took. He guided her out of the limo and onto a semi-bustling city sidewalk. Glancing around, Deja was surprised to see somewhat dilapidated shops and offices flanking a pristine-looking eating establishment that was six stories tall and made from brown brick and dark wood. A massive wooden spoon was mounted on the roof with a sign proclaiming the place to be called, unsurprisingly, "The Wooden Spoon."

"My, what a charming eatery!" Deja declared in all honesty.

"Thank you," Bastian said with a delighted smile, showing both fangs fully. "As of one year ago, it's mine. The Wooden Spoon is this province's communal kitchen and restaurant. This bistro-slash-lodging is also the source of my culinary salvation."

"I'm impressed," Deja admitted. "I'd love to see everything."

"Well, then, let's get to it!" With that, Chef Boyar led her in the front doors, which two purple Vinadroans swept open in a coordinated, smooth motion. As Bastian and Deja strolled inside, the two aliens bowed gracefully and then straightened like soldiers on parade. Inwardly, Deja was intrigued. Her date was certainly living up to his reputation as a respected chef and restauranteur.

They entered a grand dining hall with row after row of gleaming wooden tables decked out in spotless white tablecloths, napkins, and sparkling dinnerware. Deja could hardly see an empty seat anywhere, though. The room was packed. The ceiling was vaulted and gorgeous crystal chandeliers lit the spacious area. A large stage took up most of the front wall. On that stage, a motley yet sharply dressed crew of musicians were performing a beautiful ballad on the virtues of cooking with the most important ingredient of all: love.

Chef Boyar and Deja stopped at a podium behind which a middle-aged Be'Voyan stood with menus in hand, waiting to receive them. "Chef Boyar and Chef Dubois," the man proclaimed, "welcome to The Wooden Spoon! Please follow me."

"Thank you, Mr. Quint," Bastian said. He and Deja followed the golden-eyed Mr. Quint toward the front of the stage where someone had set up a special table for two. The host pulled out a plush chair for Deja, who sat down and scooted in with the Be'Voyan's assistance. Chef Boyar seated himself.

"This dining hall is simply gorgeous!" Deja said, thinking privately that Bastian must have a *lot* of clout to own and operate such a joint. Furthermore, given his performances in the cookoff and his interactions with others, Deja surmised that the Vinadroan possessed the sorts of influence and connections that could be the bread and butter of any food activist, including a certain culinary crusader named Famous Foodie. Growing up on the streets as he had, Bastian could've developed a ruthless side for sure. Excitement and anticipation coursed through Deja like fizzy champagne.

"I like to think so, too," he told her, taking a digital menu pad from Mr. Quint. The Be'Voyan also handed one to Deja. Most restaurants had holographic menus built into the tables, but she liked that Chef Boyar's eatery was more on the old-fashioned side. "Mr.

Quint, please bring some of my special green icewine for me and EvaLynn here."

"Right away, chef," said the host, moving away to find a maître d'.

Taking a napkin from the porcelain plate in front of her, Deja laid it over her lap while Bastian did likewise with his napkin. That done, Deja leaned forward to ask him something. "So how did this place come to your rescue?"

"Very good question," Boyar said, steepling his hands in front of himself. "I once tried to 'dine and dash' as they say, but Chef Lenore Swilton, the Executive Chef, caught me and dragged me back here to work off my meal. She proceeded to teach me a thing or two about the business and pleasure of feeding people's stomachs *and* souls."

"How scandalous—and interesting," Deja said, curiosity piqued.

The Vinadroan chuckled, smoothing back his blue-and-gold hair. "Isn't it, though?" he stated more than asked. "I'll introduce you to Lenny in just a bit. First, let's get started with some appetizers, shall we?"

"Sounds good," she said, eyes glancing down at her menu with great interest. To her delight, the appetizers alone occupied at least three pages of the menu. "This is going to be tough to choose," Deja admitted. This was the sort of place she and her dad had loved to frequent on their trips to various planets.

"Then we'll just have to try a little of everything," Boyar said with a chuckle.

At that moment, a short maître d' arrived holding two flutes of green icewine, which he deposited on the table with supreme grace. Bastian thanked the human server, then proceeded to order several appetizers. "Now, dear Eva, which ones would you like to try that I haven't already ordered?"

Deja promptly listed four items she wanted to taste then set down her menu.

"I'll have those dishes prepared right away, esteemed chefs," said the maître d', a young female who turned and walked off at a brisk pace.

Deja returned her attention to her escort, wondering if this pleasant yet shrewd Vinadroan was not only capable of running a tip-top establishment but also capable of murder. "So," she said, "Chef Bastian Boyar, please tell me more about your first time entering the Chef of the Galaxy Contest. I've heard you think you were cheated out of winning five years ago. And, seeing all this, I can certainly believe something untoward must have happened." The oddsbreaker finished that statement with a special smile reserved for those she wanted to garner intel from.

"I would be happy to *satisfy* your curiosity on that score," he said with a suggestive grin. "But first I would love to hear about your run-in with Judge Lukas Inciardi."

"Well, you did ask nicely," Deja began, then told him briefly about her encounter with the judge. Bastian laughed so loudly that other diners turned to look in his direction. "I was, however, wearing a disguise," Deja said, giggling herself. "And so the judge doesn't know who I am, thank goodness!"

"How clever of you," Chef Boyar said approvingly, finally able to rein in his laughter. "As for me," he continued, "I am quite certain Judge Inciardi is the reason I lost the Ultimate Chef of the Galaxy Contest those five short years ago." The blue Vinadroan leaned forward and lowered his voice. "In fact, I have all but damning evidence that he in particular is dirty."

Deja, who had begun to sip her icewine, almost spit some out at the mention of dirt. Instead, she coughed a little. Could this be Bastian's way of telling her that he was Famous Foodie?

Tread carefully, girl, Deja told herself.

"Well, that's a shame, seeing as how he's such a *delightful* human being," she said with a sarcastic chortle.

"Haha. You're not wrong," Chef Boyar agreed, his expression taking on a cunning edge. "I intend to make sure he pays for that once I have the evidence I need."

"Sounds like a noble cause," the oddsbreaker said softly and nodded. But just how far was the chef willing to go to oust Inciardi as a supposed fraud and a rascal? With any luck, Deja might soon obtain an answer for that very question.

Doctor Chipton strolled into Patricio's room in the afternoon of however many days he had been in the hospital. "How's my best patient doing?" he asked.

"*Corrección, soy un mal paciente de hospital,*" Patricio said with a laugh.

"No, you really are an excellent patient, good sir. Now, we have some weighty matters to discuss. Are you up for that?" The doctor smoothed back his yellow hair feathers and crossed his arms over his chest.

Patricio nodded wordlessly, fear seeping into his bones like a winter chill.

The surgeon pulled up a wheeled stool and sat down by the side of the bed. "First, how is your pain level?"

"Not too bad. But the drugs make me sleepy," he said.

"I'm glad your pain is under control. I'm afraid we can't help the side effects. And you need lots of sleep."

"Right, *por supuesto.*"

"So far, you have done a wonderful job with your recovery. We are pleased with your progress." The doctor took a breath. "OK, now for the tougher news. You are recovering from quite a lot, and we will need to perform several surgeries. You had a cracked skull, which we've repaired already once the swelling in your brain went down. And you know that we've already reattached your tongue. But unfortunately, your femurs and kneecaps were broken. So those all need surgery. And one hand was crushed severely. It will require a series of procedures. You'll have some residual nerve damage here and there. And your liver was bruised, so we had to take out a part of it. We had to replace one of your kidneys, too. And you'll need significant physical therapy to regain all your control. Any questions?"

All this bad news soaked into Patricio like foul grease into an old sponge. He felt so...awful, ancient, and powerless. "*Sí, yo entiendo.* What surgeries will you start with? Is there a risk I might not wake up?"

Doctor Chipton leaned forward. "Yes, there is that possibility. You were lucky to even survive as long as you did before you were transferred here via hospital ship."

"I understand," Patricio acknowledged. "Well, when do we start? May I talk to my daughter first?"

"Sure, you may. We'll take you in for surgery on your legs, knees, and hand as soon as you're ready."

"*Muchas gracias.*"

The Ractyl got up and pulled a special, wheeled table over, positioning the length of it above Patricio's torso. Then he took out a data pad and set it upright on the table. "When you're ready, issue the pad the command and it will call your daughter. I'll leave you be for now." Doctor Chipton patted Patricio on the arm before leaving the room.

Wetting his lips, Patricio tried not to let fear take root in his head. In a little while, he'd be on an operating table again. But he couldn't let his daughter see his pain or panic. He couldn't distract her from her mission, whatever it was. He'd already been the source of enough grief for his sweet daughter. Hence, he took many deep breaths and decided, finally, *not* to speak to her before he went under the knife. Instead, he summoned his surgeon.

Chef "Lenny" Swilton, a plump, silver-furred Vinadroan, strolled up to Deja and Bastian's private table with a rolling gait. Her hair was grayish silver, too, and seemed to float about her head like a halo. In one large hand, she held a formidable wooden spoon.

When she reached the table, Bastian stood and embraced the older chef.

"Executive Chef Lenore Swilton, please meet the lovely Chef EvaLynn Dubois, my worthy opponent and my companion for tonight."

"It's 'Lenny' to you, Bastian. Don't go making me look all stuck up like those snooty chefs you despise so much."

"Okay, okay, Lenny," he conceded. "Please say hello to EvaLynn here and tell her what you will of our relationship."

"I'd be happy to," said the female chef, brandishing her wooden spoon. "This here spoon can be used for more than just stirring the soup. It works quite well to knock some sense into a confused, wayward, and crafty child such as Bastian. Taught him how to make his own way in the world and how to do it with class."

"I have no doubt of that." Deja smiled and bowed at the executive chef. "Please tell me more," she invited, motioning to a nearby chair. The stout chef hauled the chair over to the table and sat. Chef Boyar then seated himself, too.

"Don't mind if I do," Lenny said with a jolly laugh. She proceeded to regale Deja with stories of Bastian's exploits, both glorious and disreputable. After that, the chef excused herself and left Bastian and Deja to their own devices. The sumptuous meal that followed made Deja's mouth water. All eight courses were as divine and sophisticated as a cloud is light and fluffy. She and Bastian talked and ate and drank the night away. When the clock reached an hour to midnight, she had to beg him to stop with the food and drink. She needed to get back to her quarters to discuss things with Geoff. With a little cajoling, Deja managed to get Bastian to again summon the red limo, which soon deposited them back at her lodging.

"Goodbye, Bastian," Deja said, then stood on tiptoe to give him a kiss on both cheeks. "Thanks for a lovely night out. I'm sure we will have more to discuss in the future, yes?"

"Oh, of course, my dear," he said, bowing. "Good night. I shall see you tomorrow."

Deja nodded and then waved as he walked away. She waited until he was out of sight to unlock her door and go inside. *Whew. What a night!*

ℓ

SEVERAL HOURS HAD PASSED since Patricio had awoken from his surgery. "Call Deja Ortega," he commanded aloud. It was late, but he knew Deja would probably still be up.

"Calling," said the gadget. It took a few minutes of suspense before Deja picked up. Again, he could not see her, but he could hear her voice, altered though it was.

"*Hola, papá. Cómo estás?*" Deja asked.

"*Estoy mas o menos,*" he replied, trying to sound somewhat brave. He knew she wouldn't believe him if he said he felt fine. "How is the mission going, *mija?*"

"*Muy bien, gracias.* I can't tell you what it is exactly. But I can say, thanks for all the cooking lessons."

That sparked his interest. "*De verdad?* Good. But now I am curious."

"*Lo siento,* but I can't say anything more. I think of you often, Papá. Focus on getting well, *sí?*"

"*Sí. Gracias, mija.*"

"Your physician said you had major surgery today," Deja said. "How did it go? And why didn't you call me before it happened?"

"Oh, I was trying to be brave like you," he answered.

She laughed. "I think I have more luck than I have bravery. But thank you."

He cleared his throat, trying to keep the fear and pain from forcing his voice higher. "*De nada.* I will talk to you again when I can, *mija. Adios.*"

ℓ

DEJA ENDED THE CALL. Her father had better recover well. Moreover, she had better perform well in the next competition if she wanted to stay in the contest as a whole. Next up was some kind of mystery challenge.

This time, Geoff would be by her side. That sure made it seem less...daunting. Of course, she couldn't let him know how much his presence meant to her. He didn't seem to understand that she had problems that were...difficult to talk about. Could he handle it if she laid everything on the table? Probably not.

Deja realized that she had taken out her flask without thinking. Now, she looked at the item and put it away in haste. She'd had *plenty* to drink while out with Bastian. Anyway, it wasn't like she couldn't *stop* drinking if she really wanted to. With that reassuring thought, she got up on unsteady feet and went to meet Geoff to discuss her "date" with Bastian.

GEOFF COULDN'T HELP but feel somewhat resentful that Deja had spent the evening with another suitor, even if it was just an undercover op. The jealousy seethed inside him like a bubbling cauldron. He was almost ready to ping her PalmStar when he heard her knock on their shared door.

He wasted no time in opening the door and ushering her in. Her breath smelled harsh but fruity and she wobbled as she walked, clearly smashed. He reached out and guided her to an overstuffed chair, frustrated and relieved at the same time.

"So what intel did you get on Boyar?" Geoff asked, still standing. "Give me a summary and then let's listen to the recording, yeah? Or do you want to do this in the morning?"

"Now's fine," she drawled, kicking off her high heels. "So get this, Boyar owns this fancy place down in the lower east side of Remla. It's a restaurant, culinary school, lodging, souvenir shop, and more. And he grew up as an orphan. Got himself into a whole bunch of trouble until an executive chef took him in and taught him how to cook. The guy wasn't always an upstanding member of society."

"Interesting. So once a ruffian, maybe always a ruffian?"

"Yep. Maybe so. And he sure has it out for Inciardi. Claims to be waiting for enough evidence to humiliate and discredit him."

"OK, so perhaps Boyar *is* Famous Foodie. But do you really think he might try to murder the judge?" Geoff asked, brow furrowed.

"I think he's got the chutzpah to do it. Just not sure if he's our bad guy," Deja said, shaking her head (and slurring her speech).

"All right. Let's get you to bed. I can listen to the recording on my own. You, boss, need to get some rest."

Some emotion—guilt, perhaps?—flickered across her face like lightning across the sky. Then it was gone. "Oh...okay. If you say so," she said, then stumbled when trying to rise.

"Hold up there, boss. I've got ya." Geoff bent down and scooped her up. He soon deposited her on her own bed and tucked her in. After a few moments, her face relaxed into sleep.

That blue, smooth-talking Vinadroan had gotten Deja drunk. And she already had trouble controlling her drinking. Geoff felt like punching a wall or, even better, Chef Boyar's face. Fighting down the urge to go have it out with the chef, he cracked his knuckles. Then he turned and went back to his room, where he listened to every painful minute of Deja and Bastian's date. Now, if only he could figure out how to break the case before it broke Deja...

Geoff sat on the edge of his bed. He had just finished updating General Trikk on the mission. So far, Deja was still in the running for the Ultimate Chef of the Galaxy. But they had no idea when or how Famous Foodie was going to strike. However, they were fairly certain that Chef Bastian Boyar was, in fact, Famous Foodie.

In just a few minutes, he and Deja would join up and head to another contest. He simply wished Deja would finally level with Geoff about her feelings for him. He had a good idea why she thought she wasn't "good enough" for him. But the lieutenant colonel didn't want to push her; she'd just shut him out again. It hadn't escaped him that she always seemed to need a drink more than just now and then. And she'd been quite knackered last night when she got back to her room. So, yeah, he'd have to be careful.

He sighed and cracked his knuckles absently.

A knock sounded on his door. "Coming," he said. He looked through the peephole. Sure enough, it was Deja. He unlocked the door and stepped out to join her, hoping they'd have luck in the next event.

"BEHOLD YOUR NEXT BATCH OF CHEFTESTANTS," said Chub, the always-jovial presenter. "We shall see if they are up for this watery contest."

Watery? thought Geoff, who stood on stage next to Deja.

The stage had been set up with rows of cooking stations for the twenty-five contestants who would compete. At the front was a huge, semicircular pantry. But in the middle of the stage stood some rectangular shapes that were enshrouded with fabric. Everybody knew the special ingredient would be under there. But what would it be? Something that lived in water, apparently.

The judges sat upon their own stages around the center dais, watching and appraising.

"Okay, audience. We have the judges, we have the chefs, and we have our secret ingredient. What could it be?" Bots wheeled out to grasp the covers over the boxy receptacles. They lifted the fabric and everyone gasped. Several five- and six-feet-long eels swam around inside twenty-five separate aquariums.

"Yes, that's right. Eels. And these are electric! They don't like being touched; we can tell you that," added Chub quite unnecessarily.

A little danger, huh? Geoff could handle that. Deja gave him a look that said, "We'd better be on our toes."

"All right, chefs. Each of you has one and a half hours to satiate the judges with some eel delicacies. Here is the equipment you'll be needing to catch and kill the eels humanely." Some other bots came out bearing gloves, pinchers, and bolt guns for each team. "You have twenty minutes to make use of the pantry and then it will be closed off. Are you ready?"

"Yes!" they all shouted.

"Time starts...NOW!"

"Pantry," said Deja. They both raced to the pantry.

"What do we need, boss?"

"We're going to make Cajun eel tacos and fresh corn salsa with dirty rice. Here's what I need you to get." She rattled off half the ingredients to him, and he set off to get what she'd specified. Cajun eel tacos. That sounded good to him. He threw a bunch of spices in his basket, dodging other contestants who'd decided to hit the pantry first too. Then he made it over to the produce and piled his basket full of fresh corn and some other vegetables. By the time he was done, Deja was already sprinting to their station to drop off her load of food. *She always did make running look extra nice*, Geoff thought. He made it to the station soon after she did and dropped his basket near the sink.

"Great," she said.

"Let's go get our electric protein," Geoff replied. She spared him a smile and they took off to their tank together. Geoff and Deja pulled on the water- and shock-resistant gloves that went up to their shoulders. Geoff now knew why their hands and arms had been measured a while back. The gloves fit perfectly. He picked up the pinchers and noted the bolt gun that had been supplied to kill the eels.

"So," he said, "shall I take the biting end?"

"Be my guest," she said.

With that, they worked to catch a slippery eel—each of which had some very impressive teeth. Those teeth curved inward, which was nature's way of making sure that prey was unable to escape once the eel's jaws had snapped shut.

"Okay, grab its head first," Deja suggested.

"Sure." He had done a lot of fishing in his day, but never like this. The purplish eels kept dodging and swimming out of the way of the pinchers. "Forget this," Geoff said, throwing the pinchers over his shoulder.

"You sure?" she asked.

"Absolutely."

At that moment, the presenter's attention shifted to them. *Perfect*, thought Geoff. *Not like I need to concentrate.*

"And what luck are you having with *your* eels, Chef Dubois?" asked Chub.

"They're being most unhelpful," Deja informed him. "But we're about to wrangle one now."

"Oooh. This should be interesting."

Geoff tried to ignore that and the other prattle from the host. "Chef Dubois, I need some extra livers from the pantry. And some butcher's twine. Can you go get that for me?"

"What could Sous Chef Blackleaf be planning?" asked Chub in dramatic overtones.

Deja gave Geoff an odd look but took off to the pantry, which would disappear in one minute and thirty seconds. They already had some goose livers for the rice, but he knew that she'd only grabbed enough for that. As she left, Geoff went to their station and grabbed a cheesecloth. Then he hustled over to the tank just as Deja came running with the livers. She handed him the package. He tore it open and dumped the contents in the middle of the cheesecloth. Then he gathered the edges of the cloth and tied off the top with the twine, leaving a long line to hold onto. He squeezed it briefly to get some of the juices flowing through the cheesecloth. Then Geoff tossed the loaded bait into the tank.

"Here we go," he said. "This trick works back home. Let's see if they have a taste for livers." In seconds, one of the eels struck the bait hard, biting into it with gusto.

"And we have a winner—or a loser depending on your viewpoint," remarked Dornack.

Geoff pulled the thick string hand over hand until the eel was up against one of the corners. Now that its curved teeth were embedded in the fabric, it couldn't shake free. "OK, chef," Geoff instructed, "I need you to be ready to grab its middle with your pinchers—or your gloves. I'm going to lift it out by the line." She nodded, and he began to pull the eel from the water.

The eel surged out of the tank and straight into Geoff. He fell backward, caught off guard. A shock of electricity coursed through his chest. Every muscle stiffened and darkness greeted him.

"MEDIC! MEDIC!" Deja shouted. She grabbed the bolt gun from the ground and lunged at the eel that was shocking and wriggling over her partner. She kicked the beast until it rolled off of Geoff. With the bolt gun, she managed to pin down the eel's head and deliver the kill shot. It went limp, and she kicked the creature farther from Geoff's body. She checked his pulse. Nothing. She locked her hands together and began chest compressions, shouting for a medic again.

"It looks like one of our sous chefs is down. Is there hope for him?" asked the host in melodramatic tones.

"Oh, shut the slag up!" she responded, still giving chest compressions. She counted the compressions in her head, then bent down and breathed into his mouth. She realized she was panting in fear and exertion.

"Ian! Come on, Ian. Wake up," she commanded, her vision warping with moisture from unshed tears.

"Move over," shouted one of the two medics who had arrived.

With reluctance, she gave up her position at Geoff's side. Just as she did, she shouted at him again. Then to her relief, her partner jerked, took in a lungful of air, and raised his head. The crowd cheered. "What just happened?" he asked, dazed.

"You got a little fried," she said, her heart swelling in gratitude. "But now that you're back, are you up for some cooking? We're gonna fry this big slagger." The crowd rumbled in delight. Deja blinked hard, realizing her hands were shaking.

"Heck, yes."

"Good. I'll even let you butcher it," she told him. He deserved to be the one to cut up the little monster. She forced herself not to think what would've happened if he hadn't woken up.

"Excellent," Geoff said, then managed to sit up. The medics tried to protest, but Geoff just pushed them away.

Chub chimed in with, "And Blackleaf is back in action. What a tough sous chef we have here, people!"

The crowd clapped as Deja helped Geoff get to his feet. After that, the two of them scooped up each end of the eel and lugged it back to their station. Other teams were carrying their own catches back to their posts. Yet quite a few teams still labored to catch their own eels.

"I'll prep the spices and get the flour tortillas going," she said. "I'll have the oil nice and hot for our friend there. Don't skin him. I want the skin to fry up nice and crisp."

"Yes, ma'am."

So Deja set out to make flour tortillas as fast as she could. Just as she was about finished kneading the dough, Chef Gaskón hurried up to her station.

"Chef Dubois. Might I trouble you for some flour? I just spilled a bunch on the floor. Bother these hands of mine!"

Lending ingredients to other contestants wasn't against the rules, but it could backfire on her if his dish outshone hers. Still, he had shown her kindness by letting her borrow something in a past contest. Besides, he had been a good teammate not too long ago. So she decided to risk it.

"Sure. You can have this right here."

"You're amazing. Thank you. I won't forget it!" His last words faded off as he ran back to his station.

♪

Meanwhile, Geoff laid the eel on the cutting board. He still felt a little wobbly, but he shrugged it off. He grabbed a suitable knife and started gutting the eel from the underside. He opened up the eel and cut out the backbone. Then he relieved the carcass of the innards and threw them in the trash. Using the movable faucet, he rinsed away the blood. He flipped the eel over and began to remove the fins on the upper and lower body. His sharp knife made quick work of it. He was no stranger to carving up game of all types. Then he cut off the head. Lastly, he sliced off a portion of the bony tail, leaving a perfect, rectangular filet of eel. He rinsed the whole carcass again.

"Eel's done. How big do you want the pieces?" he asked.

Deja looked over his work and nodded in approval. "Give me as many two-inch strips as you can."

He proceeded to do as asked, slicing up the eel that had almost taken his life. *Take that*, he thought.

"Now toss them in the flour and spice mixture," she instructed, busy cooking tortillas and prepping the salsa. Two vats of boiling oil awaited the eel bits.

At this point, the teal-furred announcer broke into their conversation. Again. "And what are you cooking for the judges, Chef Dubois? And how is your sous chef feeling?"

"Feeling good," piped up Geoff.

"We're making Cajun fried eel tacos with lime sauce, fresh corn salsa, and a side of dirty rice."

"Sounds tasty. Carry on!" Dornack said happily.

At this point, Geoff had the eel pieces ready to go. Deja grabbed the bowl from him and began placing the battered pieces in the oil. "Thanks. Start on the rice for me?"

"Sure thing." He grabbed the rice, onions, peppers, livers, sausage, celery, garlic, thyme, and paprika. First, he poured some oil in a hot pan. He rinsed the rice in a colander until the water was clear. Finding a stockpot, he filled it with the rice and some poultry stock, setting it to boil. Then he chopped up the livers and sausage. Into the frying pan they went. He was about to start chopping the vegetables when Deja moved in to take over.

⚖

"G ET OUR LIME SAUCE GOING," Deja ordered. "And turn this batch of eel." Geoff scurried off to start on the sauce and check the eel. Meanwhile, Deja chopped up the vegetables and garlic. As Geoff prepared the lime sauce, she sautéed the vegetables with the livers and sausage and then seasoned everything with thyme, garlic, paprika, salt, and pepper. She checked the rice. Almost done.

Deja looked up at the clock. They had only twenty-five minutes left. Just enough time for everything to finish cooking and then plate it all. As the rice finished, she added more stock, the meat, and the vegetables. She turned it to simmer, praying the flavors would meld in time.

"How's that sauce coming?" she asked.

"Just thickening it up. Tastes perfect."

Deja took a tasting spoon and dipped it in, capturing some sauce. The taste was smooth yet acidic and just what she had wanted. "Start getting the plates ready to go. I'll take care of the eel." As Deja inspected the eel, she smiled to herself. The seafood was crispy and smelled delicious. She used a special ladle to remove the pieces from the oil, placing them on paper towels to drain the grease. Taking one piece that had already cooled a little, she blew on the battered eel and tasted it.

"And how's that taste, Chef Dubois?" asked the host, a holocam hovering near her face.

"Divine," she said, then added this batch of eel to the previous batches and started to plot out the plating.

"But will you have time to plate?" Chub asked dubiously.

"I'll make time," Deja answered, still busy with the eel.

Side by side, Geoff and Deja worked to plate the dish. He put the tortillas down, then Deja put down some of the eel pieces while Geoff placed the salsa on top. Deja finished it off with the sauce. As soon as they finished that, Deja told Geoff to get the crescent-shaped forms for the rice. The half-moon shape would hug the curve of the plate, making it look even fancier.

Deja tasted the rice and experienced a little bliss. It turned out wonderfully. Turning off the element, she and Geoff raced the clock, pressing the rice into the special forms.

"Ten, nine, eight..." said Chub. Just as he counted down the seconds, they plated the last of the food and tossed on a little more sauce. Deja almost stopped breathing, but they had made it. Now to wait their turn to see if they had made the cut.

Deja knotted her hands behind her back. This was an elimination round. Only ten of the twenty-five chefs would make it through. She just hoped this dish would keep her and Geoff in the running. "Tiiiime to diiiiine," their host said with glee.

♪

"AND NOW," Chub announced, "we come to Chef Gaskón. What have you made for us?"

"I've made gorshun eel pie for your eating pleasure," said the porcine chef, bowing in the direction of the judges. "It has baked eel with a medley of carrots, yorbas, and devlons in a truffle gravy and a side of crisp, garlic bread sticks."

The judges sampled their pies. Deja wondered if the chef had done a good job or not. Finally, a series of chimes sounded, and the judges pushed their plates aside. Most of the culinary critics pulled out palate-cleansing sprays. Inciardi, however, reached inside his tailored blazer to retrieve something. When the camera zoomed in on him, Deja recognized the gilded, nano-equipped toothpick. Of course. The new gadget he had shown off during the trip to this planet.

"Well," Chub asked, "what do we think, judges? Is the pie to die for?"

"The gravy is a little over-seasoned for my taste," said the Rekloran judge named Greggston. "But the sweet hints of truffle make up for that. I loved the flaky pastry, and the eel was definitely the star of the show."

One Vinadroan, Chef Renthar, said, "Ah, I agree with you on the eel. But I disagree with you on the gravy. I thought its notes of truffle and white wine blended well together. What I don't get are the breadsticks. We have plenty of starchy goodness in the pie itself. We don't need more 'bread' of any kind."

Judge Inciardi was up next. "I didn't care for the breadsticks either. Not necessary. Too similar to the pie's crust. I thought the eel in my pie was a bit overdone and rubbery, though. Hence, I can't give you points for that. It's a shame, since everything else in the pie melded so well together."

On down the line, the judges provided their critique. It was too soon to tell if Chef Gaskón had made the cut. But Deja hoped he had. And then it was Deja and Geoff's turn.

"Thank you, judges. And now we will hear from Chef Dubois, whose sous chef had quite the adventure making these tacos. Tell us, are you truly feeling well, Sous Chef Blackleaf?"

"I feel a little fried, but not as fried as these suckers," Geoff quipped.

The audience and a few of the judges chuckled.

"I'm glad he's fine," said Deja. "Otherwise, I wouldn't have these delicious Cajun tacos to present with fresh corn salsa, lime sauce, and a side of dirty rice with livers and sausage. Enjoy."

The judges ate and talked amongst themselves. This time, it was Chef Inciardi's turn to start the judging. Of course, he first had to remove the golden toothpick from his mouth. "I find these tacos to be...excellent. Fiery and meaty yet delicate. The lime sauce gives us just the right amount of acidity, and the eel is fried to perfection. Even the rice is quite delicious, offering a bouquet of flavors that meld like a symphony. However, I'd say the rice is not spicy enough, but everything else about it is delectable."

"High praise! And what say you, Chef Tintillus?" asked the host, who addressed the amphibious Zoox.

The chef raised a webbed hand and waved it over the dish. "My one real complaint is that there wasn't enough of it! The eel had a depth and fire to it that hit the spot. I didn't care much for the corn salsa. But the rice had me licking my chops." He made a ribbiting noise in the back of his throat, which puffed out a little. That was quite the compliment among Zooxes.

The birdlike Ractyl, Chef Mikaw, spoke up next. "The eel was meaty and fried very nicely. The lime sauce could use some work. Even a simple squeeze of lime would've been fine. Don't overthink your dishes, Chef Dubois. I also liked the rice, which was a good counterpoint to the tacos."

After all the judges delivered their verdicts, Deja and Geoff bowed to them. Her pulse was pounding, making her head hurt. If she had figured correctly, they were still in this contest. But next up for judging was Chef Glass, who had made an array of sushi. Deja's rival stood next to her lean, black-haired sous chef.

"Now for the respectable Chef Riva Glass. What have you made for us?"

"Esteemed judges, you'll find a dragon roll with eel, crab, rice and cucumber rolled in genyun avocado slices paired with a wensly sauce. Then I prepared a runshom roll with eel and runshom tempura wrapped in rice and seaweed and complemented with a mushroom sauce. Finally, you'll see a tuna and eel roll with rice, all finished with a chili sauce."

One of the female human judges, Chef Tinhoya, spoke up first after the tasting was over. "I found the dragon roll to be exquisite. I just wish the other two were as good. Still, a solid effort."

A male human, Chef Smith, spoke next. "I found all three rolls to be brimming with a complex flavor palate. If only the rice weren't quite so cooked, it would've been flawless."

The announcer moved on to the bearish Pintrel. "What about you, Chef Routh. Do you agree?"

"I preferred the dragon roll, like Chef Tinhoya. Unlike Chef Smith, I didn't think the rice was overdone. Mine was cooked perfectly. I really enjoyed the chili sauce with the tuna and eel roll. At any rate, the dragon roll was the best of the bunch."

Deja sighed. Too bad Chef Glass was so good at what she did. Deja forced herself to pay attention to the rest of the judges' remarks. *Dang. Looks like Chef Glass is going to beat me. Again.* But she was pretty sure she and Geoff had placed in the top six. They would live to cook another day.

Two DAYS LATER, Deja and Geoff were still in the running. As exhausted as she was, Deja was excited to talk to her father again. She placed a call to his room and waited for the signal to go through.

"*Hola, Papá.* How do you feel today?"

"*Hola, Dejacita.* I feel like someone carved out my knees and replaced them. Oh, wait, that's what they did." His voice was strained.

"Aren't they giving you the good drugs?"

"*Sí. Pero no me gustan.*"

"But papá, you can't get better unless you keep the swelling and pain down."

"I know. I just hate feeling so garbled."

"I'm sure you do. But you'd better do what the doctors tell you to do. Or you'll have to answer to me."

He scratched at the stubble on his face. "Okay. But we will not be able to talk as often. The stuff puts me to sleep all the time."

"That's okay. I just want you to get better," she said. "Have they started you on physical therapy yet?"

"The torture sessions, yes. It is like the Spanish Inquisition, but they ask no questions."

She winced. "Yes, I'm sure it's hard, but you've done harder things, yes?"

He groaned. "I don't know. These days, I feel too old for all this."

"Don't give up. I'll be there as soon as I can, and we'll go through it together, okay?" Her eyes started misting.

"Okay, *mija.* I can't wait to see you. And now I had better take a dose of the 'good drugs' as you called them."

She laughed. "Good for you. Sleep well."

"*Adios, mija.*"

"*Adios.*"

She ended the call and wiped away a few tears. Her father was in such bad shape. Yet he still managed to be brave. She hoped she could be as brave in his situation. For now, she had to be fearless if she wanted to stay in this cooking contest. She went to the beverage dispenser and ordered a stiff drink. After she downed it, she went in search of a hug. She knew just who'd be happy to give her one. No kissing this time, though. She had to draw the line somewhere, right?

Many contests and many days later, she and Geoff were still in the competition. She wasn't surprised that Chef Boyar had made the cut as well. Unfortunately, so had Chef Glass and her sous chef. But at least Chef Gaskón had survived as well. Him, she liked. He had a cheery soul and a shared dislike of Chef Glass.

"OK," said Geoff. "You ready?"

"You bet. Just try to keep up with me." She grinned.

Eighteen serving bots, many-armed and equipped with carrying trays, whirred into place outside the kitchen's serving window. Deja didn't spare them more than a glance just yet, intent upon plating her first dirt-infused entrée of stuffed poultry and fried bevsnip chips.

"I need that last batch of chips *now*," she said.

Geoff hurried up with the fryer basket in hand. He dumped the chips on a towel.

"Lovely," she said, then tossed them in a bowl with some powdered balsamic vinegar and parmesan cheese. She arranged the chips on a few remaining plates as the commentator counted down the seconds. Several hovercams were filming live from various angles.

"Three, two..." said Dornack.

"Done," she and Geoff chorused, holding up their hands.

"Excellent job. Now please load the serving bots."

Together, they loaded up the gleaming bots with the aromatic plates of food and glasses of spiced punch. A low thrum of energy resonated within the bots. Her food was being scanned for any toxic contaminants. *Come on, come on,* she chanted. The humming stopped. Satisfied, the bots wheeled around and zoomed off, leaving the oddsbreaker with a smile on her face.

Using a mirror next to the kitchen's holopanel, she checked her hair and straightened her chef's jacket even though the cameras were still filming. A few minutes later, a light above the holopanel blinked a warning. Then the screen flickered on, showing a two-dimensional view of all eighteen judges on the stage. In return, she knew, the camera projected a three-dimensional hologram of her to the food critics, the coliseum's entire crowd, and trillions of absentee viewers. *Just another performance, another dare*, she urged herself. Aware of Geoff's presence off camera, she took heart. This once, she wasn't alone.

"Behold our next culinary challenger," rumbled the competition's host. "The esteemed judges acknowledge Chef EvaLynn Dubois of the Tiarr System!" Applause rained down from the spectators.

"Refined host, seasoned judges, spirited guests, thank you all." Deja bowed from the waist, smiling, all elegant warmth and confidence. As she spoke, she glanced at the judges. "Palate pleasing is my life's pursuit," she continued. "Such a pursuit could only lead me here, to the most judicious palates in the galaxy." The answering laughter and applause melted away her remaining jitters.

"Our Chef Dubois has a clever tongue," said the merry Chub. "Is her food even half as clever?" Then, stretching out his words, Chub drawled, "Tiiiiime to diiiiine!" On cue, the serving bots removed the opaque glass domes covering the plated entrées.

Deja began her spiel. "May I present pounded breasts of kurrocco bird stuffed with a paste of duxelle agabbé mushrooms and crushed wutoo nuts drizzled with gunlup sauce. On the side, you have my homey version of toasted bevsnip chips dressed in balsamic vinegar powder and parmesan cheese. To drink, spiced punch." As one, the foodies selected a preferred eating utensil and fell to sampling her dish with professional aplomb. Chub narrated their expressions and actions like a play-by-play sporting event. Deja smiled and strove to contain the worries threatening to seep through her defenses. If she didn't make it past this round, she and Geoff were out of luck. They wouldn't have time to discover Famous Foodie's underlying scheme, much less expose Chef Boyar or Chef Glass as the actual schemer. However, Deja's anxiety faded somewhat as she watched the judges unknowingly dining on dirt. Too funny. So far, Famous Foodie had not tipped his or her hand yet. The activist hadn't issued any additional commands about the dare, either.

A series of chimes sounded, and Deja snapped back to the present. The judges cleansed their palates in their preferred ways. Inciardi, predictably, used his beloved toothpick.

"Dining has ended. Judging has begun," the host said in a hushed voice. "Now we watch our seasoned experts mull over the meal from Chef Dubois. The next moments are critical. Silence please!" Soon, the judges began typing out notes to themselves and one another via their encrypted data pads. The actual rankings of all contestants would be posted at day's end. So far, Deja was in the top one-hundred competitors and she had a real shot at reaching the top fifty. Another series of chimes reverberated in the coliseum, calling a halt to the deliberation. "So," asked Dornack, "how many palates did Chef Dubois please, esteemed judges?" Deja bowed again and waited, adrenaline buzzing in her veins.

"Chef Dubois brings an earthy undertone to her marvelous, seasoned poultry," said one female Vinadroan, her ears swiveling forward in what seemed like pleasure. "The crisp bevsnips were quite unlike others I have sampled. Still, I could do with less vinegar on the chips, in truth." At this rather positive review, the crowd murmured and Deja felt hope rise inside her chest. She dipped her head in thanks.

"Thank you, Chef Roya. How about you, Chef Gorlaki?"

"Rustic. Bold yet delicate. Fit for an emperor," grunted the Tondwian, who was, in fact, an emperor. The alien's one eye blinked at her with energetic approval. Responding in kind, she fluttered her eyelashes at him.

The four-legged Zoox, Chef Tintillus, leaned back on his haunches and raised his front legs to gesture at his plate. "How Chef Dubois has captured the taste of the forest after a rain, I know not. Yet taste it I did. Magnificent indeed. Perfect? No. The chef would have done better to pair the meal with a brave Zooxian yogg. And the sauce had not the required bite to temper the dish." The criticisms didn't surprise Deja, who still took a moment to press a hand to her forehead in thanks. The Zooxes were super fond of their zesty, alcoholic yogg. And they used enough spices to practically wither the tongues of humans and many other life forms. By the time all the critics except Inciardi had passed judgment, Deja felt she could use a little yogg herself. To celebrate.

Even the snobbish Inciardi had few complaints. Before speaking, the man had to remove his lavish toothpick from his mouth, which the nanobots had no doubt scoured clean. "Chef Dubois executed a notable, robust, and sensual dish with a sleek simplicity that I like. Remarkable depth and freshness. But the somewhat uneven toasting of the chips was substandard."

Substandard, ha! If only you knew, my friend. Not for the first time, she thought back to the contest's opening ceremony wherein the judges' identities were revealed. Deja's reaction to recognizing Inciardi had been relayed to Famous Foodie via the bug planted in Deja's chef jacket. Several people in the coliseum had taken notice of her outburst, including Boyar and Glass. Moreover, Glass had been seated farther away than Boyar, so it seemed more likely that she wouldn't have been able to hear Deja—unless of course Glass had some hearing enhancements or was listening in on the bio bug's transmission.

It seemed entirely plausible that Famous Foodie was either Glass or Boyar. Boyar certainly had no love for Inciardi. And given the "eating dirt" part of the dare, Famous had a bone to pick with the judges of this contest, perhaps Inciardi most of all. If so, the grudge rated personal enough that Famous might have decided to risk being present in person to witness the payback. What, precisely, had these judges ever done to tick off the most infamous food crusader in the galaxy? Time would tell. And reveal who Famous was, hopefully.

Deja's points began showing up on the in-kitchen score panel. They were almost too good to believe.

"And that's it for this round, Chef Dubois. You made a very good showing. How do you feel?"

"Happy as could be," she said. "And very grateful to our gracious judges." It never hurt to butter up the judges a bit.

"Well, your happiness is well deserved for now. We'll see what your competitors have to offer. Next up, Chef Yurifoko. Let's see what she's up to now, shall we?"

Once Chub's attention shifted from Deja, several chefs, including Chef Boyar, turned toward her and offered congratulations. Chef Glass sniffed and looked away. Chef Gaskón, though, came in person and shook her hand. "Tremendous job, my friend." Bastian was up next to serve the judges, so she didn't blame him for not coming over.

"Why, thank you," she told Louis. "Blackleaf and I gave them quite the show, eh?"

"Yes. Let's hope I can wow them, too."

"Right. Much luck."

Deja's knees felt jiggly like gelatin.

"You've got them drooling now, boss," Geoff said with coarse laughter. The arm he wrapped about her shoulders had none of the rowdiness present in his voice, though. Aromas from the day's cooking mingled with his signature scents. After a brief squeeze, he released her, thankfully. Or not thankfully. *Ugh, get back on course,* she told herself.

"Yep," she said aloud, "don't I though?" Another chuckle from Geoff. "In fact, I think I deserve a moment off my feet."

Everyone else in the kitchen bustled about, still on their own deadlines. None of them cared that Chef Dubois and her sous chef were still there.

"By all means," he replied. Footsore, Deja shuffled over to the tall stool that resembled what else but a tropical, red toadstool with green speckles. Geoff trailed after her then leaned against the countertop. Perching on the faux fungi, she breathed a contented sigh. Yet that serenity fizzled as she viewed the unwashed dishes and general disorder in her corner of the kitchen.

Noting the direction of her gaze, Geoff shook his head. "Ah, the aftermath of culinary battle. I suppose you'll be ordering me to stay and clean up," he pouted, still in character. In sign language, he said, *Say yes. Go rest. Later, we learn our ranking. Then talk about Famous.*

It was getting tiresome, this constant, in-character parlance just so Famous Foodie wouldn't get suspicious. She followed Geoff's lead. After all, if the man wanted clean-up duty, she sure wouldn't object.

"Hey, what are sous chefs for, anyhow?" she mused. Silently, she signed, *Good plan. Thanks.*

"I'm off," she announced. Geoff held out a pale, tattooed hand to her. He helped haul her to her feet. Today, he had once again earned the right to call himself her partner, though she was too nervous to tell him so. Before he could speak again, she let the door swing shut behind her.

Staff members and competitors aplenty swarmed in the main corridors. Heading to her quarters on tired legs, Deja moved without difficulty amidst the throng even so. Once she reached the high-rise lodging building, she bore right, entering the Sea Wing. Walls and ceilings featured a continuous bas-relief of simulated fish, crustaceans, marine mammals, and corals. The sea-like hallway awakened memories of rare beach days with her parents.

Sand and sun and laughter. Or yelling. Those days could go either way.

Once, on Gessire Prime, there hadn't been much laughter that time. Esmira had stepped on some sort of razor crab. Rather typical luck for such family outings. At least Deja had gotten her first taste of candied phrum flowers while waiting for her mamá to get patched up. And her papá had served up a delicious razor crab gumbo back on the ship.

Pushing the past back where it belonged, Deja walked faster to the Jungle Wing, where her room and Geoff's room were located. She walked on, not paying much attention to the fanciful murals of plants, trees, fruits, and forest life. Stepping into the elevator, she punched the button for her floor. Arriving at her door, she keyed the code into the digital lock.

Whoosh. The door slid aside. "Lights, full." On instinct, she entered with her senses alert. But the room held no unexpected guests. Nothing had been disturbed either. After a steamy shower of indeterminate length, Deja dressed for sleep in a loose, thigh-length shirt. But despite her soothed muscles and tingling skin, she felt ill at ease. Odds were good that she and Geoff were still in the game. But try as she might, she struggled to believe the Coalition would hold up its end of the bargain with her.

Pausing by the bedroom doorway, she glanced over to the door that led to Geoff's adjoining suite. Inside, the lieutenant had hidden his GJC rucksack. Maybe she should take a peek. Find something to keep herself ahead of the Coalition's endgame. Guilt flamed to life in her chest, yet she entertained the idea anyway. After all, Geoff had charged into her dare uninvited. Maybe he *couldn't* tell her all that he knew. Before she could reconsider, Deja dashed into the bedroom to grab her gear.

Setting up her decrypter took little time. But she knew how hard it was to crack a genuine Coalition field-op unit or a "Fooper" as criminal-minded folk so endearingly called it. Minutes rolled by and her decrypter had unlocked just two of the six letters. Or characters, rather. The passcode wasn't in Common but in a logographic language. While the decrypter kept at it, she researched the two known symbols that seemed familiar somehow. In moments, she knew why, and her heart stuttered in surprise.

The characters were native to Be'Voya. The planet where she first met Geoff.

Sitting on the floor, Deja confirmed the meaning of the two characters: "exciting dare." Numb, she turned off the decrypter and sat back on her haunches. Could her chest burn more than it did now? If she still wanted to, she could unlock Geoff's personal comm device right now.

Biting her lip, she put Geoff's Fooper back where she'd found it. She didn't need to see what he'd been writing to his superiors. She touched her cheeks. They were warm. Odd. She put the rucksack back and retreated to her room, where she found solace in some rubarlo nectar with two shots of gehut.

"Plating! Plating right now," Deja bellowed. "Where are my last empanadas?" The serving bots waited just outside the service window, ready to test the food for poisons and whisk it off to the judging circle.

"Coming to the pass," Geoff bawled out. "Behind," he shouted as he raced around several other chefs. The rich, charred scent of the meat and crisp pastry reached her before he did. She turned, snatching up one empanada after another and arranging them on beds of rice and hixote peppers that rested, in turn, on spicy flatbread rounds.

Chub began to count down. "Three, two, one. Hands up!"

Deja and Geoff raised their hands, the plates looking immaculate and stunning.

"Wonderful, Chef Dubois. Now, please load the bots."

Geoff helped load the completed plates followed by glasses brimming with deep-green icewine. That done, she and her partner breathed in relief. He placed a hand on her shoulder and squeezed, then retreated off camera. Some moments later, the viewing screen powered up, and Deja stood ready to present her dish.

Greeted by the presenter, Deja watched while the bots approached their destinations. As the camera panned over to Judge Inciardi, Deja felt her breath catch in her throat. For there, in the middle of it all, Inciardi staggered upright and then collapsed on his dinner table, dark blood spewing from his mouth and nose. *Gravgummit! Famous must be making his move!*

As support staff and fellow judges clamored to assist the ailing man, Deja stepped forward in shock. But she was at the mercy of her location. The camera caught a few close-ups of the melee before the screen went dark. Geoff rushed to her side and leaned in to talk into her ear.

"I'll get over to the infirmary and find out what's happened," he whispered. "Stay put."

Before the lieutenant could move away, she caught his wrist. His blue eyes found hers as she spoke, "Like comet dust, I will." The grim yet somehow unsurprised look on his albino face made Deja glare at him.

"Right," he said. "Forgot who I was talking to."

"I'll say," she muttered. Turning back to the other contestants—all of them yammering to each other—Deja excused herself and her sous chef. It wasn't difficult, given the departure of other contestants and the general ruckus. Everyone knew a replacement judge would have to be selected from the reserve. That could take days.

After following Geoff into the hall, Deja flashed a sign that meant "play along," knowing that Famous would still be listening in using the bug in Deja's chef coat. Aloud, she said, "Gravgummit, I didn't sign up for this. How can we win a contest if one of the judges keels over?" Meanwhile, she had tapped out a message for him on her PalmStar: *Geoff, find out what's eating that judge, just like you wanted.*

He nodded, accepting her written instructions. Out loud, he said, "Maybe they'll choose a backup judge in time for tomorrow."

"They better. I'm *this* close to winning that dough. Go find out, then pack our stuff in case we have to jump outta here." She tilted the PalmStar towards him with another note: *I'll sneak into his quarters before it's swarming with investigators. Try to find the cause. Gotta be related to FF.*

His eyes thinned. "But—"

"Oh, uncork yourself. I won't leave without you. Besides, I can scare up a no-questions-asked flight better than *you* ever could"—by which she meant him to understand that *she* was quite good at sneaking in and out of places, so he'd better deal.

"True," he said nonchalantly, though his eyes told her he felt anything but nonchalant about her plans.

His disapproval didn't matter. Her nerve endings already tingled with the thought of some real action. She still wore her vest beneath her chef's jacket. Stowed inside it, she had all the equipment she needed to do some top-notch snooping. "Good. Message me when you know if we'll get another shot at this cook off. Either way, pack our gear."

"Right, boss," he said, reaching out to squeeze her lower arm. She felt a small prick.

"Ow," she said. "What do you have in your hand?"

"Oh, sorry," he said. "Must have a hangnail." Meanwhile, he signed, *Be careful.*

You, too, she signed.

Aloud, he said, "Sounds good. I don't wanna hang around anymore than you do if things go supernova."

"Agreed." Then they separated.

PALMSTAR IN HAND, she pulled up the blueprints for the Ultimate Chef of the Galaxy complex. Geoff's superiors had proven useful in that regard. First, she found the building where Inciardi was lodged and went in that direction. Without much trouble, she located a service closet with a narrow, underground power duct that, through many twists and turns, connected to Inciardi's quarters. Clearly, the passageway hadn't been built with the Vinadroan stature in mind but rather for maintenance bots.

Crap. Why is it always a duct of some sort?

Before approaching the closet, Deja activated the fabulous—and illegal—vidlooper software on her PalmStar. Staying put for a full count of fifteen, she refreshed her PalmStar hack into the system. Yep, the cameras were indeed loopy—and would remain so for almost an hour. Stowing away her handheld device, she went to the closet door and pulled on some gloves. She'd keep her skin cells and DNA to herself, thank you very much. Eyeing the locked door, she withdrew one of her favorite toys. The disk-shaped gizmo adhered to the metal door and whirred away, unscrambling the digital lock. Sadly, the physical lock proved less cooperative. Keeping an eye out for any passersby, Deja jimmied the lock open with a combination of fancy tools and even fancier language.

Slipping inside the maintenance closet, she startled, coming face to faceplate with a few inactive maintenance bots standing along one wall. Heavy-duty shelves stocked with various janitorial supplies lined another wall. Digital control panels occupied the others. Spotting one labeled *Power Access,* she stepped over to it. Without tripping any alarms, she managed to open the entrance to the power duct. Deja pulled up the blueprints again, checking her route to the judge's quarters.

Now for the annoying part.

Ow! Another bruise for my collection. Easing herself a few more feet, Deja stopped to listen. She was crawling in the power conduit that connected to the lavatory in the sick judge's quarters. Wriggling a bit, she retrieved the necessary tools to remove the panel barring her way. Once inside the well-appointed bathroom, Deja crept across the floor and peeked out the door. It opened into a bedroom. A bed masquerading as a lushly blanketed and pillowed slice of bread dominated the room. The bed's pillows resembled pats of butter large enough to give an ortoo beast a heart attack.

Rolling her eyes, she turned back to investigate the bathroom. Nothing toxic there. Unless one counted the heinous-smelling bath salts next to the jet tub. On to the kitchen then. Everything checked out fine, and she cursed. Time to look in other places.

Heading into the sleeping area, she stepped to the bedside table, which resembled a giant, crystal jelly jar capped with a brassy lid. Rapidly, she unpicked the drawers but found nothing suspect. Nothing harmful amidst the judge's immaculate wardrobe either. The desk proved fruitless, too—except it looked like a melon missing a ninety-degree wedge. The hidden safe in the floor gave her some trouble. But upon cracking it, she found expensive cufflinks, other man-jewelry, and a PalmStar not unlike her own. On a whim, she cloned the data on the pad's chip then shut the safe. She checked the time. Her mouth went dry. Minutes, she had only minutes left to find what might have caused the judge's collapse.

At that moment, her PalmStar rumbled. Fishing it out, she found a message from Geoff.

Geoff: Inciardi in critical. He has crushed glass of some kind shredding him from the inside out. He's on bypass and in surgery. No word on how it got into his system. Be safe.

Deja clutched her stomach in sympathetic reflex. Bits of glass running amuck in one's body—that was *so* not a pleasant way to go. No matter what the glass was made of, it would have little trouble destroying Inciardi in any number of ways.

No matter what it's made of, Deja repeated to herself. In a flash of clarity, an image of Inciardi's prized toothpick blazed into her brain. Then she thought about the dare. She swore.

The dirt! All that clay! By itself, in its native form, it was harmless. But add enough heat, and the clay-based soil could be fired into a glassy substance. Famous must've reprogrammed the toothpick's nanobots to act as miniature kilns. The nanos would go about their business, converting ingested soil into fatal bits of glass. Well, ceramic that is. Most likely, Famous sent Inciardi the slagging thing in the first place. "An ingenious gift from an admirer," he had said. *Hah. Some admirer.*

Deja was no doctor, but she wagered that a few batches of altered nanos would create plenty of glass to doom the average human. Surgeons were nearly magicians these days, but it might take more than magic to save the judge. Could they devise some means of treatment that would work fast enough? Some kind of substance that would seek out and coat the glass particles? Or maybe they could program some nanos to "ingest" the glass and render it safe. But then there was all the damage to repair...

"Gravgummit!" Deja swore aloud. Famous had played her, making her an accomplice to murder. Without the toothpick, Deja

and Geoff would have a hard time proving anything. So far, she hadn't found it anywhere. But she *had* noticed that he didn't have it earlier that day when Chef Gaskón had presented his dish right before hers. That was good. The judge may have forgotten it in his room somewhere. But where?

Intent on her theory, she stowed her PalmStar but then uttered a curse and pulled it back out. First time with a partner (albeit an uninvited one), and she nearly forgot to clue him in. Genius. Wasting no more time, she messaged him, explaining her suspicions about the toothpick and describing it. To finish, she typed: **Don't know if he had it on him. He collapsed before he could brandish the dang gizmo. He didn't use it earlier today when Chef Gaskón presented his dish. No luck here so far. About to leave.**

Message sent, she once again pocketed her data pad. If the judge didn't have the toothpick, where could it be? What if the demented Famous Foodie had stolen the incriminating evidence before Inciardi even reported for judging that day?

Gritting her teeth, she glanced around Inciardi's quarters once again. Another thought struck her. What if the toothpick had been programmed to malfunction after a few weeks so that the judge would throw it out? Sure, a few small gems decorated the golden-plated gadget. But the guy was rich. And he had gotten it for free.

Immediately, her gaze fell on the rubbish hatch near the kitchenette. A crazy hunch swirled to the front of her thoughts as she dashed over to the receptacle. The contents hadn't been incinerated yet, thank goodness. She dug around in the pungent refuse, thankful she had gloves.

A bit of gold flashed as she pushed aside a half-eaten pastry. Flushed with triumph, she scooped up the very thing she'd been looking for. *Bingo*! If the toothpick hadn't been covered in all manner of goop, she might've kissed it. Quickly, she cleaned it with a napkin from the counter. Then she secured it in a special pocket inside the cuff of her right glove. She sighed in relief, thinking of her father. This evidence would help seal the deal with Geoff's meddlesome superiors. Hopefully, they could connect it to Glass or Boyar. And then her papá could recuperate from his injuries as a free man.

Heart buoyed, Deja hustled to make her exit. Just in time too. Her keen ears picked up footsteps out in the corridor. Climbing inside the conduit, she put the panel back in place. With all the stealth she could muster, she scuttled away. Sweat glazed her face as she crawled onward. All the while, she considered her game plan. Once she got out of this confounded conduit, where should she go next? Back to her quarters to wait for Geoff? Over to the hospital wing to find him? Or maybe, maybe she'd go hunting for the ultimate prize: Famous Foodie. That last option was tempting. She had a good hunch that Boyar was behind this. He'd readily confessed that he thought Judge Inciardi was a bad guy. Of course, if Deja went after the activist by herself, Geoff would be furious. Still, she decided she couldn't pass up the chance to tie up this dare.

She snaked around the next corner...and Chef Glass blocked the way, a large blaster leveled at Deja's torso.

"Too many cooks in the conduit for you, Dubois?" The question echoed with metallic menace in the confined space.

"One too many blasters is more like," Deja said in an even voice. True to her training, Deja didn't let any emotion register on her face. Meanwhile, her thoughts raced. Should she play dumb? After all, the chef hadn't greeted Deja using her oddsbreaker handle. Maybe Glass wasn't Famous Foodie; maybe she had other reasons to be in the conduit outside the sick judge's quarters. *Yeah, right,* she thought. But Deja decided to play it safe, saying nothing else.

"Well," her rival flashed a brittle smile, "perhaps if we come to an agreement, I can dispense with the weapon." The other woman motioned with the blaster for Deja to place her hands flat against the floor of the duct. The oddsbreaker complied.

With an inward smile, Deja decided to activate a precautionary measure of her own. "I'm listening."

"Good. I dislike repeating myself. It's akin to eating leftovers."

Deja shrugged. "Then perhaps you should choose more tasteful things to say."

Her captor remained poised, skewering Deja with an intense gaze. "What business do you have with the judge?"

"Oh, he once propositioned me."

The woman's fingers tightened just a bit on the weapon's molded grip. "And," Deja added, "he really likes my food. Better than yours even, I dare say." For now, Deja was content to let her captor spin her wheels for a while.

"You like dares, do you? Isn't curiosity like this"—the chef made a motion to encompass Deja and the conduit—"a dangerous hobby for an oddsbreaker?"

Aww, crap. She knows who I am.

So...Glass was either Famous Foodie or at least the activist's loyal acolyte. "Curiosity? More like self-preservation," Deja said, narrowing her eyes. "I didn't sign up to put a judge *in* the dirt, just make him eat it." Several of the power nodes in the tunnel picked that moment to start humming. The sudden noise did nothing to change where the stupid blaster was pointed. And yet... Deja thought she detected regret soften the corners of the chef's mouth and eyes.

"Well, life is often unpredictable," Glass said, dismissive. "This needn't end badly for you, though. Give me what you found. It's not your concern any longer."

Well, this wouldn't do. First, if Deja gave up the toothpick, the little bargaining power she had might go poof. Second, if she couldn't bait the chef into asking for the toothpick more directly, the nifty micro-recorder in her vest, which she'd just activated, wouldn't capture anything truly incriminating.

Furrowing her brow, Deja paused. "Ah, you mean the encrypted data I swiped from his PalmStar?"

Her opponent smiled a thin smile. "No, something considerably more...flashy."

"I snatched some cuff links, too, Chef Glass," Deja lied, shrugging a shoulder.

At that, the woman leaned forward, her grin widening into one of those "I know something you don't know" smiles. "Keep them. I'm more interested in the item we both know is the culprit. Oh, and you can call me Famous Foodie."

Exhaling, Deja tried not to smile in triumph. At last she knew who Famous was. But what if Boyar was involved as well?

At the moment, she was more concerned with escaping from Famous. At least Geoff wasn't in danger. Yet.

Slowly, Deja raised her gloved hands and turned them palm up. "You may be in luck. Except, I don't like leaving empty handed. Or with blood on my hands. Or being dead for that matter," Deja said, her voice frosting over. "So how does giving you what you've asked for keep me alive and off the hook for murder? Or perhaps you're just going to stick to the 'Bylaws of Foodie Felons': flambé both enemy and accomplice alike?"

"Yes, that does sound practical, though unimaginative," Famous replied, using her free hand to draw something out from inside her crisp jacket. "You think I lack imagination, Ms. Luck Goddess?"

"No," Deja snorted with actual amusement. "Sanity? Oh, yeah." She eyed the shiny object the chef held, now realizing what it was. The recognition didn't reassure her any.

"Enough," said the activist. Maybe questioning the sanity of the blaster-toting radical wasn't such a great move. "Place this around your neck with the node at the base of your skull. Now. Or I *will* take the unimaginative route." Famous placed the collar-shaped device on the floor and slid it over to Deja.

"A sleek, new iDose! Spared no expense, I see." The iDose could be loaded with anything. Meds, recreational drugs, viruses, poisons— or all of the above.

"Just. Put. It. On. Slowly."

"Fine." Plucking the device from the floor, Deja examined what might end up killing her. An anti-tamper model often used with violent criminals or patients, it featured a remote trigger. Lovely. The securing strap unspooled from within one side of the iDose. Made from an unbreakable, cut-resistant material, the strap would lock into a slot on the opposite side. As Deja worked to put on the unwanted gift, she felt more bitterness than fear. But the fear was catching up.

"Now, Luck Goddess, what is your real name?"

"Deja Ortega," she sighed. "Now what?"

Shadows shifted across the foodie's features as the woman lowered the blaster. "Now you give me your PalmStar *and* the item I asked for earlier. Don't pull any stunts," she warned, tucking the blaster in a shoulder holster beneath her chef jacket. "That collar you're wearing contains several choice substances. It also has a voice-activation feature, not to mention the remote itself."

Oh, spectacular, she thought. Deja reached inside her own jacket to retrieve her data pad. "What I don't understand," Deja continued, giving the PalmStar a gentle shove across the floor, "is why you even came here."

Famous sighed. "You know what I came for. And although you swiped it first—"

"No," Deja said, cutting in. "I mean, why you even came to this planet. At all." With a mocking smile tugging at her mouth and eyes, Deja took her time rolling down the cuff of the glove that held the toothpick. "You had all the ingredients ready to go. The contest. The oddsbreaker. The dirt. The judge. And, of course, *this*." Deja withdrew the slender toothpick, holding it aloft as though showing off a precious heirloom. "The murder weapon: a seemingly innocuous toothpick with tweaked nanos."

"The why doesn't matter. We'll talk about that part later. Now, slide the toothpick here. You have three seconds," Famous ordered, her face just a touch paler. Or maybe it was just the crappy lighting in the conduit. Deja sent the toothpick rolling toward its original owner. *Sheesh. What'll it take to get under this blasted woman's skin?*

The blasted woman picked up the toothpick and then the PalmStar. Both disappeared into the chef's white coat. "Good. Now turn around and take a left. We'll reconvene our tête-à-tête in a friend's quarters. I believe I shall invite your inquisitive sous chef too."

Equal parts fear and wrath sizzled through Deja as if she were a fire-kissed ortoo steak. The heat of her emotions caught her off guard, and she almost flinched. In that moment, Deja knew she was *really* in trouble now. Somehow, she'd lost her slagging heart to Lt. Col. Geoff Thorne. That dare-crashing *idiot*! That fork-tongued dolt! If he hadn't barged in on her business, she wouldn't have gone nosing around.

Forcing herself to breathe normally, she bit back an angry comment. Darned if she was going to let the crazy foodie see how much she cared for a supposed rogue. Instead, she shrugged. "Fine," she agreed in her best heck-if-I-care voice. "He only started snooping around 'cuz I paid him to. Unlike me, he doesn't care if that pompous judge bites the dust." Here she smiled at her bad pun. "If you want my partner to disappear and forget all about you, just slip him some creds. *Much* easier than disposing of a body." With that, she turned around and began crawling. Famous made no reply. A good sign. Maybe. And Deja left it at that. Never oversell the lie. Or the truth, for that matter.

For all her bravado, Deja permitted herself to clench her teeth as she scuttled down the narrow passageway. Time and opportunity. That's all she needed and Famous would taste Deja's version of justice.

She steeled herself for whatever ordeal lay ahead. The faint sound of their movements mimicked a low whispering, a foreboding murmur impossible to understand.

♪

"Ah, here we are," Famous announced from several feet behind the oddsbreaker. Peering ahead, Deja saw that the panel sealing off the conduit had already been removed. This particular tunnel opened into quarters much like her own, but with a nautical theme. A view of an underwater mural peeped through the square opening. "Now," Famous continued, "when you are free of the tunnel, Ms. Ortega, make no sudden moves. My associate awaits us."

"Yes, ma'am," Deja grumbled. Associate? Blast, the odds of her surviving this dare had just plummeted once again. Perhaps Chef Boyar really *was* a part of this whole scheme.

After wriggling out of the small space, Deja looked to her left. A familiar, porcine face greeted her. Startled and irritated all at once, she glared at Chef Gaskón, the pink-skinned, tusked Orinkk who had pretended to be a friend, not just a competitor. "*Et tu*, Porky?" Deja exclaimed.

Gaskón snorted, something he did well, being so piggish. "As if I haven't heard that one before, dearie."

Famous took over. "Just move to the far wall, Ms. Ortega. Kneel, hands behind your head. Interlace your fingers, cross your ankles."

Sighing, Deja did as she was told, kneeling before a lush scene of violet seaweed. "So," she asked while Famous made her way clear of the conduit, "what do you get out of this, Chef Bacon?"

"Nothing personal, I assure you," huffed the swine-ish fellow. "I didn't want anything to do with—"

"Quiet, Gaskón. Just get her trussed up," Famous ordered. *Oh, ho!* thought Deja. Here at last was a weak spot she might be able to exploit. If she lived long enough. Gaskón approached and locked her wrists and ankles in restraints. Her skin itched where the backs of his bristly hands touched her.

"Good," Famous said, addressing Gaskón. "Did you order the food cart?"

"On its way."

"Excellent. Trot out to the main room and wait for it to arrive."

"Fine," he grumped.

"Make that 'Fine, *chef,*'" insisted Famous, "or I'll rescind our agreement."

Gaskón amended his prior statement.

"Now, close the door. When the cart arrives, wheel it in here, and load her up."

With a thud, Gaskón shut the door.

"I wonder what poor Gaskón did to get on your radar," Deja piped up. "Obviously, you enjoy getting others to do your dirty work." She turned her head to stare at Famous.

"Hardly surprising you see it that way," the foodie countered, raising a sculpted eyebrow. She pulled out Deja's PalmStar and began fiddling with it. "I specialize in performing true public service in the culinary realm, believe it or not."

"That's one way to sugarcoat what you do," Deja shrugged, barreling onward. "Of course, you've always orchestrated your 'service' projects from afar. But *this* time, you deigned to show up personally. That's dangerous for a scummy murderer like yourself."

Swwaack! Glass slapped Deja in the face. Despite the pain, Deja wanted to laugh in triumph. Oh, she had found the right bone to pick with Famous. Too bad it had to be a painful discovery, though. A groan spilled from her lips.

Famous grabbed Deja by her chef coat and jerked the oddsbreaker's face close to her own. "*Shut up,*" whispered the foodie in menacing tones. "You know nothing. This isn't even a murder. Inciardi *chose* his death. Just as you chose to be here."

Dizzy, Deja blinked. "Right, and how do you figure he wanted to die from a belly full of glass?"

"That's not what I said," Famous retorted, bringing her face closer. "I never forced him to take the bribe that killed him. Although the toothpick was merely a small piece of that bribe."

"Whatever. You still gave it to him. And bribed him to do what, exactly?"

A glint of cunning flashed in the woman's eyes. "Why, to keep you in the run—"

Just then, Deja put all her energy into headbutting her captor. Falling backwards as Famous lost her grip, the oddsbreaker landed with a grunt. Pulling her bound legs toward her chest, Deja readied herself to kick the stunned foodie in the solar plexus. But she wasn't fast enough.

"Sleep!" barked the activist.

Darkness rolled in to claim Deja.

The blow snapped Deja's head to the side. Blood oozed from a fresh split in her lip. Turning to stare up at Famous, Deja narrowed her eyes. "No. We worked together before. But I had no idea my partner was a Coat. Not until he showed up and crashed my dare." Well, he *had* butted in; that was true. A little truth always helped sell a lie. She paused to spit blood. "He threatened to lock me up. Or worse, turn me over to some lowlifes from my past."

Pain pulsed in her face and stomach. Aches rippled out from her bound wrists and ankles. Divested of her vest and everything but a tank top and undies, she sat on a chilly lavatory floor. Arms shackled around a pedestal-style sink, legs tied and linked to the restraints on her wrists, and the iDose strapped around her neck, Deja was in a lousy position to mount a counter-attack. And the situation was *really* ticking her off.

Chef Gaskón had reported finding Geoff's hidden stash of Coalition-issued gear. The interrogation had heated right up after that. Deja also wanted to smack herself when she realized she hadn't secured her PalmStar. What good reading its message history had made for the gloating foodie. If Deja *had* remembered to log out properly, she could've fed Famous a failsafe password that would've triggered a complete data wipe. But now she was enduring all kinds of abuse to soften Geoff's fate. Yep, love made you stupid.

"We will see," Famous said, wiping the small smear of blood from her hand with a towel. She tossed the towel into a corner where it landed on the pile of Deja's clothes, including her vest. "You know, I once thought to recruit you, Ms. Ortega. I still might. A woman of such pluck and culinary talent could go far in my organization. But it all depends."

Deja eyed her tormentor. "Sorry, I don't work for killers."

"Oh, but you do," Famous countered. "Not long ago, you accepted sizable deposits to three of your accounts," the chef said, motioning to Deja's PalmStar, nestled in a pocket. "And then you booked several trips, both off-planet and on-planet, under various names. Just to make it harder for Lieutenant Colonel Thorne to track down his lawless associate."

"Wow, what a double-crossing minx I am," Deja muttered, fighting a blurriness in her eyes. Tears, how pathetic. She'd just started to care deeply about Geoff, and now he might not ever trust her again. And since the Coalition had tabs on her father, she'd never be able to contact him without risking capture. Why not just throw in her lot with Famous for now? At least until she could escape and lick her wounds. Hovering on the brink of a painful choice, Deja swallowed hard but said nothing.

"As tough as bajalla scales, I see," whispered the hateful chef. "Seems like you care more about your pride than your life. But what if I were to threaten the life of your lieutenant colonel?"

Tired and hurt as she was, Deja managed to cloak her sudden terror in a sneer. "Oh, kill him and frame me for that too, huh? Well, I may've *thought* he was a friend," she said, scrunching her eyebrows in seeming anger. "But when it came to getting a shot at nailing your hide to his wall, he wasted no time in 'recruiting' me. So," she bluffed, "if you're going to stick me with two murders, go ahead. However, if you want me to take your job offer, I'd like to choose my own targets. Deal?"

Gray, unblinking eyes searched Deja's face. Famous shook her head, wisps of silver hair swaying across her face. "Why, you *are* good. I can't quite tell if you speak true or not. Let's try something else." With a brisk movement, Famous fingered a button on the white iDose remote. Amazing warmth stroked away all Deja's pains and fears. Even consciousness slipped away.

SNICK. Jolted awake, Deja blinked in the dim light. All her muscles hummed with energy. Happiness bubbled beneath her skin. Her thoughts drifted this way and that, untethered to anything in particular. Lying on some kind of cot, Deja tried to stretch, but found she couldn't move much. What did it matter? She felt fantastic. Distant worries tickled the back of her mind, but she shooed them away. So foolish to be worried about anything. She knew that now.

Reveling in the floaty happiness, Deja smiled when she noticed the striking older man leaning against the door. Trim and clean-shaven, he stood with his arms crossed. He wore an immaculate GJC uniform: dark gray slacks and jacket with silver piping. The epaulets on his collar marked him as a...her thoughts drifted. Yes, a corporal. The holographic glyphs on his jacket read "W. Kellch" in Common. His long black hair was swept into a queue at the nape of his neck. Shadows played across an odd birthmark on one cheek, and his gray eyes drew her attention. She felt she ought to know him, but her brain was foggy.

"My, my," she said, admiring the view. "Why must the handsome ones always be out of my reach?" she teased. "I can't seem to move, but maybe you can loosen me up, handsome." Just looking at him made her heart speed up. For some reason, she also felt a little ill. But she couldn't think why.

"Er—" the man spluttered, a flush spreading across his tawny complexion.

"Oh," she chortled. "I just love the innocent ones. Are you just going to stare at me? Or are you going to come get me, Corporal Kellch?"

The corners of his lips twitched as the black-haired fellow considered her words.

"But don't you remember who I am?" he queried.

"Um. Not really. But I know you look delicious enough to eat. And you can even speak in full sentences!"

Another blush warmed his face. "Yes, but that's not much of a talent."

She grinned. Seriously, she wanted to eat him up. And yet...why did a wave of disgust freeze her stomach for a minute?

At last, Kellch walked over and crouched beside her. He smelled of crushed wereth spice and fresh bread. That was strange for an officer, wasn't it? But who the heck cared? She breathed him in.

"So," he cleared his throat, "how are you feeling?"

"Hot," she insisted, unable to stop herself from a giddy laugh. Everything was so funny. And fun. All those nasty emotions like fear and anger and guilt had no hold on her now. If only the corporal would stop wasting time and have a little fun. "*Very* hot," she added.

"So I see," he said. Lightly, he reached out and touched her cheek with the back of his hand. She leaned into his touch and closed her eyes, waiting for the kiss, her heart pumping ever faster. But instead, a cool, damp cloth came to rest on her forehead.

"Ohh," she sighed. "That feels good. But you know that's not what I meant, corporal."

"Hmm," came his halting reply. "But what of Lieutenant Colonel Geoff Thorne? Have you forgotten him already, Deja?"

Deja paused. That *name*. "Oh. Him. Of course not," she said, eyes sliding open. "How could I forget the upstanding Coalition officer who thought I was worth his attention?" She babbled onward, unsure where she'd stop. "Didn't take me long to fall for him. Didn't take long for me to screw it up, either. So sweet, so honest, so stubborn, so handsome. And there's me...an oddsbreaker doing what I do. And I, well, I drink far too much. I mean, *come on*," she laughed at her foolishness. It seemed like another person had experienced all those things, not her. "I'm sure he wants to forget all about me. Now, why don't *you* help me forget *him*?"

Although, now that she had spoken of Geoff, she felt...odd. Like she was trying to keep a blistering fire at bay with a pitcher of water. And she was burning up. Somehow, she had to starve the flame of fuel, make it sputter out and die before it ruined the bliss that hummed through her body.

The dark-haired officer said nothing. He reached up and took the cloth from her forehead, dabbing her cheeks, her chin, and her neck. "I...admit I wouldn't mind that, Deja. But—"

"But what? Oh, is it the disguise? I'm not nearly as old as I look, you know, if you prefer younger women. My—"

His eyebrows rose a notch or two. "*However*," he interrupted, "although you are safe now, he is not."

She snorted. "How could he not be safe? What a joker you are, officer."

"Just pretend, then. You don't want anyone to hurt him, right?"

"You are silly, aren't you?" She rolled her eyes at him. "No, of course I don't."

"And you wouldn't want him to lose his job, would you?"

"No," she sighed, looking at the ceiling. "Why would the Coalition want to dump an officer like him?" All this talk was confusing. And boring. She wanted some action, preferably involving the interesting man and those charming lips of his.

"Just listen. What if, to keep him safe, you had to stay away from him?"

"Stay away? Can I...say goodbye?"

He shook his head. "No. No goodbyes. Understand?"

Puzzling through the question, Deja shut her eyes. She rocked her head back and forth. Thinking of Geoff made Deja feel...so many sensations. Thinking that he might get hurt made her stomach roil and her chest tighten. She opened her eyes, breathing fast. "So...to keep him safe," Deja ventured, "I couldn't get near him. Couldn't talk to him. Ever."

"That's right."

"Then, yes. I'd stay away."

"Good. He will be safe then." Her questioner pressed the cool cloth against Deja's face again, absorbing her tears. The heat receded. A little. The officer had made a promise; everything would work out. Relieved, she nodded. A wave of fatigue pressed down on Deja. "Can I sleep now?"

Kellch did something, and she heard a beep. A tide of wakefulness and renewed giddiness rolled over her.

"Not yet. First tell me why you are an oddsbreaker."

Two words reached her lips immediately. "My papá."

"*Why?* What did he do to you?"

The sharpness of the question made Deja shrink back into the pillow. "I—what do you mean? Please don't be mad."

"It's fine. You're fine. Just breathe and think hard." The cloth caressed Deja's forehead. Then the questions continued. On and on. At length, the handsome man let her sleep. As the unconsciousness began to swallow her, she remembered who he was: Chef Glass's sous chef. But why was he wearing a Coalition uniform? The question remained unanswered as she faded into sleep.

Dull pain buzzed inside Deja's head. Harsh light pressed on her eyelids. Something gripped her shoulders, and her nerve endings jangled. Honestly, she wished she were out cold again. "Ohhh, stop."

"Drink. You need to drink," said a low, male voice. Deja's eyes snapped open. An unknown enemy kneeled before her, holding a canteen. The lean but muscular man wore his dark hair long and tied back. A birthmark looking sort of like a sun adorned one cheek. What's more, he was decked out in a Coalition uniform. His pale gray eyes watched Deja from an old, but strong, face. The oddsbreaker knew him at last: He was Famous's sous chef.

"No," Deja refused, coughing. Her dry mouth was coated with a coppery taste laced with something else. Licking her lips, she found the bleeding had stopped. Someone had even applied a flesh sealant. Stranger still, she was on a mattress, not the floor. And she didn't recognize the room at all. Finding herself dressed in a long, loose shirt that hung to her knees, Deja tried to assess her injuries. Her bruises hurt, yet only a little. Her arms and legs were still bound but with manacles rather than skin-punishing cords. A chain had been secured from the restraints on her feet to a ring bolted into the floor, though. *Oh, excellent.*

Her head pounded; she couldn't ignore that. How long had she been asleep? She shifted her legs and discovered that they bore at least a few days' worth of stubble. Where was she? The last Deja remembered was... Oh, right. Trying to convince Famous that she didn't care that much about Geoff. Whatever else had happened after that, she had no slagging idea. Holding back a shudder, she hoped she'd been unconscious the whole time. Whatever had or hadn't happened, however, she was still breathing.

Unwillingly, her thoughts focused on Geoff. She swallowed a mournful sound. He could not, would not, help her now. She remembered what Famous had done, filling her accounts with supposed payoffs for the murder. Geoff and his Coalition backup must've found the deposits in her accounts already. Blood money, all funneled in as though Deja herself had accepted the transfers. No doubt they'd also discovered at least some of the transports she'd supposedly booked. She didn't want to imagine how much her seeming betrayal would hurt Geoff. Breathing deeply, she tried to calm herself.

He's better off without me.

Grimly, she wondered what the Coalition would do about her father. They might ship him back to the prison's rotten infirmary where he could die. Worse, no matter what they did with him, if she tried to find or contact him, the GJC would use that to track her down. And yet, somehow, she couldn't imagine the lieutenant colonel, the decent man she'd fallen for, just sitting by and letting the Coalition punish her father for her own screw up. Or would he?

Well, she couldn't do anything about that now. First, she just had to survive. Revenge would come later. If she managed to accomplish the survival thing. Fully awake now, she scowled at the man. "Who are you *really*?" she croaked.

"I'm the one bringing you water," the other replied, holding out the container again.

"Oh, the water boy. I just thought you were one of Famous Foodie's stooges. My mistake."

The older fellow's lips quirked in a smile, much to Deja's surprise. "Whitley," he supplied. "And I'm not her stooge; I'm her younger brother." *Her what?* Before Deja could do more than widen her eyes at the revelation, this Whitley person put the canteen to his own mouth and took a few swallows. "There, you see. Just water."

Well, so now her captor had an accomplice who also happened to be a brother—a kindhearted one at that. Okay, interesting. All things considered, Deja really was thirsty, and the water probably wasn't drugged given the man's demonstration. Experimentally, she used her elbows and stomach muscles to lever her body into a sitting position.

Taking the canteen with her shackled, awkward hands, Deja gave the man a distrustful stare anyhow, just on principle. Her body felt weak and her tongue felt half again as big as it had any right to be. Her head wouldn't quit aching. Likely because she hadn't had a stiff drink in a while. Besides, who knew what they had done to her.

One of her hands drifted to her throat where the iDose still encircled her neck. Drugged; she must've been drugged with a tranquilizer at the very least. The aging cream on her skin had started to wear off, from what she could see of her arms and legs. But that was the least of her concerns.

Her mind whirled as she looked at the thin man crouched nearby. If Whitley *was* her abductor's levelheaded counterpart, well, that *could* tilt the odds back in her favor. Deja would therefore collect what information she could and make the best of it.

As Deja drank steady sips, she looked around the room. No obvious door. And no natural light. No windows, period. Just glow panels on the ceiling to light the place. And what a boring place it was. Walls and ceiling were of a dark-looking, lacquered wood substitute, and the floor was some kind of gray material. An average-sized commode and a shallow sink stood in one corner. And, of course, she sat on a low-tech mattress. A few springs were digging into her butt at the moment. She could be just about anywhere on Vinadro or any other planet. Or even on a ship traveling through space, for that matter. *Super.*

Wiping her chin with the back of one hand, she tossed the empty canteen over her shoulder. *Clangity, bang, tang.* This earned her a dismissive shrug from Whitley. But *not* a whack on the head. Well, that was interesting too.

"Uh, is this the part where you apologize for your sister's atrocious manners and nurse me back to health as the 'good' sibling?" Deja asked.

Shaking his head, Whitley sighed. "I—my sister and I didn't pay you to bring the Coalition into this. We didn't dare you to go digging around in the judge's quarters either."

"Right," Deja said, rolling her eyes. "But your big sis forgot to mention that the dare would end up making me an accomplice to murder by dirt."

Her captor shook his head again. "I don't like this. If you had kept to your own business—" He stopped, unwilling or unsure how to go on. He rose and walked behind her to retrieve the canteen. She pivoted as best she could, tracking his movement.

With his back to her, he spoke again. "My sister is—well, we have our reasons. But I...wish you hadn't figured out what happened."

"Really? Me too," Deja said as he turned around.

He attached the canteen to his belt, looked at her, then glanced away.

Ahh. Feeling guilty, are you? Good.

"Because of your actions, we had to switch plans."

"Yeah, so sorry about that." Deja laughed, rattling her manacles for effect. "So what do those plans have in store for me?"

The guy flinched, just a little twitch in one eyelid. "I'll share that with you as soon as I can."

"And food? How about some of that?" Deja asked, patting her stomach. "Or do I get to starve some more?"

Another shake of the head from Whitley. "You've received sufficient nutrients while in our care." Deja snorted at the word "care."

"What about a stiff drink," she ventured. "I could certainly use one of those."

"Maybe later," he said with an odd look. "First, I think you should see what's happened while you slept. Then my sister and I will tell you what we know about you and let you have a say in your fate." Whitley turned to the wall nearest Deja's feet and said, "Viewscreen reveal. Local newsbeat, live stream." A large square of the dark wall went translucent and a holopanel lit up.

A male Vinadroan with peacock-blue fur stood reporting from the very kitchen where Deja had prepared her food. "...interviews in just a moment. As of today, we know this much: In the shocking attack on the renowned chef, author, and judge, Lukas Inciardi, the Coalition has identified the lead suspects as Riva Glass and EvaLynn Dubois, two assassins disguised as chefs in the Ultimate Chef of the Galaxy Contest." Contest footage of Deja began rolling in one corner of the screen. She watched herself shopping for ingredients, preparing food, yelling at Geoff in his sous chef disguise, and addressing the judges. Promises for a tidy reward in return for information scrolled across the screen's bottom.

Sitting stock still, Deja waited for a sketch of her real face to appear. Geoff knew what her real face looked like. Her own stupid fault, that. He could give a description to a Coalition sketcher. But no images of her true face ever appeared, and Deja could scarcely fathom it. Maybe Geoff hadn't given up on her completely. Despite her better judgment, Deja cradled the blaze of hope ignited by this thought. Yet a darker explanation popped into her mind seconds later. He could still think she was guilty and yet want to give her a pass because of his misguided love. Yes, that could be it. *Brilliant. The idiot could be risking his job for me.* Like she needed more guilt. Deja eyed Whitley, who was now leaning in the corner to the right of the holopanel.

The news commentary droned on. "For all those watching and listening out there, we ask that those with pertinent information on the fugitives' whereabouts come forward. The stain this atrocity has left upon our world's most beloved food contest cannot be allowed to go unpunished. Food is life, my friends. And one who threatens that, *threatens us all.*" The reporter emphasized the last three words with an irritated twitch of his ears and then railed some more about the sanctity of food. "And now," he went on, "let's speak with some of the suspects' competitors." Footage showing Chef Glass now rolled in one corner, but the majority of the viewscreen shifted to a pre-recorded interview from none other than Chef Gaskón.

What? Well this ought to be good.

"What can you tell us about EvaLynn Dubois, the lead suspect in this case, Chef Gaskón. Did you notice any warning signs?"

The pink-skinned chef bobbed his head a little. "Goodness, yes, now that I think on it. The woman had such shifty eyes and a sneaky manner. But none of us had any idea she was feeding the judges dirt—"

Whitley ordered the viewscreen to mute the sound. Captions in several languages appeared on the screen instead, but Deja didn't pay them much attention anymore.

"This," the other gestured at the screen, "isn't what we'd planned."

Deja's anger flared again. "Yeah, thanks for that, by the way. It's so hard to find real trouble these days."

Whitley paused with a look of impatience—or worry?—creasing

his forehead. "Look, Deja, if you keep...pushing like this, my sister will simply choose your fate. I doubt you'll like it."

Switching tactics, Deja put a touch of pleading in her voice. "Then why not let me go? You don't seem like a killer, Whitley. You're not like your sister. Your sister worked me over. You didn't. At least, I don't think you did."

His eye twitched again, and Deja took heart. "I'm sorry to be so 'disagreeable' and all. But can you blame me? I can't help but wonder why you're doing all this. What in the galaxy could bring you, not just your sister, to plot the death of that judge?"

"That's simple," a resonant voice piped into the room. A second later, an entry panel slid aside and Famous Foodie entered, her face bearing a brief smile.

Deja grumbled to herself. Just when she'd been making progress with Whitley, the older, meaner sibling had to show up.

"Let me explain," the zealous foodie said, waving her younger brother to silence. "All three of us have pathetic excuses for a father. Inciardi is our father."

Deja's face went slack. The judge was their *father*? And they tried to kill him? Wait. How did they know she and her papá had a few problems? "My father is not your business," she said, alarm rising.

"What, you enjoyed cleaning up after your father's gambling escapades, did you? Bailing him out on world after world, making excuses to your mother. That was enjoyable? Or how about his love for smuggling illegal foods? Didn't this habit, combined with his gambling, get you and your mother's entire crew of performers banned from several planets?"

Something inside her shriveled. They knew far, far too much. Professional oddsbreaker though she was, Deja hadn't expected this dare to get so personal. With fire in her voice, she said, "Don't project your own daddy issues on me, *chef*. None of that makes me want to *kill* him."

"Indeed, which is interesting in and of itself. Especially because he ruined your life."

"What?"

Famous moved a few paces closer to Deja. "You said as much yourself not long ago. Didn't she, Whitley?"

Whitley, nervous, shifted on his feet but nodded.

"You told my brother that you took up the high-risk life of an oddsbreaker all because of your father. He got himself locked up, and you felt obligated to play dangerous odds just for his pathetic benefit."

Fury and disbelief boiled within Deja as she spoke through clenched teeth. "Listen, I don't know what your father did to you two 'charming' kids. But my papá is none of your slaggin' concern. We both have flaws, but we love each other. He'd do the same for me."

Snorting, Famous crossed her arms. Whitley opened his mouth to speak until Famous glared at him then said, "Deja, Deja. True love, true loyalty, is so incredibly rare. Why, didn't you learn your lesson when that lieutenant colonel of yours commandeered your dare? How about when he gave you up to his beloved Coalition? Now he's hunting you down." Her slim fingers motioned to the news show. "And this is how he thanks you for saving his life during that religious coup on planet Be'Voya? He may not have released a sketch of your real face yet, but he will. Besides, *our* father deserved his fate."

Cursing herself, Deja knew that the siblings must have dosed her with a truth-speaking cocktail. They knew too much. But she wasn't about to let these crazies get the best of her in this verbal sparring. Once she found an opening, she would drive home one sharp barb deep into their psyches. For now, she had to be somewhat cautious. The iDose around her neck could be loaded with just about anything.

"Okay," Deja admitted, "so you set up the toothpick as part of a bribe; and he took it, yes. But why did he deserve to suffer so horribly?"

Famous's eyes gleamed like a predator's eyes at night. Whitley, however, frowned for a fraction of a second then looked at the floor.

"His real name is Phil Torrens. Our mother was a migrant worker in the yamallow fields on Citron Four. It was a newly settled, low-tech planet. Small. He and his younger brother were the sons of the colony's lordly founder. Like most overlords, he—and his brother—lusted for profits, good food, and pretty women above all other things. My mother had the misfortune of catching our father's eye.

"Torrens hired her to cook his meals. When she resisted, he threatened to imprison her for plotting to form a strike among the field workers. As a result, she went along with his demands, even teaching him all she knew of cooking. But,"—and here Famous seemed to look proud, her shoulders straightening—"he did not know that she began 'redistributing' his wealth as soon as he 'invited' her into his bed and gave her his trust in other matters. She helped organize the workers for protests against poor conditions and wages. But when I was fourteen and Whitley was five, Torren's father pressured him to marry a rich heiress from a neighboring colony. So he did. Then he sent me to the fields to work, and Mother was incensed."

"I see," Deja said slowly. "And what happened?"

"She upset the status quo, leading the workers in open revolt. She and others were caught planning to disable a transport ship that came to take the harvest off-world. She wound up dead, bleeding in a grove of Yamallow trees. Her skull was split open with a branch. I found a piece of my father's favorite shirt wedged in a split within the wood. After that, I took my brother and ran. I got us on a transport and away from that wretched excuse of a man."

Deja let out a breath, irked that she felt a bit a sorry for the woman who'd framed her for murder. Although she could guess the answer to the question on the tip of her tongue, Deja asked anyhow, her voice soft. "And how did you manage to secure passage on a ship?"

This time, Famous paused before speaking and Whitley broke in. "Geena, you don't need to tell her." *Geena, huh?* The foodie's eyes fluttered then glared at Whitley.

"Doesn't matter," Geena said briskly. "What matters is that many years later, we found out that our father had ascended to further fame and riches—all using skills he learned from the woman he killed.

Oddly, he divorced his rich wife, left the planet, and went on to become a celebrity foodie. He even changed how he looked—drastically. That's why it took so long to find him and be sure Lukas Inciardi was actually Phil Torrens."

With a sad grunt, Deja looked from one sibling to the other. "All right, you convinced me. He was a rotten slagger who doesn't deserve the good fortune he's had. But didn't you ever try talking to him about what happened? You know, instead of jumping right to a murder attempt?"

"Why? He was guilty of enough crimes against his workers, even without what he did to our mother."

Deja turned to address a question to Whitley. "What about you? Did you ever wish to just speak to your father?"

Lips parting in surprise, Whitley glanced over at his sister but remained silent.

"I'll take that as a yes," Deja said gently. With a sad laugh, she gestured toward the viewscreen with her chained hands. "Well, it looks like you'll get a second chance to have that chat with your dad, if you want."

Both of them whirled to look at the screen. Captions streamed across it: "...an experimental treatment has saved Judge Inciardi. He is being transported to an undisclosed location this afternoon for his safety. Relief is sweeping this planet and..."

Whitley froze, a peculiar look on his face. Geena screamed a curse so hot it could blaze through a glacier, her eyes fixed on the screen, not yet realizing that she was within Deja's reach. Deja lunged for the control in Geena's hand. If Deja could hit the release button on the control before the other woman reacted, then...

"Sleep!"

And once again, blackness seeped in. *Gravgumm—*

PATRICIO STARTLED awake at a knock on his hospital door. His body ached like a lawn mower had chewed him up, but he knew the drugs he was on were doing a fine job of keeping the worst pain at bay. With his unwounded hand, he toggled on the light above his bed using a switch on the remote in his lap. "Come in," he said, wondering if it was already time for more physical therapy. Or maybe Deja was here? He hadn't heard from her in a while.

But in walked Dr. Chipton followed by Nurse Sterling, who held a small data pad in one hand. "How are you feeling, Señor Ortega?" asked Dr. Chipton, placing his hands in the pockets of his white lab coat.

"Oh, okay, I suppose," Patricio answered. "Is my daughter on a call for me?"

"I'm afraid not. But we do have a call for you. Are you sure you are feeling up to that?"

Patricio searched the surgeon's face for clues about the call. He read sympathy in the Ractyl's eyes, and his stomach knotted up. "Who is it? Is Deja okay?"

"I don't know who it is," the physician admitted. "But I do know it's about your daughter."

"Then I'll take the call. Whoever it is," Patricio announced, holding out his good hand. Sterling walked forward and handed him the data pad.

"Okay, but please let us know if you get too distressed. We are here for you," Dr. Chipton said.

"*Gracias*," he managed, intent on the screen. He didn't wait for them to exit the room before he tapped "accept."

The face of a soldier looked back at Patricio. The man looked fairly young, with blue eyes, short brown hair, strong nose, and a cleft chin. From what Patricio could see, the man was wearing a Coalition uniform. The jacket was dark gray with black piping. And the collars bore three stripes and a star. *A lieutenant colonel*, he thought.

"Is your name Geoff?" he asked.

The man nodded. "Yes, Señor Ortega. My name is Lieutenant

Colonel Geoff Thorne. I have an update for you on your daughter's status. I'm sorry to introduce myself under such circumstances. But I figured you deserve to know what is going on."

The knot in Patricio's stomach traveled up his throat, and he could scarcely speak. "What's happened to *mija*?"

"Well, sir, your daughter and I were working undercover to prevent the potential assassinations of one or more judges in the Ultimate Chef of the Galaxy Contest. One judge is in critical condition thanks to a violent food activist. And I know that Deja recovered the implement that was used to injure him. But all we know right now is that Deja has been kidnapped by the person responsible for the assassination attempt."

Patricio spoke up, his voice low. "You are saying that my Deja was kidnapped by a murderer, and you have no idea where she is?"

"Yes, I am so sorry," the man said, taking a deep breath. "The good news is that I tagged your daughter with a tracking device without her knowledge right before she was taken. We are scouring the city and surrounding areas for her. I'm sorry I don't have better news for you. I promise that I will do everything in my power to locate and rescue her. I owe her my life, Señor Ortega. She saved me more than once. And I intend to return the favor. You have my word."

"I see," said Patricio, swallowing hard. Something in the soldier's eyes made Patricio pause. "Tell me, sir, do you care for my daughter?"

Geoff blinked a few times, and Patricio thought the man might end the communication right then and there. Instead, a small smile ghosted across his lips. "Yes, sir, I care for her very much."

That was good enough for him. "Then you better get back to searching for her, *pronto*. I expect you to keep your word and make sure she is safe."

"Yes, sir," Geoff said. "I'll keep you informed. Thank you for your time."

"You're welcome." Patricio remembered his manners just in time to add something else. "Also, thank you for getting me out of prison. Deja told me what you did for me."

"Of course, sir. It was my pleasure. Thorne signing off," and the data pad went dark.

Patricio sighed deeply. If something happened to his daughter, he wasn't sure he could face himself again. She had put herself on the line for him more times than he could count. What if Geoff couldn't find her in time? What if Geoff never found her? It was all too much. Tears coursed down his face as he wept.

Dejacita, come back to me.

The jostling woke her. She was being supported on both sides, one arm each over a set of shoulders. Her bare feet dangled, sliding along a smooth surface. Two voices talked in hushed, rapid tones.

"Can't we just leave with her right now?"

"*Listen* to me, Whitley. We'll let her go as soon as we've wiped enough of her memory."

Wipe my memory? Like heck you will!

"But are you sure she wouldn't be willing to join us?"

"Whitley, please. I admire her too. But this is the best option."

"But she seemed pretty understanding, Geena. We could offer to use our contacts to get her father away from the GJC once he's well again."

"No. I'm sorry, but she's just too liable to flip on us. If you were thinking straight, you wouldn't even be asking that."

"Still, what if she's right? What if he didn't really kill Mom?"

"Enough. If you want to chat to the *gurtler*, I'll arrange it. But right now, we have to regroup."

They lifted Deja then laid her down on something. Unable to move anything, not even her eyelids, anxiety buzzed in her chest again. Beneath the useless muscles of her body, she felt a padded table of some type, the upper section sloped a little to raise her torso. A pair of large hands secured her with soft restraints while her adrenaline scrabbled at the drugs in her system. Meanwhile, another pair of smaller hands fitted what had to be a memory halo over her head and began placing sensors on her chest, face, and neck.

"Tighten that restraint," Geena ordered.

"It's fine," Whitley said quietly.

His sister sighed and, apparently, carried out her own order. The cuff on Deja's left wrist snugged closer. *Shoot. There goes an easy escape.*

She tried to remain calm, yet panic threatened to rise like harsh bile in her throat. The siblings planned to do a *memory wipe* on her.

Wipes were bloody inexact. What if she forgot about the sketchy folks from her past? What if she couldn't remember the passwords for her cred accounts—or even where the blasted accounts were in the first place? Even worse, maybe she'd have no idea that her papá almost got beaten to death or that he was recovering in a Coalition facility. What if...what if her every memory of Geoff was ripped from her mind? Her stomach twisted and anger flared at these last two thoughts. Even worse, this memory wiper could be fourth-world junk. If so, her neural pathways would be well and truly slagged. She'd be no more intelligent than a tossed salad.

If I get out of here, Famous, I think I'll have to end you!

Hot tears of rage pooled behind her eyelids. *Ack! Stop it. Start bawling and they'll know you aren't out cold!*

She focused on slowing her heart, on taking steady breaths. An image of her mother surfaced in her thoughts. Esmira, the ever-transcendent performer. She had guided Deja through endless biofeedback exercises. Tedious tasks for a hormonal teenager with a yen for danger and drama. Lots of drama. Yet all that mandated practice had saved Deja countless times. Panicking or lashing out at the wrong time could get a person killed faster than anything else.

Thanks, mamá. I know I was a brat. But I was your brat.

Still drugged and restrained, Deja was nevertheless focused and ready to use any advantage she could get. Her ears pricked up at the sound of a zipper.

"What about her clothes and stuff?" Whitley asked.

"Just put the bag under the table." A rustling thud followed. Deja felt like cackling in glee. If her vest was in there and she could find some way to free an arm... Perhaps they would leave and wait to initialize the wipe.

Leave, dang it!

No such luck. One of the siblings began punching buttons on the machine, which powered up with several trills and beeps. "Outstanding," said Geena. "I knew we'd find some use for this device when I traded those recipes for it." The machine added a series of mysterious bloops and bleeps to the conversation.

Funny how we like our tech to make noises so we know it's working. The inane thought danced through her mind, distracting her from concocting a plan.

Whitley cleared his throat but said nothing.

"Yes? What?" Geena replied after a moment, preoccupied.

"Just...just be sure to limit the parameters as much as possible. She's got some amazing skills. And she—well, she doesn't deserve to lose a huge chunk of who she is."

Whitley, I think my firstborn shall have your name, Deja pledged with hopeful abandon.

Geena sighed. "Whitley P. Twilles, please, please understand. You know I'm not doing this out of spite. Life isn't always about what any of us deserves. We *deserved* a decent childhood. We *deserved* a father who wouldn't smash our mother's head in. However, we didn't get that, did we?"

"No, but—"

"Right. But we *do* deserve justice. That, Whitley, is more important than a few memories of an oddsbreaker, talented as she is. If all goes well, she'll lose just a month or so of memories. Nothing that will really harm her."

Says you, thought the talented oddsbreaker. Her face and fingertips began to tingle. She rejoiced. Her feeling was beginning to return!

The brother huffed in resignation, and Deja heard a shuffling of feet—Whitley's, she presumed. "Don't we need to wait until she's awake?" he ventured after a moment.

"No. Most minds are more active during sleep anyway. The process will make her black out. The deeper she is asleep, the better the wipe works. In fact..." she trailed off. "Yes, it looks like she'll need more sedative soon. Come, I'll retrieve it while you do a final check on our engines."

"OK, one second," Whitley replied. "I saw this gadget of hers that I wouldn't mind snagging. Can I...?"

Geena's answering laugh was...warm, not malignant. "See, that's the spirit. For all the trouble she has caused, Deja Ortega is lucky we aren't taking *all* of her toys."

At that moment, Deja Ortega wasn't feeling too lucky. But that changed as the chef's footsteps faded away.

A warm breath tickled her ear. In shock, she nearly forced her eyes open.

"Deja," Whitley whispered, "I wish you could hear me. I'm so sorry. My sister...she hurts so much. I once felt as she did. I *hated* him —the father who treated us like slaves and then killed our mother. But then, well, we were so *young*, you know? And then I began to wonder. Is her quest for vengeance blurred by 'facts' based on half-remembered events? What happened? Did he kill our mother for sure?"

His hand, warm and broad, came to rest on her right arm. He rushed onward, "You have only tried to save your father. You forgave him. I think forgiving someone who wounded you so deeply takes more courage than a dozen dares." His breath continued to brush her ear, and she again found herself tempted to open her eyes and plead for escape. But...no. Best to hear him out first.

"Deja, I can't let you free. The iDose collar would sound an alarm and she might k—do something drastic."

Ugh. "Kill." That's the word you're looking for. Yeah, that would be bad.

"But," he said, "I can alter the wipe program even further without her knowing. You should forget just the last few days and the, uh, horrible things we did to you."

OK, yes, please. Let's do that. NOW.

He couldn't hear her, of course. And he wasn't done talking. "I hope you find your lieutenant colonel again. I wish—"

He stopped himself, though, and his hand lifted. At the mention of Geoff, Deja fought down a traitorous sob. *Oh, Geoff. I've tried so hard to prove you shouldn't want me. But if I lose all memory of you, I might just lose myself too.*

She heard Whitley pop open a console and mess around inside. Not long after, the machine produced a cheerful chime. Whitley snapped the console back into place and, without another word, hustled from the room.

Deja made no effort to stop him.

If what he said was true, she had to find a way to get off the table and get the drop on Geena. Whitley seemed somewhat unlikely to team up with Deja to kick his sister's butt. A pity.

Forcing her eyelids open, she took in her surroundings. Some kind of warehouse or hanger? The room was bare except for a small crate of old electrical parts. Okay, possible weapons. But the entrance was broad and doorless. No good places to hide. Too bad shrink rays didn't exist. Too bad she didn't have one. Heck, too bad she'd been kidnapped by a space-traveling, whacked-out Ahab hunting a white whale.

Papá would be proud of that allusion, she told herself.

He was the bookworm of the family. Deja sighed. Maybe...maybe she should just let them slice away a few unpleasant days and drop her off somewhere. And yet... Deja would have the Coalition after her and, worse, those idiots might ship her dad back to the prison's medical ward. Oh, and one other galling detail: "Chef Glass" wouldn't get one ounce of what was coming to her. Right. Yes, staying put was Plan B.

So, testing her muscles once more, Deja started working on Plan A: Get the heck away from Crazy Chef & Co.

Exerting herself, she tried to move her hand, which cramped most unhelpfully. Precious minutes passed as she struggled. Still, her arms merely tingled. Her legs were lifeless weight. Now what? Keep trying? Vision blurred and body still immobile, she wondered if she had a choice. Hot tears sluiced down her cheeks and, naturally, right into her ears.

Gah! Just what I need. An itch I can't scratch.

And that's when a low buzzing joined the rumbling hum of the memory wiper. It was a metallic whine. Her mind groped for a comparison. The buzz sounded like...like a hull slicer used at scrap yards. A chill sliced through her as she discarded that absurd possibility and another reared its ugly snout.

Gravgummit, the wiper is having a meltdown! Whitley must've screwed it up!

With all her effort, she willed her fingers to move. They twitched and then, to her joy, flexed open and closed.

"Awake! She's awake," Geena yelled, striding toward Deja.

"Darn right, I am! And when I get free, you'll be fricassee," Deja growled. She had just managed to dislocate her left thumb and was working that hand free.

Whitley rushed in, too, right on his sister's heels--which is why both siblings went down in a tangle. A section of the wall shrieked, gave up the good fight, and slammed to the floor. The ground shuddered on impact, plasticrete dust and rubble spraying in all directions. Deja blinked and coughed, searching the debris cloud for what had better be her rescuers.

And there he was. Lieutenant Colonel Geoff Thorne. No tattoos, no albino skin, no alien mask; just Geoff. Well, Geoff and a whole squad of fierce-looking officers decked out with a mega-load of weapons and riot gear.

Behind a protective riot helmet, her lieutenant's bright eyes were already locked on her. The savage determination in his eyes washed over her like a cloudburst in a desert.

"Geoff!" she croaked. "Two hostiles—your ten. Pharm restraint on board."

And that was all she could manage before Geena lurched to her feet, the iDose control held high. Geoff pivoted in Geena's direction, raising his blaster.

"Stop! Or she's dead!" Geena barked.

"Okay, okay." He obeyed, making a sharp signal to his crew. Eleven high-powered blasters lowered slowly.

Whitley! Deja strained her neck, trying to see if he still breathed. She could see...yes, that was blood on his face and chest. And a leg seemed crooked. *Crap. The guy must've shielded Famous from the worst of the blast.* Muscles in her neck spasmed, and she groaned, swinging her head forward.

"Deja? What—"

"She's fine, for now," Geena rasped, blotting a head wound with her sleeve.

"Deja, hang in there," Geoff said, his gaze flickering to her and back to her kidnapper. "What now, Famous? We let you go free and you let her live?"

"No. You let *us* go free"—the chef motioned toward Whitley —"and I let Deja keep her life *and* her memories."

Quick as anything, Geoff's expression knotted into a snarl. Exhausted as she was, Deja could not remember him ever looking *that* enraged. Despite her predicament, a smile drifted across her face.

She breathed deep, tugging her hand again, trying to get free. She couldn't do a thing about the iDose. But she hated lying there trussed up like a baked turkey. Then a thought occurred to her.

"Geoff, the judge is their father!" The lieutenant's eyes widened but he kept his raptor gaze on Geena. Ignoring Deja's outburst, the crazed chef looked down at her brother, nudging him with her foot. Whitley, stretched on his side, didn't respond. But Deja thought she saw him breathing. Barely.

Hang in there, mister. I'd like you to meet your future namesake one day. If, you know, your sister doesn't kill me or melt my brain.

"My brother," Geena said, enunciating clearly, "is hurt. He dies and the deal's off."

"Well, let's say I have a counter offer, hmm?" Geoff said, voice hot and cutting as a blowtorch. "Famous Foodie, I am Lt. Col. Geoffrey Thorne. You are charged with attempted murder of a judge, kidnapping and torture of an undercover CI, and, oh, about a hundred other crimes. If we let you leave, we keep your brother for insurance."

"Famous Foodie?" she replied, smirking. "Why, there are hundreds of food lovers who use that moniker in our righteous cause. How will you ever prove who did what?"

Deja's eyes widened in disbelief.

"And I had nothing to do with the judge, who is certainly not my father," Geena continued. "Your girlfriend here stole several of my prized recipes. I wanted to erase them from her thieving mind, that's all."

Geoff, tension telegraphed in every angle of his body, exhaled a big breath. "Ah, the 'she said, she said' defense, huh?"

"Not a defense, just the truth. And my brother comes with me."

Deja's sudden laughter drew the gaze of Geoff and Geena alike. "Playback Delta-Eight-Niner-Victor-Ten," Deja said loudly. Beneath the table, a muffled beep sounded.

"Good. I dislike repeating myself. It's akin to eating leftovers."

"Then perhaps you should choose more tasteful things to say."

"Pause Whiskey-Seven-Papa-Tango," Deja said.

The activist's face turned the color of a ripe tomato. "You tricky, meddling—"

"Oh, *puh-leeze!*" the oddsbreaker snapped, aching and tired and brimming with wrath. "*You*, Geena, are the interplanetary meddler—and murderer—not me, lady. You didn't have the guts to shove dirt down your father's throat—to kill him yourself. Instead, you played the coward and set me up to do the dirty work, literally."

Geoff chimed in. "Yes. Speaking of which, your *father* wants to have a chat with you, Geena. He's been listening this whole time." Geoff pressed a contact on his matte-black helmet. A life-size hologram of the judge, ashen and bedridden, flashed into view. Famous staggered as if slapped, her features glazed with a riot of emotions. Still, she clutched the blasted iDose remote.

"No! Nobody move," she ordered, steadying herself.

Deja and Geoff cursed in unison.

The judge's image shifted, and he began to speak, his halting voice projected from Geoff's comm gear.

"G-Geena? Is that you? Whitley? I've heard...everything. I didn't ever think to...see you b-both again. Please, I can—"

"Explain?" Famous screeched. "You *killed* our mother and treated us and my people like slaves. You should be dead too. If you hadn't been hiding who you were so well, I would have hunted and killed you long ago."

"Please, Geenie," he coughed, spitting scarlet blood. "No. My b-brother...he killed her. He learned of my alliance with the r-rebel movement. He blamed your...mom. Said I'd g-gone soft. I took a blow try-trying to stop him. Put me in a blasted c-coma. You two left b-before I even—" he wheezed, then erupted into a coughing fit.

The woman shuddered and cried out, doubled over like she'd been kicked by an ortoo beast.

"That...can't be!" Geena declared. Her head teetered back and forth, her face graying in shock. "But you took the bribe. The toothpick. Everything."

"Had to. I'm...a d-double agent for the Coalition."

"No. How can all this be. I know you. You're evil. You ruined my life! You ruined Whitley's life!"

"Speaking of Whitley," Deja blurted out, spotting some

interesting movement, "it looks like you got your baby brother killed, not your old man." A bluff? Yes. But a gravgummit awesome one.

The stupefied activist took the bait, her eyes darting down to look at her fallen brother.

Geoff took the shot—but Whitley rose up on one arm and rammed his shoulder into the side of Geena's knees. The blaster shot missed as Famous Foodie collapsed, iDose control spinning across the floor.

Geoff's team rushed forward to secure the prisoners and the remote. But Geoff himself sprinted to Deja. Energy gone, she panted in relief. Tearing off his helmet, the lieutenant leaned down and pressed fevered lips over hers. His passion awoke her own, shoving all her pain onto a back burner that seemed quite far away.

When at last he broke away, she sucked in a deep breath. Without a word, Geoff closed his eyes and buried his tawny head on her shoulder. His shoulders heaved and his breath gasped. Was he...crying?

"Geoff, it's—"

And then the machine, the one that everyone had forgotten, burbled a few notes in the sudden silence.

Deja saw black spots and then just...black.

"Medic! Medic!" Geoff hollered, frantic, as he cupped Deja's face. He didn't dare yank off the memory halo or sensors. But each second counted. Horror pounded in his every heartbeat as he stared at the thin metal probes pressing against Deja's precious skull.

The unit's medic joined him, pushing Geoff out of the way. Geoff let himself be pushed, but grasped Deja's limp hand. The soldier produced a lightwand, then pried open both of Deja's eyes in turn, flicking the light to gauge responsiveness.

"Please, Char," Geoff asked. "Can you stop it?" The probes, tipped with lasers, seemed to be firing now. Or maybe they had stopped for a moment? He just couldn't tell.

Char glanced back at Geoff, her mocha skin slicked with sweat. "Deja's pupils are responsive, sir. The wiper hasn't blown either of 'em. That said, I'm not an expert with this sort of tech."

His heart crumpled a bit more. "We can't just take off the halo, right?" he ventured, walling off everything but his concern for Deja. *She's suffered so much. Stars, please let her come back to me.*

"No, sir. Bad move. *That*, I know, could damage her hippocampus or—"

"Got it, but what do we do? Can we hack the system?" He forced himself to start unstrapping Deja's legs, then arms. He noticed the dislocated thumb with a flash of fleeting pride. She'd almost gotten one hand free. In a gentle motion, he pulled the thumb back into alignment.

"Yeah, we can try," the medic said, two fingers pressed to Deja's carotid, timing her pulse.

"Geary," Geoff yelled, looking around for their chief tech specialist.

"Right here, boss. Already on it."

Geoff startled, aware now that Geary was crouched by the machine, examining its innards. The lieutenant blinked then gazed back at Deja, whose eyes moved behind closed eyelids. REM sleep. She was dreaming. Of what, he wondered?

Feeling helpless as a newborn, Geoff fought a sharp urge to smash something. Instead, he stripped off his gloves and sandwiched Deja's uninjured hand with his own, squeezing as though the pressure would keep her memories intact. Char was rigging Deja with an oxygen mask when he realized that someone else was trying —no, begging—to get his attention.

"Sir! My brother, *please.*"

He knew that voice. Geoff swung a frigid glare toward the manacled prisoner. His unit's junior medic, Dobbs, was tending to the activist's brother, who stretched unmoving on the floor. Geoff breathed deep, speaking in a low voice colored with rage. "What would you have me do? Let a *criminal* suffer a while longer or let an innocent woman lose who knows how much of her memory? All because you loathed your father for something he never did?"

Famous dropped her eyes. "I'm...sorry. This was *my* idea, though. *He* wanted to let her go. Please, I can stop the wipe if you'll let me. Just take care of Whitley. He is not doing so well."

"Look at me," Geoff barked. She did, and he saw the defeat and fear in her eyes.

"First, what's the code to unlock this pharm collar?"

"The iDose?" Without a pause, Geena reeled off the code phrase. Char looked to Geoff, awaiting permission. He nodded and she entered the code into the remote.

The iDose clicked open. Geoff nudged the medic's hand out of the way, seizing the collar. Which he dropped, smashed with a booted foot, then slagged with his blaster. That sure felt good.

"Fine," he told Geena. "Get over here. But you had better work fast," he cautioned, ice shards still coating his words. "Sooz, watch the boy. Yates and Takeshi, stay at the prisoner's sides at all times."

Trusting his crew to do as ordered, Geoff looked back at Deja. How much time did they have? How many memories were being burned from her brilliant mind while he watched? The pulse in her wrist raced. Her face felt too hot, feverish, when he brushed his fingers over her cheek. His own face was cold, the skin tight from the tears he'd shed moments before. Hope and fear, pride and anger kept new tears at bay. Just barely. Without her he wouldn't even be alive today. Without her, he might never feel alive again.

"Char, go help stabilize the brother," Geoff said. Char couldn't do much else for Deja anyway. And, well, the injured young man *had* helped subdue his sister. "Dobbs, come take over for Char." Refocusing, he listened as the prisoner told Geary what to do. Moments later, the machine chimed, and Geoff held his breath.

The laser probes stopped doing whatever they were doing and withdrew. The lights on the halo blinked blue instead of red. The lieutenant fixed a sharp glare on Famous. "Is the machine off?"

"Yes. It's powered down."

Geary nodded in agreement.

"Th—good," he said gruffly, correcting himself. He'd almost *thanked* the crazy chef. He turned to his junior medic. "How is she, Dobbs? Should we wake her? Or let her sleep? Is the med bus in route?"

Geoff waited, stock still, as the backup doc did a quick evaluation, including blood pressure.

"Sir, her vitals look good. Pupils still reactive. Don't think we want her waking up, though. Not after *that*." The man carefully removed the halo.

"Okay, give her a mild sedative?" Geoff asked.

"Yessir. Also, the bus should be here—ah, there it is." Dobbs touched a comm node in his ear and issued some instructions to the incoming vehicle. Then the medic stretched out a hand to remove the sensors stuck all over Deja, including under her clothes. But Geoff stopped him, a flare of possessiveness catching him off guard. "Uh, I'll do that." Forcing his fingers not to linger over her soft skin, he removed the sensors against her chest first and then those on her face and neck.

"Lt. Col. Thorne?" It was Famous Foodie again.

"Silence. You have the right to remain silent," he snapped, skewering Geena with an icy stare. "I suggest you exercise your right because, otherwise, I'll have you gagged."

The chef frowned a bit yet quieted down as the med bus approached.

The reinforced, double-decker vehicle lumbered to a halt beyond the gaping hole in the wall. *MEDICAL TRANSPORT* said the sign on its roof and side. Teams were unloading two rolling gurneys as Geoff bent down to whisper in Deja's ear. "Deja, I'm here. I love you. I've got you. Just rest. You'll be okay." *Heavens, she had* better *be okay*. Cold anxiety swirled inside him, but he refused to let it win.

"Excellent work, everyone," he said hoarsely, looking at each of his team members in turn. "Dobbs and Geary, with me and Deja. Char, Yates, and Sooz, guard the wounded male on the med bus with me. The rest of you, stay guarding the female perp. The prison transport should be here soon. *Lethal action*," he added.

"And *you*," he told Geena darkly, "you are going to behave yourself. Try to escape and my crew will drop you."

One gurney team reached Deja's bedside as he finished issuing orders. Geoff helped them hoist her onto the gurney and then clasped her hand again, trotting alongside as the paramedics rushed her to the bus. The other team brought the injured man right behind.

Geoff prayed all the way to the med facility, holding the oddsbreaker's hand in his big paws.

SHIFTING in the chair by Deja's bed, Geoff rubbed the back of his neck. Then he reached up to touch his blackened eye. *Stars above, she has crazy good reflexes, even when she's half asleep.* He hoped the swing Deja had taken at him was indeed a reflex, driven by confusion and drowsiness. But, when it came down to it, he deserved the shiner. Geoff should never have gotten the Coalition involved. He should've protected her better. He should've done a lot of things. All things considered, he'd told the nurses to leave him be. The black eye would heal when it healed.

Geoff mapped the shape of her face with his eyes. Already, her olive-brown skin looked brighter than it had since she'd been admitted two days ago. Finally, he sat back. The doctors had said she should awaken soon. But they hadn't been able to tell him much of anything about her memory. "Tests look good. Brain waves are strong" was just about all they would commit to, gravgummit. The brain was so...tricky. Mysterious.

He let his thoughts drift to when he first met Deja, the perfect stranger who had saved his life. Yet would he be a stranger to her again when she awoke after the aborted memory wipe? He *knew* they could build a life together, a wonderful life. If, that is, Deja still knew who he was. If she could forgive him. If she still cared for him.

CHEF BASTIAN BOYAR sat in a chair on the other side of the table from Geoff in a brightly lit interrogation room. The dark-blue Vinadroan looked...worried. His brow was creased and he kept fiddling with an earring in one ear. But was Boyar worried about his own fate or Deja's or both? Geoff had already interrogated Chef Gaskón, who had come forward and readily admitted his part in the plot. Apparently, the "pork-eschewing" Orinkk had once dined on a deceased uncle in secret, and Geena had found out and used that damning information against the porcine chef.

"So, Chef Boyar," Geoff began. "why do you think you are here?"

The alien smiled briefly, flashing his fangs. "Because I had an...'unhealthy' fixation on Judge Lukas Inciardi. And because I showed interest in Chef EvaLynn Dubois, which I doubt is her real name."

"That is correct, chef. You have been entirely too obsessed with the now-convalescing judge, not to mention your competitor. And, no, EvaLynn Dubois is not her real name. But her true name is not for you to know at this point." Geoff narrowed his eyes. He was one of many to interrogate the culinary star, but he would hopefully be the last. "Did you play any part in the plot to assassinate Inciardi or capture Dubois?"

"No to both," said Bastian, clasping his hands in front of himself. "I never tried to harm either of them. But how is EvaLynn or whatever her name is? Was she hurt?"

"Yes, she was...injured in more ways than one," Geoff said haltingly. He hated admitting this. But he felt that the other man deserved to know at least that much.

"Will she recover?"

"No one knows at this point," Geoff said. "Now, I need you to tell me everything you have on Inciardi. First, I will tell you something that might change your perception of him. The judge is a double agent, working as a confidential informant for the Coalition. He has been feeding information on dangerous culinary criminals to the Coalition for years—even as far back as your involvement in the Ultimate Chef of the Galaxy Contest five years ago."

"He *what*?" Boyar exclaimed. "So the man was only *pretending* to be dirty?" The alien's deep-blue eyes opened wider.

"Precisely. Do you still have doubts as to Inciardi's actions in the past or present?"

"I...do not know," answered Bastian, shifting positions in his chair.

"OK. Give me the 'evidence' you have on him, and I will be able to confirm or deny whether he acted on behalf of the Coalition or not."

"Sure, I will tell you everything that I know." And then the Vinadroan began to detail what he knew about the judge's past. "And that is all the information I have, truly," Bastian finished. "I swear on my mother's table."

Geoff leaned back in his chair, pleased. "I am happy to tell you that nothing you said incriminates the judge. Inciardi is *not* the reason you lost the contest five years ago. Furthermore, you are now cleared to re-enter the current competition. If you want to, that is."

"Oh, I do, I do," Boyar assured Geoff. "Thank you very much. But I wonder...is there nothing I can do to help EvaLynn recover?"

"I'm afraid not," Geoff sighed. "Thank you for asking, however. You are excused. Good luck to you."

⚬

GEOFF STRODE toward Deja's room after questioning Chef Boyar and then meeting with Deja's team of doctors once again. If the oddsbreaker didn't awake in the next few hours, they'd give her a stimulant. He nodded to the guards charged with protecting Deja from prying eyes, especially all the reporters vying to interview her. His CO had held a press conference stating the facts of the case. If there hadn't been a leak in the first place, no one would've known that it was Deja who had fed the judges dirt. Anyhow, the contest had resumed without three of its contestants: Deja, Geena, and Gaskón. But the media was almost more interested in the Famous Foodie drama than the Ultimate Chef of the Galaxy Contest.

He was about to plop himself down in the chair but started pacing in front of her bed instead. Out of habit, he straightened his uniform and clasped his hands behind his back. Then he walked.

Back and forth, back and forth.

Until...a groan from the bed brought him up short.

He swung his head toward Deja as her eyes fluttered open. He opened his mouth. Yet as she spoke, his greeting died on his lips.

"What... Who the slag are you?" She took in his uniform and swore. "You're Coalition. I'm...under arrest, aren't I?" she groaned again.

Something cracked inside him. She didn't remember him. His heart crumpled into ash.

"No, no, you're not," he managed, struggling to keep his feelings in check. "You were injured during a Coalition operation—under my purview. But you're safe. And thanks to you, we caught the people involved in a high-profile murder plot. I'm...my name is Lieutenant Colonel Geoff Thorne." He paused, searching her face for a hint of recognition. He found none.

She raised her eyebrows. "Geoff Thorne, huh? Well, if I'm not under arrest, lieutenant colonel, why are those guards outside my room? Why the heck would I even work with a Coat such as yourself? And what the slag happened to me? Why can't I remember stopping a murderer?"

He chuckled a bit. "The guards? They're just here to keep *you* safe from reporters and other annoying folks, Miss Ortega. Please don't worry about it. You're important to—to the Coalition," he caught himself. "We just want to be sure you recover as soon as possible."

She rolled her eyes in that charming way she had. "Fine. Go on. Tell me how I ended up here."

"Of course." His knees felt wobbly, so he walked over to the chair and sat. He clung to his training as a soldier, working to find that dispassionate center of calm within. This was just another battle, he reminded himself. He could make it through. "A food activist subjected you to a memory wipe because you learned about her plot to assassinate a judge in the Ultimate Chef of the Galaxy competition. I'm afraid you were hurt because of me. I'm beyond sorry. I tagged you with a bio tracker that would leave faint traces of a certain radioactive signature in your wake. You went hunting the murder weapon. Then the suspect found you and kidnapped you. We had drones out scouring likely sites for signs of the tracker. But I didn't...get to you in time. I regret that more than you can ever know, Miss Ortega," he finished, forcing his face not to show any inappropriate concern.

For several moments, she said nothing. Then she looked up at him with soft eyes and whispered, "Call me 'nurse'."

Geoff's jaw went slack.

The expression on his face must have been priceless. She hid a laugh with a cough, then held out her arms. "Oh, stop gawking and get over here, Geoff," she teased. "I'm a bit fuzzy on some stuff, like how Famous got the drop on me. Yet I haven't forgotten everything. But you *did* deserve a little payback. Hey, where did you get that black—"

But she couldn't continue; his lips were firmly pressed over hers. After a gentle but long kiss, he pulled back, brushing her cheek with the back of his hand. His hopes for the future shone bright again, soothing the ache in his chest. She remembered enough to love him.

"Nurse," he sighed. "You came back."

EPILOGUE

Deja squeezed Geoff's hand as the holopanel powered up. He was trying to pull her in for a proper kiss when the screen revealed a 3D image of Whitley, who lay convalescing in a bed and propped up with pillows. Straightening, Deja nodded at him. She'd been the one to request a conference with the older man. From what she could remember, if it hadn't been for him, a whole lot more of her memories would've been zapped. Also, from what Geoff told her, Whitley had been a great help in getting his sister to cooperate with the Coalition, aiding them in tracking down other dangerous criminals in return for a lighter sentence.

"Ahoy, Whitley. How are you feeling?"

"Fine," he said quickly. "I'm just glad you're okay, too." He took a breath, hesitating, then plowed onward. "Did you lose any memories? I'm so sorry. What I did—"

"Was not so great," she finished for him. "But stop apologizing, would you?" she insisted, waving a dismissive hand. "You were a jerk. But with a sister so, er, disturbed, I'm amazed you didn't do worse. In fact," she added with a wicked grin, "I think what you did to help me took more courage than, oh, a dozen dares."

The man's gray eyes widened, embarrassment coloring his face red. *That's right,* she thought, *I heard and remember every word you said before you reprogrammed that memory wiper. I just don't remember what else you and your sister did to me.* Anyhow, now he knew that she knew that he was a little sweet on her. Whew. What a sentence.

At her side, Geoff leaned in close. "What's that about?" he asked, although the request sounded a bit too much like a demand. Jealous, was he? Well, that might have annoyed her in the past, but now it gave her great amusement, not to mention satisfaction.

"Odds are you'll never know," she replied, and Geoff gave a little shrug.

Whitley continued. "Uh, well, thank you, Dej—Miss Ortega. I still don't think I did right by you. If it weren't for you, I would've never known the truth about my father. I would've never been able to even talk to him." He paused, looking a bit choked up. "And my sister —okay, she's going to need a *lot* of help before she can face him. But I never dreamed she'd be able to stop hating him so much. Basically, I'm glad we got caught." He nodded. "Best thing that could've happened."

"Yes, I think so, too," Deja said.

♪

THE HOLOPANEL LIT UP, showing an image of her papá tucked in a hospital bed with a fuzzy, yellow blanket.

"¡Hola, Papá!" Deja exclaimed. "*¿Como te sientes? Que tal la mano?*" The surgeon had operated on his hand again that morning.

"*Mas o menos,*" he replied. "But I'm better just looking at you, *mija.*"

"Silly, Papá," she told him, smiling. "I will come see you as soon as I can."

"I know. And I know something else." He paused to cough, and Deja's forehead crinkled. "Geoff," Patricio said, "don't you have something to say to *mija?*"

Deja turned to look at Geoff, curious.

"Yes, I sure do, Señor Ortega." Geoff lowered himself onto one knee, holding up a shiny ring in one hand. A rare, Tuvian fire opal flanked by two diamonds topped the ring, flashing in the light. Deja's stomach shuddered in surprise. Her mouth dried out like the desert planet her papá had been trapped on.

Geoff spoke, trembling, "Deja Ortega, I have never wanted

someone like I want you. You've never been unworthy of me. Your past, present, and future are all I could ever ask for in a mate. You think I don't know that you have flaws—like how much you rely on a stiff drink. But I know we can get through that. Together. You're like this opal: fiery, mercurial, and so very precious. I love you. *All* of you. Please, be my wife?" His head dipped to the side in suspense as she stared at him.

He knows the best and worst things about me. Yet he still loves me. And I love him. I've loved him this whole time.

She raised a hand to caress his face and said, "Yes, on one condition."

He would've fallen over, but she steadied him. "Just name it," he told her, breathless.

"I marry you. Then you help me find the slaggin' scum who murdered my mamá and the rest of our troupe."

"Deal!" He grinned, jumping up and jamming the ring on her finger as if she'd change her mind.

"Good," she said.

"So, can I kiss you or what?" he asked, color returning to his face.

"How about 'or what'?" she said, smirking up at him.

ACKNOWLEDGMENTS

People ask me how long it took to write this novel. The thing is, I really couldn't tell you. The ideas have been in my head for so long. Moreover, it took me years of writing off and on to actually finish it—first as a novella and then as a full-blown novel. At first, it started out as a short story that I wanted to enter in the L. Ron Hubbard's Writers of the Future Contest. But, well, my characters refused to be contained in a measly short story! I often felt as though I would never finish it or it would never be good enough. But I managed to finish it and find someone who wanted to take a chance on it.

Speaking of which, I feel incredibly lucky to have found a home for my book at Immortal Works Press. I am grateful for my editor, Holli Anderson, who not only listened to my pitch but also asked to read my book, which was only a novella at the time. When she devoured it in about two weeks and asked if I could write more, I was both thrilled and humbled. I also wish to thank the whole team at IW for their assistance.

Long have I been fascinated by food and its myriad facets of meaning. I wrote my entire master's thesis at BYU about the power that food and consumption have in defining or shaping gender, culture, religion, psychology, and so on. "Animals eat," the French gourmand Jean-Anthelme Brillat-Savarin once declared, but only "men and women dine. And men and women of discrimination dine well."

Naturally, I'll always be grateful to the *Life, The Universe, and Everything Symposium* (a sci-fi/fantasy con also known as LTUE), which is the whole reason my manuscript was picked up in the first place. Back in February 2020, the con offered pitch sessions. Without that, my book may never have found its way out of the slush pile.

Many other people have given me feedback and encouragement throughout the years. The first people to really workshop my story were the members of my (now-defunct) writing group, Type & Gripe. (Yes, that awesome name was my suggestion.) Oh, what crazy fun we had! I'd like to personally thank them all: Vanessa Christenson, Jana S. Brown, Kristin McAlear May, Kathleen Dorsey Sanderson, and Jeffrey Creer.

Carrie Parker, an alpha reader and sweet friend, read it quickly several times and helped me a great deal. She was the very first person to read the book in its finished form as a novella and then as a novel. Aunt Marcella Bolzenius is my other alpha reader—the first of anyone in my family to read the book and offer this kind praise: "Cute slaggin' book, gravgummit!"

I also have some beta readers to thank for their highly helpful feedback: Kathleen Dorsey Sanderson, Ryan Hayes, (Aunt) Ron Nelson, and (Cousin) Karilee Gardner. In addition, I want to thank some of my favorite authors for their influence on me: Terry Brooks, Brandon Sanderson, John Scalzi, Jim Butcher, Patricia Briggs, Dan Wells, Brandon Mull, Eric James Stone, and so many others. A special thanks to the awesome Allyson Bylund for the book ad she created. A big thanks to Guy Larson for his help with the big math in my mortadella chapter.

Moreover, I need to mention my honorary sister, Mandy Stock Bylund, who has become one of my dearest friends. In fact, she let me read my book aloud to her whilst she was extremely ill with her third pregnancy. Her suggestions, questions, and support along the way were invaluable. Love you, Mandy!

When I pondered who I should dedicate this book to, it didn't take me long to decide on Mandy—and, indirectly, Aaron, the brother who still has no clue how he managed to win her hand in marriage. My brothers are all so dear to me. Incidentally, all of them are "present" in my book as names for three different characters.

In general, I have my mom, Tessie Bylund, to thank for my love of reading and writing. She introduced me to the magic and wonder of books at a young age. One day when I was in junior high, I was home sick. A lover of libraries, Mom brought me a special book that day: *The Druid of Shannara* by Terry Brooks. Now, I'd read fantasy and sci-fi before (Lewis's *Chronicles of Narnia*, Alexander's *Chronicles of Prydain*, etc.).

However, Brooks's book transported me into a whole new mindset. From that moment on, I dared to hope that I, too, might one day create new worlds and new peoples in awesome universes. For that, I will always be deeply thankful to my mom—and to Terry Brooks. Love you, Mom. And thanks, Dad (Alan Bylund), for believing in me and for being the dad you didn't have to be. And thanks to my Heavenly Father because I couldn't have done any of it without Him.

ABOUT THE AUTHOR

A hopeless bookworm and native Utahn, Sarah Bylund enjoys a variety of nerdy and not-so-nerdy pursuits such as reading, writing, collecting antique inkwells and poison bottles, prowling museums, taking photographs, cooking, traveling, and playing board games and card games. As for books, she particularly enjoys science-fiction and fantasy as well as historical romance, mysteries, and suspense/thrillers. By day, she works as a customer service representative in the genealogy field, and by night, she works as a freelance writer and editor. She has two master's degrees: one in Publishing and Writing from Emerson College (Boston, MA) and one in American Literature from Brigham Young University (Provo, UT). One day she hopes to own two or three dogs. She resides in Utah, and *Deja Ortega: Oddsbreaker* will be her first novel.

This has been an
Immortal Production